A. N. Donaldson studied Philosophy and Economics at New College, Oxford. He trained as a barrister and works for the British Council. His other published works include *Prospero's Mirror* (2013).

Visit his website at:
www.andonaldson.co.uk

'Absolutely brilliant… I can't recommend it enough. A Day in the Life of Ivan Denisovich meets Call of Cthulhu.'

Mike Taylor, *A Podcast to the Curious*

The Devil's Atlas:

Dark Tales from a Scholar's Study

A N Donaldson

ISBN-10: 1984334727

ISBN-13: 978-1984334725

Published in association with Endeavour Press Ltd

Many thanks to T, T and my family.

Contents

The Devil's Atlas:

Dark Tales from a Scholar's Study

Prologue

For many years, I have collected nasty stories. The Devil finds work for idle minds. Here is a small selection for you to enjoy.

Leviathan

Contents

Leviathan

"To do evil a human being must first of all believe that what he is doing is good"

The Gulag Archipelago

Preface: Sketches from an Album of the Hunted

This is a true story. On 27th January 1959 several cross-country skiers went missing in Russia. They had set off from a remote region of the Urals called Sverdlovsk. All nine were experienced and well-equipped. The investigating authorities confirmed they had stuck to their planned route for three days. But then they had reached the shore of Lake Syakhl, which feeds into the deepest tributary of the Ob. There for some reason they had deviated, and made camp high on the east shoulder of Kholat Syakhl.

In the local Mansi language Kholat Syakhl means 'Mountain of the Dead'.

No-one has suggested any plausible reason for why they went up there. Nor has it ever become clear why they chose to camp a mile above the treeline, in weather that was challenging even for that far North. Yet this was where the rescue party found their tents. They were empty and had been shredded open.

The first three bodies were discovered a few hundred yards downhill. They had died before they made it to the treeline.

Two more were found together beneath a large pine tree at the edge of the forest. Several branches of this tree were broken, as if one of them had for some reason attempted - and for some reason failed - to climb it.

The remains of the final four were discovered some way away, at the base of a ravine. It was not clear whether they had fallen into it, been pushed - or thrown themselves in to escape from whatever they were running from.

The temperature that night was minus thirty. Yet none of the nine were properly clothed. One of them had managed to put on a single shoe. In other words they had left their tents in frantic haste. They had clearly been running for their lives. Or rather to postpone their deaths. For they must have known it would be impossible to survive in such temperatures for more than a few desperate minutes. It seems they preferred that fate to whatever was chasing them. But the coroners concluded they had not died of hypothermia. Instead their bodies displayed strange crushing injuries: fractured skulls, broken ribs, ruptured organs.

One of them was missing her tongue.

There were no other human beings in the area and no other tracks in the snow. The official investigation was supressed until after the fall of Communism. It recorded an open verdict, concluding they had been killed 'by an unknown force'.

Their deaths have never been convincingly explained.

1 - Diary of a Sane Man (from a Traveller's Journal)

I was on the Trans-Siberian railway when I learned the terrible truth. This was a few years after Russia opened up and there was a real sense of hope. The horrors of the past were half-unknown, half-forgotten. For the first time it was easy to do the greatest train journey in the World: ten thousand kilometres from Moscow to the Pacific. I'd read a couple of Russian novels (in translation), so I considered myself something of an expert on the country. I had started a travel journal of considerable tedium and self-seriousness. It would end up looking like the ravings of a madman. It's amazing how much can change in one night.

I travelled second class, which meant 4-berth compartments. It was off-season and still well off the beaten track. But of course I ended up being made to share with the only other back-packers on the train: an American student couple who were going round the World without, it would seem, paying it the slightest attention.

The other occupant of our carriage was an old Russian lady who got on at Kirov and didn't say a word for the next four thousand kilometres. We all assumed she didn't speak English. Mostly she ignored us. Though when I took out my tattered old Red Army hat - a romantic Communist relic bought in Moscow – she watched me intently over the horned rim of her glasses.

She spent most of the next three days smoking in the corridor – much to the Americans' disgust - and the nights forcing air into her lungs in short, gasping snores.

On the second evening we crossed the frozen Urals into Siberia. Siberia! – so vast and empty it might have been the dark side of the moon. Nothing can quite prepare you for its remoteness. For day after day the train slogged on through a wasteland of steppe, forest, and taiga.

The signs of habitation, though infrequent, were more desolate still. We headed further East through settlements blighted by rotting industry. The guidebook would warn us of chronic iodine deficiency in one place, of clusters of terrible cancers in another. Some were abandoned altogether: all that was left as the train pulled through would be a few square miles of concrete and rusting metal, haunted by packs of wild dogs. We tended to slow down to an apologetic crawl as we approached these awful places, as if we were deliberately pausing to take a good long look at the devastation. Or perhaps the drivers were reluctant to disturb the ghosts of these shattered towns, and felt it best to roll past as quietly as possible.

Eventually the tracks turned north-east, into really wild country. We chugged relentlessly through a vast frozen landscape of mountain and forest. It seemed inconceivable they'd somehow laid a railway here.

On the fourth night out from Moscow the snow - which had been falling since the Urals - got thicker, and the train strained, slowed, and finally, in a cutting deep in a conifer forest, rolled stiffly to a halt.

At first we all felt twitchy and irritable at the unscheduled stop, as you always do on a train that won't move: there's something about that wait for the jolt of the engine pulling away that builds a tension in your chest that's like a torture - I suppose it's the unpleasant feeling of expectation, of waiting for something to happen, like listening for a starting gun that won't fire.

Eventually the terrifying *Provodnitsa* came round with tea from the Samovar and generally fussed at us. Our room-mate asked her a question in Russian which she answered brusquely before moving off. Then our companion turned to us and spoke – of course! - in flawless, barely-accented English:

'The track ahead is blocked' she said, 'I think we'll be here for the night. They're waiting for a heavy snow-clearer to come up from Usolye-Sibirskoye. I hope you have a good supply of vodka.'

Feeling somewhat mortified I got out my secret stash: a bottle of ultra-filtered Stolichnaya I'd bought at the GUM store to take home with me. I cracked it open and passed it round.

'I'm Polina', said the Russian, pouring herself a couple of small cups and drinking them down with great relish in polite little gulps. She herself got out some savoury snacks – I couldn't tell you what they were, but they were delicious, and even the Americans overcame their scepticism and tucked in.

Now that – to everyone's relief - the awkward silence had been breached, Polina was suddenly talkative. She had one of those delicious voices whose soft resonances produce goose bumps and a sort of hypnotic ticklishness at the back of the neck. There was something particularly mesmerising the way she pronounced her 'w's' and 'ch's'. She had the patient but authoritative manner of a natural story-teller. She said she'd been a teacher (retired now), and it was easy to imagine her holding a classroom of children enthralled as she told them a cautionary tale.

We ended up slightly drunk and started swapping silly stories. I told them a bizarre story that I'd heard in India about a vampire. Then eventually, quite late into the evening, I made some comments about the Soviet Union, perhaps partly to provoke an interesting reaction for my journal. Polina seemed to ignore me and asked instead to see the Americans' guide book, which she leafed through with an amused but slightly sad expression. Then she said:

'I see there's nothing in here about the Vegohzi.'

'What's that?' asked the female student. She was slightly irritated at the implicit slight on her book, which I believe her father had bought her as a gift.

'Well tonight, if you wish, I'll tell you a story about a real devil. I actually heard it myself on this very train.'

The Americans looked at each other uncertainly.

'It is a nice story.' she said, and then as an afterthought added: 'Like something from Gogol, but it really happened. It's really uncanny, bloody, and horrible...' Which of course made us all determined to hear it.

Also, mercifully, no-one wanted the evening to end. There was a sort of spell cast by the vodka, and the forest, and the snow thudding softly against the window. So we sat there in our cosy compartment, with the lights on low and the heater on full, picking contentedly at the wreckage of our boozy picnic, listening to the great muffled silence outside, and the creaks as the carriage cooled, and the occasional distant shouts from the drivers and guards at the front of the train. As the locomotive was slowly entombed in snow, time itself seemed to grind to a halt, and then, into that expectant silence, in a voice at once soft and amused, Polina told her terrible tale:

2 – A Nice Story

'It was decades ago, before I believed in evil. I was a young woman then, travelling to take up a teaching post at Novosibirsk. And back then, funnily enough, there was another Englishman on the train. He was an academic from Cambridge – a charming and intelligent man. And a fool, too, as I discovered, as only an educated man can be. He was travelling to a conference in Akademgorodok about industrial economics and central planning. He was probably the only man in the Soviet Union who still believed in our system.

Akademgorodok, by the way, means 'City of Academics'. Stalin had it built in the early Fifties for thousands of scientists, but it was still going strong now that Brezhnev was General Secretary. The idea was to round up all the intellectuals you could and send them into exile in the same place, safely out of the way. They'd be like a factory for ideas. That was the theory anyway. They had similar cities for athletes, I believe, and for various industries. Magnetogorsk, Chemichovo, Electrograd... Quite large cities you've probably never even heard of in the West, and some whose very existence was a secret. Many of them are abandoned now. Whole cities can be lost in Siberia. Imagine what else there could be out here.

This Englishman had somehow got a permit to take the train.

'I want to look at the country', he said.

Well, he looked at plenty of it, but I'm not sure how much he really saw.

'It's good to see the workers happy', he would announce. In fact of course we were nothing of the sort – we grumbled constantly about everything, though in those days you had to be careful what you said - and he took our guarded responses at face value. People see what they want to see. He appeared not to have the slightest idea of the nature of some of the places we were passing through, or why, as a regular train, we did not stop at them.

Still, to me he seemed rather glamorous. I'd just finished my modern languages course and I suppose I wanted to practise my English. So I sat up with him one night in the restaurant car, where he'd go to drink and feel a glow of self-importance and solidarity. As you know, they keep the restaurant car on Moscow time even when you're seven time zones to the East. So it was about two in the morning by the time they served us dinner. That's Russian logic for you. My Englishman seemed to think this was the essence of scientific good sense. Though by the middle of the fifth night even he baulked a little at the goulash.

Anyway, he got drunk and started making a ludicrous speech about trade unionism and the decline of the bourgeois West. 'Here's to the benevolence of the General Committee', things like that.

Finally it was too much for someone and I heard a low voice from the next table saying:

'Here's to you shutting the hell up.'

The others in the restaurant car all laughed at this. The Englishman was rather put out and retreated to his compartment shortly afterwards, which I now realise was exactly what had been intended. He had the best compartment on the train, of course, and had it to himself too, for all his comradeship. He asked me to join him so we could continue our conversation.

But, as soon as we'd settled, the light from the corridor was blocked out by the figure of a man, who now stepped in without invitation. He sat down on the seat next to me and grinned at the Englishman opposite. Sure enough, it was the man who'd insulted him in the restaurant.

He was an old man – over seventy, I'd say, and his body was half-broken with ill-health. But it looked like there had once been a wiry strength in it, and that he'd been tall and able to handle himself. His face was intelligent and heavily lined, and covered in a grizzly white stubble. He wore a grey overcoat that swamped him, and for all the warmth of the carriage he kept on huddling into it as though he was outside in the howling snow. It was as if the angry cold of Siberia had got into him and wounded him, so that no heat - even if it burned his skin - would ever truly warm him through again.

The Englishman looked at him indignantly, but our uninvited guest just sat and stared back. Then, after a minute or so of unbearable silence, he chuckled to himself and without any other introduction started to say:

'I was born in Novgorod in 1897-'

But just then the Englishman stirred himself and cried out:

'Look here, who the hell are you, and what are you doing in my compartment?'

'I am Gorobets,' said the man, simply, 'and I've come to tell you something.'

This was so unexpected that the Englishman fell silent for a moment.

'Gorobets' opened his mouth and said again:

'I was born in Novgorod in 1897-'

'Oh Christ!' the Englishman again interrupted: 'Don't think you're going to bore us with your life story!'

'I am not going to tell you my life story' said Gorobets. 'Though I think that wouldn't bore you. And with all the things I've seen you might learn a lot, even from a humble man like me. But it's not your business. The story I've come to tell you is not about life, but about death. You must listen to me.'

'Pfah, why should I listen to you?'

'Because you've no idea, have you – no idea at all - what this is' (here he waved vaguely around him) 'And every conversation you've had here has been horse-shit.'

He said this without the least venom.

'How dare you! I'm a Cambridge Professor of Economics. Who are you, and why should we listen to you?'

Gorobets shrugged and said:

'I'm a murderer.'

3 - The Ace of Spades

That shut the Englishman up good and proper. And there was something about the simple way he said it – not as a threat but as an embarrassed revelation – that made you know immediately it was true. Sure enough Gorobets now rolled up the great sleeve of his coat and showed us his prison tattoos: the Devil's skull in the square, the inverted Orthodox cross, the quincunx.

On the underside of his right wrist there was the Ace of Spades with the letters 'M.I.R.'. Gorobets explained that this was the mark of the political clan of the *ubiicha v zakone* – the Murderers-in-Law, or union of murderers. (Yes - in Russia there was even a monopoly for murder.) No man dared to carry those tattoos who wasn't a convicted killer. And no-one would dare insult such a man, unless he carried them too. M.I.R. stands for *menya ispravit rasstrel.* It means 'Never Rehabilitated'.

I doubt the Englishman knew of the *ubiicha* brotherhood; but he was so astonished that he just sat there, wide eyed. Gorobets, satisfied, leant back in his seat and started speaking, in a voice that was quiet but implacable. It was thirty years ago, as I say, but I remember ever ghastly word, and I shall for as long as I live.

This is what he said:

'I was born in Novgorod in 1897. Mine was a good family, though they never had much money. My mother was killed by the Tsar's soldiers on Bloody Sunday, right beneath that bronze horseman in Peter's Square. My father was a doctor. He wanted me to be a doctor too, and he sent me to study at the Imperial University of Medicine and Dentistry. This was before the wars. It was the autumn of 1913 when I first arrived at the University. I was lonely and homesick but also impatient. I hated the old ways and was hungry to change things. I didn't know then how much worse things could get. At that time Petersburg was seething. The Socialist Revolutionaries and the Bolsheviks and the Syndicalists and the Black Hundreds were all plotting and spying and informing on each other. The secret police were everywhere. I fell in with a bad crowd.

Most of it was drinking and wild talk, but Bryollov and Glinka were more serious. They said they were part of a secret group called the Grey Fist. It was the proudest moment of my life when they let me join. 'You've been chosen specially', they said; and I thought it a great honour. I was in awe of Bryollov's supposed success with women. Perhaps I hoped that by joining them some of that might come my way too. Politically, they seemed to express what I'd felt but never dared think. 'Anarcho-Mensheviks', we liked to call ourselves. Tear everything down to start again. That was the idea anyway.

I was desperate to impress my new friends. I told Bryollov: 'I want to do something good for Russia – something people would remember me for.'

Bryollov laughed. I thought at first he was laughing at my simplicity. I grew angry but he hushed me and let me in on their plan:

'It mightn't be a big enough task,' he said, 'for a hero like young Gorobets. But we've got to start somewhere. The first step is simple. We're going to kill the Tsar.

To kill the Tsar. As soon as he said it I knew it was my destiny. To me this man was a blood-drenched tyrant. A man who'd continued to party on the night of his coronation, when a thousand of his subjects lay dead outside from the crush in Khodynka Fields. Whose Cossacks had charged with their sabres drawn against unarmed petitioners. Whose soldiers had shot my Mother in cold blood. I was never quite sure what was supposed to rise up after we'd killed him. No doubt much energy was expended planning the new society. But I barely listened to that. I just wanted him dead. And I was obsessed by the thought that I, Gorobets, would be part of this great undertaking - the greatest in the history of Russia. How brave it was of me to want to kill a man in cold blood. A man I'd never met and who'd never even heard of me. How *selfless* of me to risk everything in such an endeavour. Yes, they'd remember me forever, I was sure of it.

At the end of term Tsar Nicholas was going to visit the University to open a new block of science laboratories. Glinka said he'd got a gun from somewhere and volunteered for the great task. Bryollov would then lead the students and hopefully some of the steel workers to the militia arsenal at the 'Peter and Paul', and after that do Christ alone knows what. My job would be to give the signal to Glinka and, if he missed, act as second assassin. Unfortunately we only had one gun (not that they let me see it). I was armed with a home-made grenade and, rather pathetically, a long knife Bryollov had taken from the canteen kitchen. I prayed I'd have the chance to use them.

That seems odd, doesn't it? To pray to God to break His most sacred commandment. To pray to kill His appointed representative. To pray for the success of a group that didn't believe in Him and were sworn to destroy His church in Russia. But the night before the Tsar came that's exactly what I did.

I couldn't sleep, of course. I was in a sort of delirium: drunk with feverish expectation. And frightened too, but that seemed right - such a great task *should* require self-mastery. It was winter and dark for most of the day in Petersburg. There was no sun that morning anyway. Even after dawn it never got beyond a bright grey haze, as if Nature herself was waiting for something magnificent and terrible.

Bryollov fetched me early and came with me to the new laboratories. There was already quite a crowd, including guards along the façade of the building where the Tsar would get out of his carriage and be welcomed by the University Chancellor. I stood behind them, just above the foot of the main steps. From there I'd have a good view of the carriage as it approached along the avenue in front of the labs, coming from the main university buildings. As the hours passed the number of on-lookers swelled and the guards formed a line to hold us back. I spotted Glinka several times on the other side of the avenue in the thickest of the crowd. I hoped he'd be able to see me waving my grey handkerchief as we'd arranged. I realised too late I was in a much better position than he was for a clean shot. There was only one line of policemen between me and the place where the official party would stop to get out of their car.

I forced myself to run through all the scenarios in my mind. I must have thought of everything except what actually happened. The Tsar was over an hour late – the bells of the nearby monasteries chimed midday before he arrived. Then suddenly there was an excitement in the crowd at the far end of the road and a carriage turned into view, with two Cossack outriders. They passed slowly up the Avenue. The crowds cheered and a few students heckled. The trees shook in the breeze and the faces of the crowd craned to look, but only we knew that the World was about to change. All the men and women around me, though they didn't yet know it, were relics of the old century. I was the man of the new one. How I exalted at that, and how jealous I was of Glinka. They pulled level with where he was standing. Frantically I waved the grey handkerchief above my head. The great moment of fate had arrived. It seemed incredible that nobody noticed me straining every nerve for the shot.

'And then?' asked the Englishman, in spite of himself.

'And then: nothing happened. No shot rang out. The procession rode on unharmed.
They were coming towards *me*.

'I didn't think of what might have gone wrong. Though I knew I could now easily walk away and blame it all on Glinka. But I was too busy watching the carriage. There were three people in it. Two facing backwards away from me: a woman in a white dress whose face I couldn't see and the Dean of the University. He was a fat Volga German who ran the place like a boyar and who we all hated.

But I didn't think about them for a moment. Because now I could see the Tsar himself. He was in a crisp white uniform covered with medals and epaulets. He was smaller than I expected. He sat very straight, waving occasionally at the crowd.

So, I thought: this was the monster who stood between his people and their future. How absurd that this little man should wield so much power.

His carriage came to a stop at the foot of the steps. It was just beyond where I stood: no more than ten feet away. As he passed I could see his eyes scanning the crowd. For a moment they met mine. It was then that I made up my mind.

4 – Black Days

I think a sort of demon possessed me. Because my mind exalted as I decided to kill and to die. At this range I calculated there was no chance of surviving the explosion. Even if I did, the guards would be sure to kill me on the spot. But I didn't mind that at all. As I say, I was a man possessed.

I tried to shout 'down with the tyrant', like Brutus when he killed the first Caesar. But my mouth was dry and the words caught in my throat and were drowned by the cheering of the crowd.

I lifted my bomb and heaved it over the shoulder of the guard on the step below me. It landed on the folded cover at the back of the carriage and then, bouncing, it fell forwards, jumping up into the carriage itself, and tumbling down at last between the passengers' feet. For a second nothing happened. The Dean bent down to examine it. Then there was a roar like the end of the World.

Explosions are curious things. Unpredictable. The force of the blast actually sucked the policeman in front of me forwards under the carriage. I believe he was blinded (though whether by the flash or by splinters of wood I can't say). One of the horses was killed outright and the other, maddened by pain, careered off into the crowd, dragging the front half of the coach with it and scattering anyone still standing. Both of the Cossack outriders had been thrown by their mounts and were badly injured, as were most of the guards nearest the blast. The arm and breasts of the girl standing next to me had been blown right off. But I myself felt no pain. For a second I thought I'd been killed. Perhaps it would've been better if I had. But I found myself unharmed. I rushed forwards to the wreckage of the carriage.

The coach's axles had broken and its wheels collapsed outwards, leaving its ruined carcass on the road. Of its three passengers, the Dean was simply gone. His head, neck, and left shoulder had been blown up onto the top of the front of the carriage. The rest of him was spread about all over the road. However, in bending over, he'd partially shielded the blast and directed it sideways. The Tsar himself was mortally wounded:

his legs destroyed. But above the waist he was intact and moving. His torso was drenched in blood but most of that was probably the Dean's. The woman, who'd been entirely protected by the once-impressive bulk of her companion, was also miraculously unharmed. I noticed she was far too young to be the Tsarina.

I was the first to reach them. I seemed to be the only person who wasn't dying or reeling from shock. The woman got to her feet just as I came up.

'Oh no', she said, in the tenderest voice, and reached out to the broken man opposite her.

For his part he looked at her and said:

'It is nothing, Anna, tell the children I love them.'

Then he looked at me. He alone had seen me throw the grenade. And now he saw me reach in my coat for the knife. He calmly unbuttoned his jacket to bear his chest for the thrust. I stared at him in amazement. He was quite calm. He said:

'Why?'

The first guards were running up to us at last. Flustered, I shouted:

'The Tsar is Dead!'

He smiled and said:

'I am not the Tsar.'

I dropped the knife back in my pocket.

'You fool', he said, 'God forgive you.'

Then he crossed himself.

Then he died.

I'd expected to be sabred by then but I was just barged out of the way by the officials who were rushing up from all sides. No-one else had seen I was the killer, or paid any attention to my triumphant shout. No-one, that is, except the woman. Fearlessly she turned her back on me, bent over her husband, and kissed his lips. Then she stood up and stared at me. She was very still and very beautiful. She didn't point or say a word to the men who crowded around her.

In that moment something incredible happened. I still can't really explain it. It was like being re-born. The feverish daze of the previous days evaporated and I felt suddenly calm. I realised in an instant the enormity of what I'd done. I seemed to stand at the very centre of the World and be able to look round and see it properly for the first time. I'd changed it - torn a hole in it - broken some covenant with Nature. I made a show of helping up one of the injured. Don't misunderstand: I didn't yet feel regret, or wonder who he was that I'd killed, if he wasn't the Tsar. There was no time for that. But I understood now what violence was and the power of it. This was all *my doing*. I saw every detail of the coach and the bodies and the screaming horse at my feet and the place where its fur had been burnt. I felt the crowd that ran round me, towards and away from the carnage. I saw the noblewoman looking at me and felt we'd shared a private understanding. I nodded to her before the crowd surged between us and I allowed myself to disappear into it. Then I just walked away.

I didn't have any thought of escaping, particularly. I just wanted time with this new feeling, this euphoria. This realisation that I was a man and had acted as a man and had struck a blow for my fellow men.

Well, after all, I was seventeen.

It didn't take long to find out who they were – the streets were full of it. The dead man was Count Varovsky: the Tsar's second cousin and one of his ministers. He'd stood in for the ceremony as the Tsar was indisposed. It was only much later that I realised he wasn't important. Of all the political assassinations at that time he was probably the most minor. Apart from seasoned revolutionaries, who considered it a bungled operation that had set back the cause, most people haven't even heard of him. Worse, he was known to sympathise with the liberals. His young wife the Countess Anna was one of Petersburg's celebrated beauties. I believe she joined a convent afterwards, and dedicated herself to charity. They say she was shot in the Revolution.

For three days - black days when the sun barely rose – I staggered aimlessly around the city. Then I went back to the campus. Of course my friends hadn't gone through with their part of the plan. Instead they'd sold me to the Okhrana – the secret police - who were waiting to pick me up.

I pleaded guilty, of course. Because I was guilty. I was determined to be true to my actions and take the consequences. But I began to realise now it was a pointless act. Banal. I should never have done it. I deserved to die for those deaths. I'd acted out of a desire to do good - or so I told myself. But in fact I'd let myself be possessed by evil ideas. When you kill a monster you become a monster. And it turned out I hadn't even killed a monster, just murdered an ordinary man. Nor was he the only one whose life I'd destroyed. There was the Dean. Well the Dean was the Dean. But don't forget several bystanders had also died of their wounds. And for some reason I felt terrible about the horses. So I pleaded guilty.

That didn't save me from torture, of course. They wanted names and they wanted revenge. I won't describe their methods. You just have to believe me that there are things they can do to a man that will make him forget all his principles. And when they were bored of that they would lock me in a box full of bed-bugs. Look: I still have the scars. I gave them Glinka, I'm ashamed to say. I tried to tell myself afterwards it was because I blamed him for setting me up like that (sometimes I wonder whether there ever was a gun). But, after all, that had given me the chance I had prayed for. I've no idea what happened to him or if they believed me. But I always made myself count his blood too on my hands. And even he wasn't the last.

They held me at Fontanka for four months while they questioned me. It was there I got the letter saying that my father had died. Of grief, it said. Of all the people I'd killed his death was the hardest to face. That was the moment I gave up pretending I'd done something glorious. I no longer felt anything for myself but disgust.

So I was relieved when they came to my cell and dragged me off to the courtyard and showed me the firing squad. I even thanked them when they put the blindfold on me and tied me to the post. It was my father's name that was on my lips when they shouted out to take aim. But it was the Countess's face that I saw in my mind. My only sadness at that moment, I remember, was that I'd never loved a woman, and that no one would remember me. Then they shouted 'fire'.

5 – Moscow to the End of the World

The volley echoed round the courtyard and died away. I had no idea if I'd been hit or not. I thought I could still hear myself breathing. But I felt nothing at all until a cold metal mouth kissed my forehead. It was the sergeant's revolver for the coup de grace. This time my mind was empty as he pulled the trigger.

Then there was laughter and I realised they'd fired blanks. Mock executions were the Okhrana's favourite sport. But do you think I was happy? No! Please take my word for it: dying is no terrible thing. It's living with regret that men should fear. I raved at them to do it properly. But the sergeant just spat at me and said:

'You're too low to waste a bullet on, Gorobets. The Countess pleaded for clemency. We've just received your pardon from the Tsar.'

Which, of course, was why they'd decided to treat me to these amateur dramatics. I'm ashamed to say I cried when I heard it. Not from relief, you understand, but from shame. I'd been pardoned by the monster I'd tried to kill. I didn't want his mercy. But under the Tsar it was rarer than you'd think to be sentenced to death (it only got common after the Revolution, when Lenin 'abolished' the death penalty). I was a traitor, yes, and there could be no forgiveness. But then the Tsar had no great love for the Count. And his government's policy was against making martyrs of us. Besides, I was technically a minor. So I wasn't to die.

I got something worse. I got Siberia.

My crime was serious enough for a 'twenty five'. People said a twenty five was as good as a death sentence, just colder. Then they put me on the train out East.

I'd tried to kill one monster but instead I found a worse one. I'd sinned and they sent me to hell. But I didn't know that the worst thing about the camps were the people who lived there. Hell is a beast with other beasts inside it.

You see I'd never really met the people before. I mean the peasants and the workers I'd been fighting for. I suppose you could say I idealised them. I never realised they hated us.

Hated us worse than we hated the nobility. And their criminals, who we were going to release as one of our first acts of the revolution, turned out to be the most depraved people on Earth. It was no good telling them you were a revolutionary: that made it worse. 'We can look after ourselves, thanks', they'd say. 'You'll never be one of us'. And they meant it, too. It seemed that no matter how long you'd served you were always a bourgeois intellectual. The more you protested about your common roots the more they despised you. They actually had more respect for the noblemen and the guards than for people like me. They hated them too, but at least they respected them.

And they saw violence differently. For me it was an extreme and dreadful resort, to be used only in self-defence or the noblest cause. For them it was endemic, chronic, *normal*. It was just the way they settled disputes, established hierarchies, or let off steam. They were the products of a cruel system so they themselves were cruel.

My first encounter with the zeks - the other convicts - was on the train from Moscow to Siberia. There were sixteen of us in a compartment this size. Oh that's nothing: after the revolution there'd be twenty or thirty.

At this point the Englishman interrupted with an incredulous comment. Gorobets laughed and said:

'How do you know there isn't a *vagonzak* at the back of *this* train? They don't have windows, you know – they look just like baggage carts.'

The Englishman protested:

'Such things couldn't happen in Russia today.'

''Such things don't happen in Russia today'' said Gorobets. 'That should be our nation's motto. It's been heard in every period of our history since Ivan the Terrible. It's never been true yet. I wonder if they'll still be saying it in fifty years from now - and if it will still be a lie.

'It's not so nice sharing a compartment with fifteen men who hate you. First they took my remaining possessions. Then they took my food. Then they beat me and made me lie on the floor like a dog.

By the time that train reached Tomsk two weeks later I'd learned a lesson. It was the law of the taiga out here: only the strong would survive.

Thank God there were other politicals in the camps who took me in as one of their own. That's when I got this tattoo. I was something of a hero to them for what I'd done. The first praise I got came after I no longer believed it myself.

I was in the transit camp that summer when the Archduke was shot, and my class-mates marched off to their deaths at the Masurian Lakes. I was still in that camp three years later when the workers at the Putilov came out on strike, and for the July Days when Kerensky gave the orders to fire on the Reds, and for that October when they had their revenge. I was still there when they shot the Tsar, along with the Tsarina, their servants, their daughters, and the little Tsarevich in the 'House of Special Purpose' in Sverdlovsk.

We heard about it all, of course, in the end, as our numbers in the camps continually swelled. But to us it was like news from cloud cuckoo land. This was not our fight any more. We were legally dead, after all. From now on even our loved ones wouldn't know if we were alive (not that there was anyone left back West who loved me). We'd been sent down to frozen circles of Hell so far beneath our old lives that the events that shook Russia in those years were to us just distant echoes of the World above to a man at the bottom of a well.

All that changed when they started the amnesties. When the Bolsheviks took charge they let most of the non-politicals out. I allowed myself the dangerous luxury of hope. They should have released me too, except that they were already purging the Anarchists, and my name was still on that list, thanks to my 'friends' in the Grey Fist. So the revolution we'd prayed for didn't free me after all, just sent me to an even harsher servitude. I was tainted with Kropotkinism. So instead of letting me out they moved me deeper into Siberia.

Those months were a time of chaos. The war in Europe ended (only Russia could manage to lose to the losing side). But the fighting didn't stop, it just came home with the troops. In Siberia the Civil War was very nasty. Unger-Sternberg, the mad Baron, took Urga, where his men raped the women to death and roasted their children in ovens and the boilers of trains. He proclaimed himself the re-incarnation of the great Khan, creating an 'eternal empire' to honour the ghastly Buddhist demons that he worshipped.

He wasn't the only devil in Siberia. One of the politicals in our camp was a Red commander from the Belorussian front who'd performed his duties with such zealous cruelty that his own officers had grown frightened and disgusted. They denounced him as a traitor for fear that they'd be next. Becoming a victim of his own terror baffled him. But far from re-appraising his actions, it merely strengthened his zeal: he concluded he hadn't purged hard or deep enough. He told me with great relish how he'd fed captured Whites and their families to the animals in Minsk zoo. There weren't enough animals to eat all his prisoners, so he loaded the rest onto barges and sank them in the Dnieper.

Anyway, Sternberg's Whites moved north to Ulan Ude and were within 30 versts of cutting the railway. Some of the guards ran away and the system almost broke down. In the confusion I got on a transfer detail by pretending to be someone else. But then I was recognised by a snitch: a dirty Don Cossack from Rostov. He hated me because I'd beaten him in a fight that spring over a helping of cabbage soup, of all things. Amazing what your life turns on. That cabbage soup was what finally did for me, because they took his word and stopped me. I got 100 lashes for attempted escape. You can see it on my skin. There was no chance of them letting me out after that. I was a murderer, after all, and if the act was political it was the wrong sort of political. Also, I was a bourgeois. Worst, I was trained as a doctor. Which meant they had a special use for me.

They needed doctors for the hard labour camp they were building around the deep-level Mica mines at Cape Kotelnikovsky, two versts in-land from Lake Baikal. The worst place in Siberia. What am I saying? – it was the worst place on Earth.

The Decembrists used to say that Christ visited Siberia when he was blessing all the different lands of men. But when he got to the Southern shore of Baikal He refused to go any further. He just waved his hand at the North and said 'beyond this there is nothing'.

He was wrong: beyond this there was Ubiichogorsk. Even God would not tread there.

6 - The City of the Dead

'But you said it yourself,' the Englishman said: 'you weren't innocent.'

'Who said anything about innocent?' replied Gorobets. 'No-one in Russia was innocent. Almost everyone had killed, or denounced, or stood aside whilst the killing went on. But no, I don't mean what I say: poor Russia didn't deserve it. In fact we were the only men in Siberia who deserved to be there. The only guilty men in a sea of innocent martyrs. That's why we hated each other and why most of all we hated ourselves. I was a murderer. And like all murderers I deserved punishment. And like all murderers I was sent to Ubiichogorsk.

That's what Ubiichogorsk means, you see: 'City of Murderers'. 'Killer-ville', if you like. And that's exactly what it was. 'Special category'. Only murderers were sent there. There were other secret cities, of course. Like this precious Akademgorodok of yours (who shovels the shit there, I wonder? Probably a professor of gastrology). The idea was to hold all the convicted killers together in one place. What sick sort of theory lay behind that? That's town planning by fanatics. You can see why they screwed the economy. Let's put all the tractor factories together here, all the wheel-rubber plants together here, and all the murderers together here.

But they found a use for us; you have to give them that. That's the thing about murderers: no-one cares what happens to them. So they can be put to work. Hard, dangerous work that no-one else will do. So they fettered our legs and worked us to death in the mines, whilst the dissidents from 'Journalistgrad' crawled towards us with the branch-line they were building-'

'That isn't true', interrupted the Englishman.

'Oh really? Who do you think built it, then? Gnomes? No, it was zeks: prisoners, slaves, like me.'

'Yes, but in the days of the Tsars.'

'Ha, they really taught you that, did they?' he lowered his voice: 'To think of the stories I could tell you, but-' and here he glanced suspiciously at me 'a man must be careful what he says. Just listen carefully to my story and you might begin to understand.'

'We were put to work on the mica mine on the North West shore of Lake Baikal. Our job was to scratch out the crystals and carry them two versts through the wilderness to a warm-weather dock on the lake. There we'd pile them up. And in summer, when the ice had cleared, barges would come and take it away to make into Muscovite for electrical insulators. It was madness, in that place and climate. But no doubt it looked good on the map of some villainous adolescent in Moscow.

You can't believe how remote it was, particularly back then. We're talking here about the back of the back of beyond. Siberia is bigger than the Antarctic. Colder, too, when it wants to be. It's the biggest wilderness in the World. You know it was Ivan the Terrible who first conquered Siberia, from the last of the Mongol Hordes. Only a madman like him would have thought that was a good idea. We were five thousand versts east of the Urals, and twenty days' walk beyond the railhead. Twenty days if you lived, which you wouldn't – in summer you'd starve and in winter you'd freeze to death.

There were no other settlements in the region, except perhaps the odd secret village of *Skoptsy* Old Believers, hiding out in their beards in the woods, poisoning their kids with in-breeding and self-castrating to purge their sins. And there were still some Buryat people around in those days – aboriginal reindeer herders. But the nearest settlement of them was way off on the far shore of the lake. It was maybe two hundred versts away if you went round by land; though only twenty if you sledged across the lake. They used to come into town once every few months to trade with the guards. Furs for metal and vodka. They were in a dreadful state by then: they'd been forced into collective farms, but they only knew nomadism and it was killing them. They were starving, and drunk, and dying off like flies.

Not as fast as we were, though. Eighteen months, give or take, was how long a man would last in the mines, if he wasn't killed by a rock-fall. And no-one in Ubiichogorsk had less than a tenner to serve. So you didn't have to be a mathematician to see it was a death camp. A few did serve out their time - those who were strong enough, or who were excused full shifts underground. Thank Christ they made me camp doctor, after the last one had died of despair. That was the only reason I survived so long: it kept me out of the mine.

You might ask why we let ourselves to be worked to death. I used to think it was fear. But now I realise it was actually hope. It's hope makes a man a coward. Random amnesties and mock executions were bad enough to live through, but they had a worse effect. They meant people would go meekly to their deaths, clinging on to the end to that hope of reprieve. They didn't even struggle as they knelt by the ditch they would die in. What craven creatures we are: do you think all that's happened in Russia could've happened if we weren't? Or the camps? There were millions of us, after all. If we rose up together many would be killed, yes, but the rest would be free. And anyone's chances would be better in a revolt than rotting in the camp waiting to die, one by one, of exhaustion. So why didn't we try, even once? It was the cowardice of hope. No-one had the balls to take the risk. Needless to say we all knew this. It only served to increase our self-hatred.

There wasn't a single woman in the city. I don't say there were no murderesses in Russia. I'm sure there were plenty. But no doubt it was felt that the husband-killers, abortionists and infanticides were better off elsewhere.

Another unusual thing about Ubiichogorsk was that there was no money. Any that was brought into camp was immediately confiscated by the guards. This was decreed, as it were, by order of the management. They were able to do for us here what they were never able to do for the rest of Russia.

But here again I found my prejudices over-turned. Because far from a liberation from materialism this was another step to destroying our individuality. Without money it was harder to collect or trade possessions, and without possessions we were all the same. But of course it turned out that money isn't so easy to abolish. We soon learned to use other things as currency. There was a roaring trade in cigarette-stubs, for example, that we picked up where they were discarded by the guards. For a while laundry tokens were exchanged (until the commandant found out and closed the laundry). And then there was the inflation caused by Mirza the Uzbek. The poor man couldn't understand the delighted cheers when he first arrived and flashed a smile revealing a set of gold teeth. Needless to say within half an hour he'd been relieved of the burden of those teeth with the end of a rock-needle. Miners are good excavators. I'm not sure it made much difference to Mirza, since they never gave us any proper food to chew anyway. But he didn't smile much after that, I can tell you. This gave him an air of sadness, as if he was always in mourning for those teeth.

That was Ubiichogorsk. Sixty below in the winter, and the earth as hard as rock, and the rock as hard as iron. And that was when you got through the ice. On the northern slopes of the mountains there were many places where the snow was so deep it never thawed. In one of the high valleys one of the teams dug a mammoth up out of the tundra. A huge beast from an age before time, just lying there, under the ice. It even still had its hair. It was so cold that nothing had bothered to eat it before then. We were in Hell all right, and we spent our days digging further down into it. And that was before we knew what was to come. Though there were rumours even then that this place was home to a nameless evil. Of course it was, I used to say: it was home to us.

There was only one way out, which was death, and many men found that road quickly. Some of us died of exhaustion, some of cold. Some hanged themselves and others threw themselves in the lake. At first I prayed to join them.

And I would have done, thinking like that. Despair will kill you faster than anything. You needed a reason to live, if you were going to survive in Ubiichogorsk. At first I couldn't think of one. I had no life to get back to and there was no-one waiting for me to get out. I didn't even have illusions to cling to: I'd realised by then that ideology is not the cure for evil but its source. Without hope or illusions I was doomed – perhaps we all are. Yet here I am talking to you now. Does that sound impossible to you, Englishman, that a murderer like me could find redemption, out on the haunted shores of Lake Baikal? But I found I had one skill that made me useful to my fellow man. As so-called camp doctor I was no good at saving lives, but I became an expert at solving deaths.

That's where this story really starts. With those terrible killings.

7 – From the Notebook of a Country 'Doctor'

The commandant didn't usually care when the workers killed each other. It was just one of those things that happened from time to time, as it must happen in all prisons. And it was hardly surprising in a city of murderers. It was rarer than you'd think, though. We were all so weak and there was so little to gain from it. You see, most of us were normal murderers, not psychopaths. The psychopaths were mostly working for the government-

'What nonsense', muttered the Englishman.
Gorobets, sensing he'd gone too far, continued:

'What I mean is that our commandant was more evil than most of the inmates. The average man in camp had killed his woman for sleeping around, or been unlucky in a bar-room brawl. It was the commandant who seemed to kill for the hell of it.

So he didn't care when normal zeks were murdered. But he did care when his engineers were killed. And one winter that's exactly what started to happen. It was a few days before Christmas Eve in '26 – my ninth year at Ubiichogorsk and the thirteenth of my sentence. Believe me, I'd been counting every day.

The engineers were making trips out of town for geological surveys on the cliffs by the Cape. It was a useful spot because there you could see the different strata of granite that lay beneath the land, and get a better idea of where to find the mica.

Cliffs? Yes! Baikal is the only lake I ever heard of to have cliffs – there's so much water in it that it has a tide, and storms come up from the North that send huge waves against the shore. Over the ages they've gouged out real cliffs from the mountains that arc around the lake. Anyway one day two engineers - Borisovsky and Ivanov - had headed out to these cliffs. By evening they'd failed to return. That was a serious matter – they'd been expected back hours earlier and been missed by the guards. Furthermore they had no camping equipment, so they'd be lucky to survive the night, given it was now December and colder than death.

I'd also been out of the camp that day, and been out alone, collecting birch bark for the infirmary (it was supposed to numb pain, which it didn't, but it was almost the only 'medicine' they allowed us). As I was returning through the woods I ran into three men coming back from a search party sent out to look for the engineers. They were almost beside themselves. Rather than tell me clearly what they'd found - and talking over each other in their excitement - they doubled back the way they'd come so I could see for myself.

There's a spot on the cliffs where the forest peters out in a clearing by the edge of the lake. That's where they'd found the missing men. Borisovsky had been fully eviscerated. By which I mean to say that the entire contents of his torso had been removed. I'd seen plenty in my time, but nothing prepared me for this. Not even the Dean of the Imperial University of Medicine and Dentistry, and believe me he had a lot of guts. But that was nothing to the innards Borisovsky had in him. Or rather, I should say, out of him. Because they were spread all over the clearing. I've studied anatomy but I was still astonished by the length of the duodenum, particularly when you see it unravelled like that. He'd have needed a better anatomist than me to put him back together.

The situation with Ivanov was somewhat worse.

He'd been dragged up a tree, from which he was hanging limply, upside-down. The trunk and the snow at its base were drenched black with his blood. As your eyes made sense of it you suddenly understood why. He had been partially *skinned.* Some of the flayed skin was still tenuously attached, hanging down from his limbs in sheets, with parts of his clothing still stuck to the outside of it. And where this skin had once been, the angry red and orange of muscle and fat were clearly exposed.

'He was still breathing when we found him,' said one of the zeks, 'but when we asked him who'd done it, he just shook his head and died.'

Could this be true? Perhaps these men were lying and had done it themselves. In which case I realised that things looked bad for me. I took hold of the lower branches of the tree and hoisted myself up. Sure enough the body was still warm, even on that cold Siberian evening. At least they were telling the truth about that. Given the scale of his injuries, that meant they must've only just been inflicted.

'Perhaps they killed each other, or one killed the other and then himself', the second zek volunteered, hopefully.

'No', I said, 'from the look of him Borisovsky's been dead for some time. Perhaps an hour or more. Ivanov's injuries were made long after Borisovsky was killed - and they can hardly be self-inflicted, can they? – he probably witnessed the murder. But for some reason he didn't want to run away. Or couldn't.'

'So he had plenty of time to contemplate what was about to happen to him…' the third man muttered.

'Yes,' I said. 'And you must've stumbled onto them just moments later. Whoever – or whatever – did this must still be close by. Perhaps watching us right now.'

I stopped and scanned the dense forest around us. Then I looked more closely at the men in the search party. They'd already stripped what clothes they could from Borisovsky (he didn't need them anymore, after all, and no-one was sentimental about things like that in Ubiichogorsk, where good shoes could be life-or-death). Now they looked around themselves, obviously terrified. The first man whispered:

'Let's get out of here!'

It was clear they'd stumbled onto this scene unexpectedly rather than caused it. Everything in their demeanour acquitted them of the killings. How did I know? Well, I am a murderer, after all. I've seen shocked on-lookers and I've pretended to be one, and to the trained eye there's all the difference in the World.

These were no normal murders. Killings like this were new, even here - even in Hell.

Sure enough, the authorities were appalled: here was sadism more cruel and elaborate than any they'd yet thought of themselves. It insulted their creativity. It was a clear threat to their state monopoly on torture.'

Here again, Gorobets thought better of going on in this line and changed tack:

'My real job as camp doctor was to keep scurvy and cholera and night-blindness to acceptable levels, and to stop the zeks from dying before they'd completely used up their strength. In the end it was about maximising productivity. It was no good telling them that the only courses I'd taken were 'Basic Anatomy', 'Hippocratic Ethics', and the first third of 'Kidneys and Pancreas'. Besides, they didn't want a doctor to cure people, just one that could sign off plausible death certificates for inmates who were worked or starved to death. You wouldn't believe how many men who'd been given a hundred too many strokes of the birch, or too many hours chopping trees in the cold, were signed off by me as 'dead of acute Pancreatitis'.

And as camp doctor, I had the delightful task of scraping together the bodies and conducting some make-shift autopsies. Not that I was any sort of expert, you understand, with only two terms of medical training. But I was the best they had. And whatever I said, there was no way these two could be marked down as 'acute Pancreatitis'.

There was something that already made me uneasy. It's no simple thing to drag a man up a tree, even if you'd ever want to. Harder still to follow him up and skin him alive at the top. This didn't seem like the work of a man. Perhaps it was an animal? There were bears in the area, of course, though they should've been hibernating by now. More likely a large Siberian tiger. A man-eater could've killed Borisovsky, mauled Ivanov, and been disturbed by the search party before it could finish him off. Attacks by tigers on humans weren't uncommon. And they play with their victims for hours before they kill them, like a house cat with a mouse. They'll kill for fun, you see, even when they're not hungry. Nature is cruel like that. These tigers were a constant risk for the men building the railway to the south. They weren't the most likely thing to kill you. Siberia is the only place in the World where you can just as easily die of malaria as hypothermia, and just as likely be eaten by tigers as by arctic wolves. We were a long way north for a tiger, here, but perhaps one had wandered into the area out of its usual territory.

These were my first thoughts as I examined the bodies. It was clear both men had died slowly and died hard. They'd both been bruised trying to fight their attacker. But apart from some black filth that I couldn't identify, there was nothing under their fingernails in the way of hair or blood. And on closer inspection an animal attack now looked less likely: Borisovsky had deep stab injuries, which seemed inconsistent with any animal I'd ever heard of.

There were small knives in the camp, and stolen mining tools. It was relatively easy to get hold of a murder weapon. Harder, though, to get the sort of blade that could've done this. And harder still to hide such a weapon and have no one miss it. In Ubiichogorsk you were never alone for a minute and someone was always watching you.

As for Ivanov, he'd had most of his ribcage broken, as if by a great impact or pressure. Perhaps he'd jumped or fallen from the tree and then been dragged back up it? There were strange marks on his head that I couldn't make sense of. Also, he had no tongue. And large parts of his skin were missing altogether.

In all my life I've never seen anything like it, and when I'd finished the autopsies I puked like a schoolboy. I didn't know there was worse to come.

8 - Murder and Retribution

The question of killing is a delicate matter. As Lenin would say it all comes down to: 'Who? - Whom?'. The injunction against murder must be the most fundamental moral principle of man. The one shared by every Society, in every period of history, wherever humanity has spread his poisonous presence. Without it no society could exist. But I'm here to tell you that it's no universal imperative. Or if it is then the grace of God really did stop at Baikal.

Because murder was not a taboo in Ubiichogorsk.

It was *celebrated.*

The Manslaughterers, for example, were looked down on by the rest of the town. A value system had arisen which actually despised inadvertent killing as sort of weak - and even faintly ludicrous. It doesn't take much to reveal the cruelty in man. It doesn't take much for him to justify that cruelty - to say that good is bad and bad is good. Anything's easier than admitting you were wrong.

For me all this raised interesting questions. My student days were over but still I was hungry to learn. There was nothing else to study so I decided to study murder. After all, we must've been the biggest collection of murderers in the World. And I had some vague sense that - if I looked into it deeply enough - I might understand what lay behind man's desire to kill, and maybe even somehow learn how to stop it.

I had plenty of material. The others were surprisingly willing to discuss their murders. I think we were all, somewhere in our souls, trying to work out why our lives had brought us here. Also, boasting about it did you no harm. Indeed, most of the zeks were completely unashamed.

So I must've heard about hundreds of murders, in all their exquisite details. From the most banal and pointless to the most elaborate and debauched. Murders of fathers by their sons and sons by their fathers. Murders of wives and sweethearts, cruel bosses and abject workers, nobles and low prostitutes and little babies in their cots. Murders from Poland to the Pacific, from the White Sea to the Caucasus. Murders described with wild laughter or raved about in nightmarish sleep. Murders boasted about for face - or sobbed out in death-bed confessions. Murders as tragic accidents and murders as work of art. Eventually I was an expert, so surrounded was I by murder. Morning, noon, and night: murder was all that I saw.

My interest in the topic didn't go unnoticed. I got a reputation, due to a few unpleasant incidents I won't bore you with, of being good at finding out about murders, if there was ever one that someone wanted solved. And if the commandant didn't usually care who'd done it, the friends of the victim or the bosses of their barracks often did. The vengeance they meted out, not the commandant's random 'justice', was what really kept the peace in Ubiichogorsk.

I should say something at this point about the barracks and the 'union'. You see, by a capricious whim of the commandant, we had at first been segregated according to class of crime. This proved impossible to keep up as the camp's population changed. The new prisoners were never the right sort to fill the gaps required: even Russia's murderers refused to work to predictable quotas.

Furthermore, interestingly, we died at different rates. This would've made a fascinating medical study. I noticed that the wife-killers, for example, seemed to have less stamina than the rest of us, and their numbers were constantly depleted. No doubt this was as much statistical variation as violence of zek against zek. Though putting all the Dagestani bandits in together wasn't clever. They all came from different tribes, and had been killing each other longer than they'd been killing Russians. Eventually the survivors had to be separated.

So new arrivals were often assigned to a barrack because it was less full, rather than because of the nature of their crime. This somewhat diluted the purity of the commandant's vision. But the names of the barracks stuck, and so did certain traditions associated with them. A new convict would adopt this name and these traditions. He'd be considered as belonging to them whether or not they fitted him. Someone put in 'Rapists', for example, would always be referred to as a Rapist, regardless of whether he'd ever committed a sex-murder. The same with 'Child-killers' and so on.

The different barracks gave themselves different tattoos. The spades were for 'Politicals'. The higher the number the greater your number of victims. I doubt you'll never see another 'ace'. You have to kill a high-ranking noble for that. In my day it was very rare to do that and live to tell the tale. And later, when it became government policy, they gave you a promotion and a medal rather than a twenty five and a tattoo.

Believe it or not there was a sort of a hierarchy between these barracks, as well as within them. The more depraved your crime the higher up you found yourself. 'Mass Murderers', for example, had a certain glamour attached to it. 'Politicals', on the other hand, was pretty much the bottom of the pile. Even the commandant agreed with the zeks about that one. After all: they were criminals, but we were traitors. It seemed that even in Ubiichogorsk a perverted class system had risen up.

There were wars between the barracks, but mostly the bosses stopped them. There may not be honour amongst thieves but there must be a way to keep peace amongst murderers.

This way was the *ubiicha ponyatiya*: the murderers' code. In a city of killers we were all 'murderers-in-law'. All brothers together in the union, all respecting its code of honour. The membership requirement was simple: you had to have killed another human being.

The other rules of the murderers-in-law were these:

1. Swear loyalty to the union and its hierarchy and know your place within it;
2. Forsake all who aren't murderers, including your own father and mother;
3. Never co-operate with the authorities, or grass about anything;
4. Purge your emotions.

To forsake your own parents is a terrible thing. Now I'd already done that the moment I threw my bomb. So for me the last rule was the hardest. But it's easier when you're hungry. Did you know you can be so hungry that you lose all compassion for your fellow men? And the rule entrenched a sort of fatalism that despised affection or pity. There was a logic to it, though. In the gulag pity can ruin your chances of survival.

So the union wasn't a society for mutual support. But if they cast you out or caught you talking to a guard then you'd become a 'Bitch' and your life was worth nothing. Men who 'allowed themselves' to be raped also became 'Bitches', and from then on were seen as fair game and the lowest sort of scum. There were rapes in the camp, but not so many: most of the inmates were too weak from exhaustion to think of it. Years later the Bitches got themselves organised and fought back in the 'Bitch Wars'. So many died they had to segregate the prisons. That was after my time. As camp doctor I only escaped being seen as a Bitch because the zeks thought I kept them healthy. But the point is you couldn't collaborate without becoming a Bitch. And becoming a Bitch in the gulag was a fate even worse than death.

The authorities tolerated the union it because it kept order. It meant less for them to do and a lower chance of riots. It kept the murder rate down to levels which I'd describe as chronic rather than a bloodbath. And they saw it as a sort of collective, which satisfied them politically.

Now when Ivanov and Borisovsky were killed it was felt on both sides of the fence that there had to be a reckoning. It was a matter of honour to us, and of administrative necessity to them. Each side wanted to be the one to punish the culprit. It was just a question of who found him first.

But the authorities knew that no-one would answer their questions. That's why, whilst they tried and failed to solve it from their barracks, they appointed me to play detective around the camp. Me and ex-police sergeant Yuri, who I'll come to in a minute. Now they let me and Yuri off our duties, and gave us free passage anywhere we wanted to go. It was a relief from the hospital and the mine. But it was an unenviable task.

The worst part of it was this. I was *also* chosen by the barracks bosses to find out what had happened (not for payment, you understand, but if I valued my own life). And they made it clear it'd be more than our lives were worth to conspire with the authorities.

As I investigated my life would be in as much danger from the union as from the killer himself. But on the other hand, if I didn't find the culprit and inform the commandant at once, I'd be in for it from him for abetting criminality. And the final straw was this: he made it quite clear we'd better find him before they sent a Government Inspector who'd give him shit for missing his quotas. If I found the guilty man that was a bonus, but the important thing was to find someone. If I didn't he said he'd assume it was me (after all, he said, hadn't I been out alone in the forest myself at the time of the killings?). But no-one likes to be framed for murder, even a murderer, and if I set someone up his friends would surely come for me. So pretty much any way you looked at it I was screwed.

That's how I got told to investigate the most incredible murder case I ever heard of. Because who do you suspect of murder in a city full of murderers? A population of twenty three hundred and fifty six, and every single one of us a killer.

Besides us there was the commandant, his secretary and two deputies, and a detachment of sixty eight guards. Their style was usually less elaborate than what had happened here. But I can tell you that none of them were beyond killing either. They'd kill *me* if I made the wrong move. And there would be plenty of the other zeks who would kill me for bitching out if I made the right one.

It was the middle of winter - we were completely cut off. A supply boat would come through when the ice cleared in April.

Until then we were on our own.

9 - A Villain of Our Time

Yuri was my only friend in Ubiichogorsk and I think the only man there who was truly innocent. I don't mean he hadn't killed. I remember asking him about that on his first day. I'd gone to watch the new arrivals. One of the guards brought their bags back from being 'searched' (the real purpose of which, of course, was to remove anything left of value). He threw the bags over the fence into the mud where the new men were waiting. Most of them cursed, but Yuri, as if the man were a railway porter, grinned and said:

'Thanks Comrade – but I'm afraid I've got nothing to tip you with!'

The crowd all laughed. I decided to go up and welcome him. He'd been assigned to the 'Politicals', which was ludicrous if you knew how un-political Yuri was (in Russia being un-political was itself a political act). He'd only been assigned to us because his victim was a party official.

'How long did they give you?' I asked.

'A twenty.'

'What for?'

'For doing nothing wrong!'

'Don't be a fool,' I said, 'the penalty for doing 'nothing wrong' is a tenner'.

At that he roared with laughter, which immediately endeared him to me.

'Go on,' I said, 'tell me. Why are you in here?'

He shrugged and said:

'A woman.'

You'd be amazed how many men in the camp said that. It covered a very broad range of crimes. But from the lining of his coat Yuri took a photo of a young woman. She looked like a real stunner.

'That's Mariya. My wife. Obraztsov tried to take her by force – he's the party man in our village. I caught him at it and killed him with a coal scuttle.'

'Good work.'

'They thought so too: they awarded me a long holiday to Ubiichogorsk. How's the weather here?'

‘Delightful!’

‘Oh well’, he said, ‘Pushkin went into exile. And Dostoevsky did time inside. If it’s good enough for them it’s good enough for me.’

That was his attitude to everything. Even here he was unstoppably cheerful. He had a sort of naturally positive character - an apparent refusal to see the horror around him, or believe the worst of anyone. It was either naiveté or genius, or a strange mix of the two. He wasn’t a terribly intelligent man, but he more than made up for this with his humour and common sense. Within a few months I knew him better than I’d ever known anyone. He was good for me, too. His presence somehow gave me some hope that I could survive.

He was also determined to escape. One night, a few months before the killing of the engineers, he hadn’t returned before curfew. After searching all over I found him hiding behind some bins in ‘Laundry Street’. He was standing by a corner of the fence and sobbing.

‘What’s happened?’ I asked him.

‘It’s no good, my friend’, he said, ‘I thought I could brass this one out but I can’t. I don’t doubt she’ll wait for me like she promised, but who’ll look after her? She always says what she thinks to people, which seems to be the wrong thing to do nowadays. If it wasn’t for her I could stick this place fine. But the thought of not seeing her for twenty years. Or of her saying something she shouldn’t and them sending her somewhere like this... I just can’t do it anymore.’

‘You have to, Yuri’, I said. I couldn’t bear to see him like this – it lessened my own resolve. ‘What choice do you have?’

‘We always have a choice’, he said. ‘I’m going to escape.’

‘You’ll be killed’, I said.

‘I know. That’s why I’m crying.’

Escape from Ubiichogorsk was impossible, everyone knew that. They didn’t make much effort to lock us in – they didn’t need to. There was simply nowhere to go. You didn’t try to escape because there were five hundred versts of frozen waste between you and safety. Even if you made it, the new convicts had stopped calling the world outside ‘freedom’, and started calling it ‘*bolshaya zona*’ – ‘the bigger prison’. Spies and informants were everywhere, they said. Movement without papers was impossible. And you couldn't bribe your way to getting new ones anymore. Even vagrancy was no longer tolerated and would get you shot as a spy. It seemed everything had changed in Russia except the things that needed changing.

Anyway, with regular roll-calls you'd never get enough head-start on the dogs. And if the dogs caught you they let them tear you to pieces. Several times we'd watched them being brought back from pursuits, the white fur of their cheeks stained with red.

'What's your plan?' I asked.

'I'll save some food and just bloody run for it', he said.

'It won't work. I'm not going to let you.'

'Then help me think of a better plan and come with me. You're the one with the brains.'

'No amount of brains can get a man out of Ubiichogorsk', I said, and dragged him back to Politicals.

This was probably true. But I'm still not sure if it was also fear that held me back. And I don't just mean fear of dying in the attempt. I mean cowardice about living if we got through. I'd spent all my adult life in Ubiichogorsk. And with all the blood on my hands I didn't think I deserved to be out. The only thing I knew about was murder, and the World didn't need any more of that.

In the end Yuri didn't listen to me. He went on with his preparations in secret, but he wasn't as careful as he should've been. One of the engineers caught him coming away from the mine with some tools to help him break through the fence. They decided to shop him, doubtless anxious for some tit bit from the commandant for turning stool pigeon.

At first I thought the authorities would shoot him. But I'd underestimated the sadism of the commandant. Instead he got two months in the Isolator. That was practically a death sentence, particularly in winter, as they were unheated. Also there was no human contact. Which might be fine for a few days – a relief, even, after living in a town where you were literally never alone. But even if you weren't frozen or tubercular, weeks of it on end could send you insane: we'd all seen it happen.

For my sins I'd developed a good relationship with the commandant. Or as good as I could, given that the man was a maniac and I was his slave. He tolerated me because I treated his 'skin complaint'. [Which I was pretty sure was secondary syphilis, though I wasn't about to tell him that, since I'd made a bet with myself that even if I didn't survive I'd make damn sure I lived longer than him. And I was right about that too, by the way.] But he fancied himself an educated man, trapped by his duties in this god-forsaken place. His deputies were party thugs and most of the convicts couldn't read. He saw in me, in a guarded way, a sort of fellow intellectual. He'd sometimes request my company when he was bored, so he could tell me about his asinine theories of criminology, and his conquests in the whorehouses of Kiev.

So I resolved to use whatever influence I had to get Yuri out. I flattered him more than ever the next time I saw him, and made a great show of pretending not to have heard his stories. Then I changed tack:

'How are production levels?' I asked (I knew the commandant was always anxious about them, as he was answerable for them to his lunatic party bosses in Moscow). Sure enough he said:

'If you must know we're behind on the quotas. You zek scum never do a proper day's work.'

It didn't occur to him that this might be connected to the fact he was starving us to death.

'Ah what a shame about Yuri Melnik' I said, 'I hear he is one of the most productive shock-workers – a real Stakhanovite.'

This was true, thank God: Yuri worked harder than anyone, and certainly harder than he could've got away with. It was typical of him that he viewed it not as murderous torture, but rather as a healthy distraction from the torment of being inside. The commandant, hearing this, seemed to waiver. I seized the moment:

'Instead of solitary, why not give him a couple of months of extra-hard labour?'

It was a risk, as that was enough to finish most men off. But it was better than freezing or going mad in solitary. And if I could call in some favours and get him some extra food, a strong man like Yuri could hope to make it. It would also take his mind off Mariya, which he'd have to do anyway if he wasn't going to lose his will and become a *dokhodyaga* – a goner.

Sure enough the commandant relented, and swapped Yuri's solitary for fifty lashes and eight weeks of 'storm-work' punishment shifts in the mine. When he came out of the Isolator, dishevelled and shivering, he grinned at me broadly:

'I never thought I'd say this, Gorobets, but thanks for getting me flogged!'

'Any time.'

'Seriously, though. You saved my life. I hope I'll be able to repay you some day.'

Which in an odd sort of way he did, when we got face-to-face with the killer.

10 – The Gulag Ocean

'Anyway, news travels fast in the gulag. By the day after we'd been asked to investigate the murders of Ivanov and Borisovsky we were swamped with denunciations. There was hardly anyone in town who hadn't been accused by someone else. And as for alibis: every witness was also a suspect. It'd take months to sort through that labyrinth of false reports. That is if the men I was questioning let us live that long.

That afternoon Yuri and I returned to the crime scene. But with all the comings and goings the previous night there was nothing useful I could make out from the tracks. Anyone could've followed the men from the camp or the mine and killed them in the forest, then returned before he was missed. [It wasn't that hard to slip out unnoticed during the day. There were headcounts every few hours, and it was mainly these not the fence that prevented escape. The town was locked-up much tighter at night when you had a chance of getting a head-start on the dogs.]

The tiger theory looked doubtful, though, for we couldn't see any animal tracks. There were some strange scuff-marks here and there, as if something had been dragged towards the water. But this probably had to do with the engineers' surveying kit, which was strewn all around the fore-shore near their bodies. Some of it might have showed signs of damage, but from what I could tell there was nothing obvious missing. Not even quite big metal spikes on the tripod legs, which might've been detached for use or barter as tools or weapons back in town.

I climbed to the top of the cliff overlooking the clearing and stared out at the landscape. From here, between the tree-line and the shore, there was a spectacular view of that whole vast wilderness of mountain and forest, which I knew stretched for thousands of versts in every direction. And because the cape formed a headland that projected out into the lake, this cliff-top gave an incredible vista over the whole coast. As far as the eye could see a serried line of dead rocks and cliffs, the colour of broken teeth gone bad, looped out in both directions to infinity. And in all that immensity, I thought, there might not be another living person.

Then I turned to look at the lake itself. Its still surface reflected the leaden sky. It had hardly bothered to get light that day. But you could see the thin Arctic Sun, which hadn't shone on us all week, breaking through the high clouds near the horizon, and glistening here and there on the lake many versts to the South, where the deeper water hadn't yet frozen over. Nearer to shore great ice sheets were spreading from the coast, but they hadn't quite coalesced into a single whole. In a couple of days, though, I knew the ice would be a metre thick and more, and by the end of the week a man might walk over it all the way to Irkutsk. A whole army had walked across in the Civil War, when the Whites were retreating to Novoselenginsk, though most of them had died from exposure in the teeth of the terrible wind that howled straight down from the Arctic over the ice.

As it was a clear day I could see dim glimpses of the further shore. Baikal is narrow from West to East, though it's seven hundred versts long from South to North. It's the largest lake on Earth, and also the deepest: fully six thousand feet. The Mongols, who never understood water and were afraid of it, called it 'the cursed Ocean'. Three hundred rivers flow into it but only one flows out: the mighty Yenisei – greater than the Rhine and Danube put together, and navigable all the way to the arctic. That's how so many sea species find their way into the lake.

As I looked over it now I noticed to the South a small hidden cove on the other side of the Cape. Spread along the shingle there were the bones of hundreds of seals. Over the years they'd been picked clean by scavengers and the elements: it looked as if an entire colony had died here, though how or why I couldn't say. Directly opposite, about half a mile from shore, loomed the dark mass of Dianda Island – the forested top of a mountain that rose sheer up from the bottom of the deepest water. Amongst the convicts it had a strange reputation. Its name means 'Devil's Saddle'. The shamans of the remaining indigenous tribes believed it was haunted by demons. Against the backdrop of the lake it was a forbidding presence.

The cold wind was starting to burn my face. Turning back, I shrugged at Yuri and looked one last time at the scene of the killings. Then he said:

'Come on, back to the 'meat-grinder'.'

'Any thoughts?' I asked, as we trudged back to the camp, feeling exhausted and hollow.

'My thought is that what happened here wasn't very nice,' said Yuri.

'Well thanks for that flash of genius!' I laughed. 'It's a good job I got you out of the mines'

'What I mean is: this isn't the normal run of killing. Whoever did this took a lot of time and effort over it. And spending that time was taking a risk. No I reckon this was done for pleasure... '

'For *pleasure*', I repeated.

It made sense. There certainly were men in Ubiichogorsk who were known to kill purely for pleasure. Most of them were in 'Mass Murderers' barracks. In the absence of anything else, that seemed like the best place to start. With a word in the right ear we arranged to meet Vaska, the boss of Mass Murderers.

Vaska was a giant of a man, a Crimean Tartar, who'd once been a wrestler. He'd also been a violent drunk, and was convicted of several killings in tavern fights in Kazan. He kept the peace in 'Mass Murderers' by his sheer size. There was probably no-one in Ubiichogorsk who could beat him in a fight, and as boss of the top barracks he was like a king amongst the zeks. Deprived of his old poison, he still lived to fight, and loved nothing more than settling the hard way some real or perceived challenge to his supremacy. Even the other Mass Murderers were afraid of him. But for all his ultra-violent ways, without access to booze he was straight enough. He enforced a sort of bastardised, inverted moral code that at least had the benefit of predictability. Now he professed to be horrified by what had happened at the lake.

'We can't have this sort of thing,' he said to us when we shuffled into the Mass Murderers' building. 'Have you found who it is yet? Because if you don't find him soon I'll do to you what he did to them.'

I was slightly surprised at this. But I guess the killings had, by their brutality, implicitly challenged the terror he held over the camp.

'Not yet, Boss,' said Yuri. 'We're working on it. We wondered if we could ask you who came in late last night?'

'Are you saying it was someone from Mass Murderers?' he raised his voice, 'because if you are – and it sounds like you are – I'll personally tear off your ears.'

The men around him moved forward slightly, delighted at the prospect.

'No Boss,' I said, as coolly as I could: 'we're trying to rule Mass Murderers out of the investigation. That's why we came to you first.'

He grunted and motioned us over to him. We stepped reluctantly forwards, exchanging glances. Suddenly he thrust his great arms out round our heads and dragged us down into his reeking chest. That's it, I thought, he's going to break our necks.

11 – The Possessor

I believe Vaska thought about killing us, but decided against. Instead he said, in a whisper only we could hear:

'We covered for the Perm Ripper last night: he didn't come back til after curfew.'

Then he shoved us away laughing and, for the benefit of his barracks-mates, shouted:

'Now get out!'

We thanked him and backed away slowly.

I can't now remember our suspect's real name. Perhaps I never knew it. Everyone just called him the Perm Ripper. He'd been convicted of a notorious and particularly unpleasant spate of murders in Perm before the war, and had continued to kill regularly when he was inside. The man was clearly insane. He killed at random and without thought of the consequences, apparently for pleasure. When anyone asked him why, he'd say the Devil spoke in his head and made him do it. He liked to keep his victims' heads as trophies. There's nothing new in that: Tsar Peter kept his lover's head pickled in his bedroom. But the Ripper liked to *play* with them like toys.

At first the others in 'Mass Murderers' treated him as something of a mascot. But even most of them quickly grew afraid: he was so unpredictable, one minute quite normal and the next a violent lunatic.

Vaska wasn't afraid of him. But then Vaska didn't fear anyone. He'd always protected him before now, even when everyone knew he'd killed someone. But now for whatever reason he seemed to have turned against him. Maybe he knew something we didn't. Or maybe he thought, like we did, that there was one of only a handful of men in Ubiichogorsk who might have done something like this for no reason other than their own amusement, and knew that the commandant wouldn't be satisfied until a plausible suspect was presented. The Ripper was without friends, and could be offered up safely without disturbing the peace.

We found him in the canteen, lounging at one of the long benches, picking drowned cockroaches out of his soup and eating them whole. He seemed to be in one of his calm moods, and had not drunk too much *chifir* – the extra strong tea he liked to use as a stimulant. There was nothing for it but to ask him where he'd been last night.

'I went to buy some cigarettes from a guard I know', he answered, sullenly. He wouldn't say which one, and didn't reveal what he'd been selling.

Yuri and I looked at each other. This was a surprising revelation, as the Ripper wasn't known to be friendly with any of the guards.

'Where exactly did you go?' I asked, expecting an evasive answer. But to my surprise he replied as follows:

'I was supposed to meet him out in the woods beyond Lake Street. He never turned up. But it wasn't me who killed those engineers', he suddenly brightened. 'Who did, eh? Wouldn't you like to know! *I* know because I saw him. Give me some cigarettes and I might even tell you...'

There didn't seem much alternative. With a shrug I handed over my precious collection of half-smoked stubs along with my tin of rough Makhorka tobacco.

'So who was it?'

The Ripper stopped laughing and said:

'It was the *Vodyanoy*.''

'*Vodyanoy*?' asked the Englishman.

'I'm afraid it doesn't really translate. You might say: the old man of the lake.'

When we got back outside Yuri said: 'That was easy. And I think asking him any more questions might've been bad for our health.'

'Yes,' I said, 'a new variation on his old story of 'Satanic possession'. We haven't found the murder weapon. But it all sort of makes sense. He must've somehow bribed his way past the guard, killed the engineers just for the hell of it, and snuck back into Ubiichogorsk in the ensuing confusion.'

'Well even if we're wrong, it would be good to have that devil off the streets.'

'Not if it means there's another 'devil' still walking around with no-one suspecting.'

The next challenge was informing without being seen breaking the code. After squaring things with Vaska, I pleaded some medical duty and sneaked off to the guard hut to suggest they bring in my suspect for questioning.

But the commandant wasn't interested in the facts. The Ripper was simply seized and dragged through Ubiichogorsk to the permanent punishment cells. This was terrible news for us. If he ever got out he wouldn't forget who'd grassed him up. Needless to say, none of the guards were punished for colluding with him in the first place.

Unlike the Isolator, the permanent punishment cells were a set of small heated rooms in a building on the Eastern edge of town. You're wrong if you think a heated cell to yourself sounds like luxury after the barracks. Because in these cells you were permanently manacled to the wall. We were all shackled with leg irons round our ankles anyway. But these fetters didn't much impede us. Besides, we quickly learned how to take them on and off, so we generally only wore them when the guards were around. But the prospect of being tied to a wall by your ankles and wrists was said to be so horrid that those who survived it thought the torture of normal camp life was nothing by comparison.

Even so, it was surprising how desperately the Ripper screamed as they dragged him away. He pleaded and threatened and raved all the way to the cells. He kept shouting over and over:

'Don't leave me where he can get me.'

Next morning the story went round that the men in 'Parricides' had heard unearthly screaming in the night. At first no-one knew what to make of this. Finally someone thought to check on the punishment cells, which was the only building beyond their block to the East.

Sure enough the entrance, which faced out to the fence and the woods, was found hanging splintered in its frame where the lock had been torn out of the jamb. By the time I got there a large crowd had gathered inside. But the Ripper was no longer there.'

‘What do you mean, ‘wasn’t there’?’ asked the Englishman.

‘I mean he wasn’t there.’

‘You mean he got away? How had he freed his arms and legs?’

‘He hadn’t. Those were still attached to the manacles.’

12 – Non-attendance at a Beheading

There was a silence in the carriage.
'You mean?'

'Yes. The rest of him was... gone. The cuts where his limbs had been severed were relatively clean, as if something very sharp had been used. Not the sort of small razors that circulated as weapons in the town. In any case it didn't bear thinking about: being chained, helpless, to the wall, whilst you were hacked away from your limbs one by one. I never thought I'd feel sorry for a mass murderer.

They searched the town and even dragged the cesspit. But if he'd been buried somewhere in the mud of Ubiichogorsk there was little hope of finding the rest of him.

It seemed that Borisovsky and Ivanov's deaths had been avenged in a brutal manner, with the body mutilated as reprisal. As for the Ripper, no-one was going to mourn his passing. Even the guards were relieved to see the back of him, after the way he'd threatened them when they took him in. Most of the zeks naturally suspected the remaining engineers. Nor did people blame them much in the circumstances – everyone was pretty disgusted with what the Ripper had done. And given that the engineers were necessary for the functioning of the mine, it was inconceivable that they'd be harshly punished by the authorities. Anyway, they were bound to cover for each other.

The question on everyone's lips, though, was this: would the Mass Murderers take vengeance for the death of one of their own? It was one thing to consent in secret to the confinement of a barracks-mate who'd got out of control. It was quite another for everyone to see the killing of one of your own go un-avenged. That was enough to undermine your authority. But if the Mass Murderers were going to go after the engineers it would disrupt the mine - indeed it would be tantamount to a camp revolt. One way or another that affected everyone. People started arguing about it all over, and small scuffles were beginning to break out.

Fortunately the cold wind I'd felt start up the previous day now threatened to bring an ice storm in its teeth. This alone chased people indoors and stopped a riot breaking out then and there.

Sure enough, as the evening wore on a terrible blizzard got up and we were confined to our quarters. It was so cold that the oil froze in the drill motors and piss froze before it hit the ground. The dogs in the pens up by the guard house howled all night. What sleep I had was disturbed by monstrous dreams.

Next day three more of the engineers were missing.

Originally there'd been six of them – that's counting the first two victims. Of the remaining four just one – Nikolayevich - had proper form (he'd drowned his daughter in a jealous rage). So far as I know the other three were innocent men, but, being educated, were suspected of being Whites, and were accused of various incidents of lethal industrial sabotage. Which really meant they'd probably been sent to Ubiichogorsk to take the blame for someone else's incompetence. We never knew whose bright idea it was to have saboteurs construct a mine.

The engineers lived in a separate block near the commandant's house and offices. They usually kept themselves to themselves. They got extra rations, for a start, for reasons that are beyond me, since they didn't have to do the actual mining. And they were allowed much freer movement than most of the rest of us, as their duties regularly took them away from the camp. They didn't even have to wear fetters. They were hated by the prisoners, who complained about all this. The real reason they were hated, though, was that they were innocent. Their lives were ruined too, of course, but even moral superiority is resented when all other sources of jealousy are stripped away.

That day reveille was, as usual, at five (though by November that was five hours before dawn). Even so three of them had gone out an hour earlier to clear the worst of the ice from the equipment at the mine shaft, and get things ready for the next day's work. When the main shift arrived they found the men had never got there. It was a couple of hours before the gale subsided a little and they found one of them out in the woods.

Or rather, they found half of him.

Everything was gone below the chest. And his nose, too, had been ripped out. The only strange thing was that there was hardly any blood, either in him (which wasn't surprising with wounds like that), or on the snow around him, which was more problematic. If he'd been killed on that spot it would have left a bloody quagmire for yards around. So it seemed he'd been carried some distance from the site of the murder. And the blizzard had covered all the tracks.

The head of a second man was eventually found out by the lake-shore. We never found the rest of him. But I think it was safe to say he was no longer a suspect. The only thing I could tell by examining him was this: from his expression he'd clearly been caught by surprise.

Of the third man, Nikolayevich, there was no sign at all, which of course made some people assume he was guilty. At first some people said Nikolayevich must have done all the killings: the result of some unknown feud within the engineers. But I didn't buy that. Nikolayevich had been serving in the canteen on the evening of the first deaths (they gave the engineers cushy jobs like that when their services weren't needed). As such he had a cast-iron alibi. Unless of course more than one man was involved. But in that case who, and why? It was conceivable that Nikolayevich had brought in the Ripper to kill Borisovsky and Ivanov, and then silenced him so he couldn't talk. But why go to all that trouble if you were then going to hack up two other men yourself?

The more convincing and widely-held belief was that this was the expected revenge by the Mass Murderers for the killing of the Ripper. The idea was that the Ripper had killed Borisovsky and Ivanov - for pleasure or because he'd been told to by some devil in his soul. The remaining engineers had agreed between themselves to kill the Ripper. (With the tools at their disposal, breaking into the punishment barracks would've been easy.) Then the Mass Murderers had collectively punished the engineers.

The only problem with this interpretation, to my mind, was the similarity between the types of killing. They could've all been copycats, of course. But all my experience told me that murderers - like artists - have their own different styles. And these killings all bore the same signature.

This led me to consider one final theory: that the entire thing was in fact a disguised rebellion. An attack on the authorities and the mine, by a party or group that was smart enough to realise two things. First, that that this was much easier than physical sabotage or an all-out attack on the guards. Second, that everyone would be distracted by the killing of the Ripper into dismissing the whole thing as an inter-barracks feud.

The commandant, though, wasn't subtle enough to think of that possibility. He simply had the guards search for Nikolayevich. Finally someone found a man's shoes caught in a thicket, about three hundred yards from the quarry. If they were Nikolayevich's that didn't bode well for him. It was forty below by now - colder in the wind. How far could a man go in that weather with no shoes? Eventually the blizzard strengthened again, and the search was called off.

I went to see the one remaining engineer, who I supposed was now also a suspect. But he was a pathetic old man cowering in bed in the sick-bay where he'd been for days. He was rolling around in his sheets, moaning that he was bound to be next.

Nikolayevich stumbled into camp a few hours later, in the last stages of hypothermia. His feet were ruined, of course, and at the very least he was going to lose his toes. More seriously, he appeared to have gone insane. He was mumbling incoherently that there was 'something in the lake'. They'd gone to look but been suddenly attacked in the dark. When he'd realised that his companions were dead he'd run for his life into the blizzard. He hadn't got a proper look at his attacker. But he'd heard a terrible high-pitched cry. And one other thing he kept saying: that the attacker was fast. Much faster than any man.

13 – From the Lower Depths

Yuri thought the 'high-pitched cry' was a clue. Some parties of 'Manslaughterers' gathering timber in the previous weeks spoke of hearing what they called 'the Screaming', deep out in the woods. It hadn't seemed important at the time, just the sort of stupid story that was always going round. But Yuri thought it fitted with what Nikolayevich had said, and that it might've been some sort of signal. It might even tie in with the screams that had been heard from the direction of the punishment block the previous night, which everyone had assumed was the Ripper dying. I thought it was inconclusive.

The detail about the killers' speed was more interesting. Eye-witnesses commonly exaggerate such things in their mind, especially when they don't get a proper look because they are themselves running for their lives. And after all Nikolayevich had managed to get away from his pursuer. But what struck me (though I'd no time to think it through properly) was the similarity of the description to something I'd read that spring.

As I said earlier, I was a favourite of the commandant. He would sometimes invite me round to his house for medical advice and conversation. He allowed me, in turn, to read from his 'library'. This ridiculous affectation consisted of Das Kapital and a few volumes of Lenin and Gorky, some well-thumbed pornographic French novels, an out-of-date almanac, and the last two parts of a three-volume 'Encyclopaedia of Siberia', which had clearly been issued as standard. Still, it was better than nothing - they were the only books for several hundred versts. It was the Encyclopaedia that fascinated me. It had long essays on the history and folklore of the region.

One of these essays concerned a mysterious incident in the Eighteen Sixties. That was the time when they exiled the Polish dissidents before the liquidation of the January Revolt. Of course their ringleaders had been dispatched by Muravyov the Hangman. But the rest were all sent to Siberia. Eighty thousand of them, poor buggers.

Anyway a group of the first of them out there – Polish and Lithuanian officers they were - had crossed from Port Baikal to the wild far shore of the lake to go prospecting for gold. There were six men in the expedition. They'd got lost in bad weather up near the north end of the lake, their boat had been crushed in the ice, and they had to make camp high up on an exposed plateau. First they ate the dogs and then they started to eat each other.'

The Englishman, who'd sat silent for a long while, at this point muttered something in disbelief.

'There's nothing like hunger to overcome scruples when it comes to cuisine.' Gorobets chuckled, 'I could tell you some stories from when I was in Leningrad, during the siege, that would make you shit yourself. And what do you think happened to your Captain Oates? I don't believe a word of Scott's journal. You can't understand: you've never felt real hunger.'

The Englishman made a disgusted groan.

'When it got down to the last four men, two of them – who were weaker than the others – could see the way things were going and didn't want to hang around long enough to end up in the pot. So they decided to make a break for it. They left early one morning and somehow got as far as the line of the forest up near the Selenga delta. There one of them could go no further. They'd heard strange sounds and were convinced something was following them through the woods. At first they thought it was the companions they'd left up on the plateau, but it can't have been: the other two were found in their camp the next spring, frozen to death. One of the escapees, though, in the last stages of exhaustion, somehow got back to Port Baikal. He said he'd hidden in a tree and watched as something - a devil he said - came out of the lake and ran after them, *much faster than they could out-run it.* It had killed his companion, mutilated him, and dragged his remains away. Naturally this was dismissed as the ravings of a dying madman. But what he said was so bizarre, and so vivid, that it stuck in my mind. And now it seemed similar to the case in hand, though I couldn't work out for the life of me what it meant.'

At this I finally summoned up the courage to speak. 'Could it have been the result of hallucinations? I've heard these are common amongst victims of exposure…'

Gorobets now fixed me with an intense stare, as if only then noticing me for the first time. The Englishman, too, seemed surprised. Gorobets was silent for a second or two as he weighed me up. Then he said:

'Yes, of course that's just what I thought - at first. Or perhaps derangement from liver-poisoning, brought about by the cannibalism. But it seemed worth following every lead, so I did some more research. And sure enough it wasn't the only story like that I found. The Encyclopaedia was written long before Ubiichogorsk was built, of course. But it had lots of information on the other, older settlements, down at the southern end of the lake. As I started to read into it I realised there were unexplained deaths going back even earlier. At least to the time of the Decembrists – the first generation sacrificed to Siberia. The cold killed hundreds of them, of course, and the crushing of all hope no doubt killed more. But when they were moved out to Baikal there were other deaths that were harder to explain. Hunting parties that went missing. Fishing boats that didn't come back, or were found deserted. The local Buryats had warned them not to build settlements by the lake, but they had no choice. It stopped at the end of their first full winter there. 1827, that was.

Before that, back in the days when Siberia was first explored, there were plenty of dark stories. Half-remembered, half-believed stories of expeditions that were lost. Expeditions which must've descended into exposure, cannibalism, and madness, out in the endless snow.

1827, 1860, and now 1926. Perhaps it was a coincidence or perhaps it was a pattern. I looked for anything similar in 1893. But that was the terrible winter when the line to the south was blocked and the ice-breakers frozen into port. That year they even laid tracks across the lake-ice to keep the trains running. Until the *Russiya* crashed through with the loss of everyone on it.

These disasters every generation surely can't just be coincidence. They suggest something that goes much deeper.

A pattern of monstrosity. As if the very land out here was cursed...

Anyway, the commandant was now furious. He had five bodies on his hands. (Well, parts of five bodies…). And with four of his engineers dead and the last two incapacitated, there was no way he'd be able to hit his mining quotas. This put him personally on the block. Worse still it seemed the killer was unafraid to strike every night. There was no telling where it would all end.

His instinctive response, as always, was collective punishment. Someone must know something, he reasoned, and if he applied enough pressure that someone would come forward. So he brought forward the curfew and reduced the food ration. Of course, what this actually invited was ridiculous denunciations between feuding barracks. Not to mention the beginnings of a serious hunger panic, which only inflamed the situation.

As for the prisoners, paranoia had set in. Men who thought they'd gone beyond fear now found themselves afraid of the dark. Two and a half thousand of the hardest men in Russia, and they were all scared now. Every man in there had a different theory. Most blamed the 'Mass Murderers', but they'd closed ranks. The different clans within the union were now at loggerheads. Fights were starting to break out, and order to break down.

One of the bosses of 'Rapists' threatened to kill me, saying he'd heard I was bitching out to the authorities. He told me to frame someone quickly to take the blame for it all - a low-life that no-one cared about. This would at least give the real killer a perfect chance to stop, and would prevent Ubiichogorsk from descending into civil war.

I gently tried to point out these dangers to the commandant. But my own stock with him had fallen considerably since locking up the Perm Ripper had made things worse. So I decided not to tell him that these weren't normal murders by normal murderers. That I was starting to doubt the killer was from Ubiichogorsk at all.

14 - A Night in the Death of Pyotr Petrovich

I decided on a different strategy. If we went wading back into the denouncements and theories in the camp we'd likely be lost in them for days, and we'd probably get our throats slit for our pains. Having talked it over with Yuri I decided instead to take a risk. I asked the commandant for permission to be let off the new curfew so we could move around camp that night. We would of course be happy to be under armed guard. This final suggestion, by the way, was as much to reassure us of our safety as to reassure the commandant of our good faith.

'You can have one man with you all night,' he eventually conceded. 'I need the rest with me to make sure there's no funny business from 'Mass Murderers', or whoever else was out killing last night. See what you can come up with. But if I don't have answers soon I'll give you both a hundred lashes.'

'A hundred this time?' said Yuri later. 'It's always nice to get a raise from the boss.'

Sure enough we were both issued with extra-thick bushlat jackets, that the guards had for night patrols in winter. We were also issued with Pyotr Petrovich. Pyotr was the most sullen and stupid of the guards. He viewed the whole idea with the same suspicion he viewed us. And he was understandably unhappy at the prospect of a freezing night babysitting two zeks. He'd doubtless have been even less pleased if he'd known what was in store.

Ubiichogorsk was more like a town surrounded by a fence than what you might think of a prison. There were streets of the single-storey barracks where we lived. There were other buildings which held the kitchens and canteens, the punishment cells, laundry, workshops, guardhouses, and so on. The commandant's house and the hospital stood some way further off, at the North and South ends of the town.

Soon after dark the other zeks disappeared into their barracks for the curfew. After that the only people on the streets were the guards on patrol. Naturally Ubiichogorsk had no electric lighting. So the streets were lit only by dim oil lamps in the barracks, and the lamps that the guards themselves carried with them. Through a combination of the visibility of these lights, and the stupid regularity of the guards' patrols, it was both quite easy and quite common for zeks to go about the town at night. But it was much harder to do so without your barracks mates knowing about it. The barracks themselves were long wooden buildings, with tiny gauze windows that let in the cold but never the light. They were hot in the summer and unbearably cold in the winter. They weren't properly ventilated so they stank. Needless to say they were infested with fleas, midges, bed-bugs and all sorts of other vermin. We lived communally in these barracks. Instead of beds they had long raised shelves down their length. The upper shelf was considered preferable and so reserved for the stronger men. The toilets were in outhouses round the back, so at night we had to use a bucket. All this meant that it was impossible to leave your barracks without being seen by dozens of people.

Of course it was harder still to get beyond the fence into the woods. Nor was it ever attempted, since there was really nowhere out there to go.

Once the coast was clear Yuri and I left the guardhouse and began to lead Pyotr on what he complained were crazy twists and turns around town. We avoided the main patrol routes and poked round the spots where we knew people might actually go at night. We spent time crouched and listening in dark corners from which we could see the blind spot between 'Rapists' and 'Military Murderers', the alleyways behind Laundry Street where the washing blocks abutted 'Manslaughterers' and 'Fratricides', and the dark space behind the canteen bins and 'Honour Killers North' that was often used for certain midnight dealings, particularly in summer. Finally, we crept up on the ring of guards keeping watch on 'Mass Murderers'.

Yuri puffed and whispered, under his breath: 'Isn't it funny how easily you can see them all. And they're not even covering the route over the roof of 'Bandits'!'

By midnight we'd trudged all the way down to the hospital, where we'd gone inside for half an hour to rest and warm up. We'd only been challenged once, and that was because Pyotr slipped over and cursed loudly. We'd neither seen nor heard anything suspicious. Once we were warm we went back outside and picked our way right round the other side of the permanent punishment block. A deeper blackness showed where its shattered door still stood open. After what we knew had happened in there, nothing on Earth would have made us go inside at night. Finally we crept all the way past the commandant's house to the very north side of the town. We crouched there in the silent darkness until the cold became unbearable.

'Right', I said, with us much authority as I could, 'now let's go through the gate and walk to the mine.'

Yuri looked at me but was smart enough to play along as if this was indeed an obvious next step.

To my surprise Pyotr merely grunted and cocked his rifle, but didn't object. I think he thought that at least a brisk walk would be warmer than all this creeping and crouching. He led us through the gate and then followed us North towards the mine, keeping ten yards behind us with his gun trained on our backs. He did, however, insist on us re-attaching our fetters, which we'd been allowed to loosen whilst moving silently around the camp, but which now reduced us to a slow and noisy walk. He also made Yuri carry his paraffin lamp, though he agreed we could keep it turned off.

'Phew! If I'd realised how easy this was I wouldn't have tried such a stupid escape plan', said Yuri. 'It seems a man can practically walk out of Ubiichogorsk at leisure.'

'Maybe we should.'

'Yes,' he said, 'but how far would we get before we were missed and the dogs were sent after us? Besides, where is there to go?'

'If we overwhelmed Pyotr we could run to the lake, walk back backwards in our own footsteps, hide in a deep chamber of the mine til they called off the dogs, and walk out next night at our own leisure.'

'Fair enough if we had accomplices outside', said Yuri, 'or if only we'd had the foresight to stash some food. But they searched us so thoroughly earlier they'd have found a tiny morsel, even if I'd hidden it in my stomach.'

'Yes I'm starving too. At least we're let off normal duties.'

'Well, you know what they say: 'You can't both have the lambs alive and the wolf full.' Still, this jaunt is better than lying in 'Politicals', scratching our fleas.'

I'd been taking us north through the woods towards the mine, keeping the main path about twenty yards to our left. To our right, where the coastline bowed somewhat in-land, we could see a silver streak where the moonlight shone on the ice of the lake. We were effectively re-tracing the route the engineers had taken the previous night. There was nothing unusual that I could see or hear. But then I wasn't entirely sure what we were looking for. Already we could see ahead of us the deeper blackness that marked out the entrance to the mine. It was just a large open mineshaft angled into a slight swelling of the ground, with a clearing around it where the zeks had chopped back the trees. I knew that inside there was a small flat area where equipment was stored and then the entrances to various shafts that led off and down in different directions.

I hated the mine more than anything, and always did everything I could to stay out of it. It was bad enough when I had to go down to help victims of bad air. Worse still when I had to treat men they pulled out from a deep tunnel collapse. Of all the things I hated about Ubiichogorsk, it was the mine I most feared. I suppose it was the horror of being closed in. Down there in the dark a man simply couldn't *breathe*.

When we were about a hundred yards short of the entrance Pyotr called out to us to wait: he'd stopped for a piss. He'd first allowed us to walk a bit further on. He no doubt wanted to keep a greater distance between us than before, so that he'd have time to take up his rifle again if we rushed him. This meant we were probably forty or fifty yards ahead. It was almost pitch black in the forest. We could barely make out the deeper shadow that showed where he was standing. Once we stopped walking there was no noise except the occasional creaking of fir trees under the snow.

Yuri looked at me and tutted (this was the third time Pyotr had needed a piss that night). He'd just opened his mouth to say something when suddenly there was a scream from behind us.

15 – The Ninth Circle

In fact there were three screams. I could distinguish them by their pitch and intensity as one turned into another. The first was a scream of extreme terror and pain. Then there was the death-scream. Then finally the animal scream of tidal air escaping from ruptured lungs. Pyotr was clearly a goner – by the sound of it beheaded.

'Shit!' cried Yuri. 'Quick! Into the mine!'

What he didn't think of, though, were his fetters. These ruled out anything faster than a jog. I decided I had to get mine off. So I didn't immediately set off after Yuri. Instead I dropped down and took the pin out of its hiding place in my shoe. I tried to slide it into the clasp of the fetter where it attached round my right ankle. The screams behind us were cut off in a fury of wet crunching sounds that were presumably the mutilation of Pyotr's body. I fumbled in the dark and dropped the damned pin. Yuri was already half-way to the mine shaft. Too late for a change of plan. By now I was panicking like a child and swearing like a sailor. I threw off my gloves and felt on the ground at my feet. Finally I found the pin and picked it up again. The sounds behind me suddenly stopped. I looked up. My fingers, numb with the cold, were almost useless as I tried to get the pin into the clasp. A black shadow I couldn't make out now rose up where Pyotr had stood. I somehow managed to free the clasp. Looking up again I saw it turn and start running towards me.

I slid my right ankle out of the fetter and - without bothering to undo my left – I charged after Yuri. I had to run legs apart to avoid tripping over the fetter that was still attached to my left foot. But still I overtook Yuri just as we got to the mine. The figure behind us, though, seemed to move with dreadful speed. In spite of our head-start it was already right behind us. I couldn't turn round to look at him, but there was something weird in the way that he moved. He clearly had no intention of stopping at the entrance to the mine. This meant that even when we got there we had to run straight on in at full speed. The utter blackness of the mine came over us. Our eyesight was now useless. We were like men who were suddenly blinded and then forced to charge down a mountain. And now he was on us.

It was weeks since I'd been in the mine. My memory of spaces has never been good. Yuri worked here every day and knew the layout of the entrance by instinct. But my fetters were half off. In the end it was this advantage that saved me, and doomed Yuri. Running blindly on with my arms outstretched, I veered right - partly in the hope that a last-minute change in direction might save me from our pursuer - partly because I remembered there was a side tunnel somewhere that led off almost horizontal.

Yuri did the same - no doubt on the same instinct. But I was a couple of paces ahead of him when our pursuer caught up with us. I tripped on some boxes or some sort of equipment but managed to recover. But Yuri - either because his fetters had caught on the same obstacle, or because he'd been hit from behind - went straight over, careered into me and sent us both flying into a wall. I struck my head hard on something and then the ground disappeared beneath me. Either I'd forgotten the layout of the mine or a new shaft had been sunk from the side of the main chamber, because suddenly we were falling. I landed, very painfully, on my arse. Yuri landed on top of me, and more awkwardly. He was somehow still clutching the lamp, which hit me in the face. In fact, I later realised, we'd only fallen a couple of yards. But these things are much worse in the dark.

We were on a sloping floor but by now I was completely disorientated. I stood up and felt a shooting pain in my ankle which made me sink back on one knee. As I did this I looked up. It was pitch black so God knows what I expected to see. But to my horror there a few feet above me I could see two eyes staring down at me. Worse still, they were getting bigger. Whoever they belonged to was lowering himself down the shaft towards us. I grabbed Yuri, who felt wet and was moaning. But in spite of the fact he was clearly injured, he growled:

'This way, into the tunnel.'

Half scrabbling, half rolling down the slope we came to what seemed like a wall of rock. But Yuri, now behind me, grabbed my hair and pushed me down into it face-first. Sure enough there was a tiny cleft at ground-level. It was too low to crawl into on hands and knees. But by lowering myself onto my belly and reaching forwards I realised I might just get my head in. I begged Yuri to find another way but he shoved me hard from behind. I *swam* forward into it, with the ceiling scraping my back. I kept going in face-first until my head got jammed into the crevice and I couldn't go any further. Behind me Yuri kept coming, trapping me and grinding my face into the rock. I screamed at this and Yuri stopped pushing. But I could still hear our pursuer, right behind us. I was now completely stuck, with Yuri's weight blocking me in. It was impossible to move or breathe. Then it was Yuri's turn to scream, loud and continuous, whilst I sobbed with panic and tried but failed to turn round. The back of my leg touched something cold and damp with what felt like slicked-down hair.

Just then there was a sudden blinding light and a third scream – guttural and unearthly – that seemed to split the very rock. This was followed by a desperate scrabbling and a final cry, further off above us. Then we were alone.

After a few seconds my eyes adjusted to the brightness. Yuri had somehow managed to use his cigarette lighter to light up the lamp. The brightness must've shocked and blinded our assailant even more than it did us, and he'd retreated at least as far as the first chamber of the mine.

I could now see where we were. There was a long very low tunnel that led off from the lower chamber we'd fallen into. In fact it went some way. If I'd crawled further to the left we'd have been in the tunnel proper and I could have kept going. Instead I'd pressed myself into the very end of it where it shallowed out and formed a corner with the wall of the chamber and got stuck. This trapped Yuri behind me between me and our attacker, who had in turn had been unable or unwilling to follow us into this tight spot, but had somehow lashed out in malice or frustration into the space we were crouched in. He'd caught Yuri full in the stomach with something very sharp, which had pierced him right the way through his abdomen. Blood was pouring from the wound, and from others on his back that looked like deep scratch or stab marks. I could see at once that he would die within at most a few hours.

Fortunately so could he:

'Gorobets - the bastard got me.'

'Yes.'

'I'm for it, aren't I?'

'Yes.'

'Tell me at least he didn't get you?'

'No', I said, 'I'm fine apart from my ankle. I'm sorry. You saved me. Until he comes back.'

'Don't worry, we can go further down there – I don't think he'd come after us into the tunnel.'

'Why not? Did you see who it was?'

'It was… black… *so fast!*'

'Yes.'

'He got me pretty bad. It really hurts.'

'I know. I'm sorry. But even if we could get you back to the sickbay…'

'Oh I'm not going back out there with that devil around. Will you wait here with me?'

'Yes.'

Not that I was likely to go anywhere – given who was waiting for me above.

I could see there was enough oil in the lamp to last until morning. There seemed to be nothing for it but to lie there in that hellish tunnel with Yuri whilst he bled out, and then hope help would arrive from the camp when it got light. We lay there together in silence for a moment. Then Yuri said:

'I feel cold.'

'It's because of the bleeding.'

'Did you see its *eyes*?'

'Yes.'

'But how could we?'

'I don't know. I don't understand it. They were somehow reflecting the sheen of the mica. Did you see who he was?'

'Oh it wasn't human.'

He was rambling now – his mind was wandering.

'I want you to take this', he said.

He reached into his pocket and took out his cigarette lighter. This was a valuable object in Ubiichogorsk.

‘I can’t take this’, I said, holding my hand out for it. I instinctively started to calculate how much food it was worth. Starving men are rarely sentimental. The next thing did make me pause, though. He opened up the secret pocket stitched into the seam of his coat and took out the photo of his wife.

‘And this’, he said. ‘It won’t be any use to me where I’m going. I won’t ever see her again now. It might sound stupid but I’d like someone to be thinking of her from time to time.’

He absolutely insisted I take it, pressing it into my hands. I promised to keep it safe. Thank God I did, as you’ll see. Then we embraced and wished each other good luck.

He was silent for a long time and I thought he’d lost consciousness. Then some time later he smiled and said, weakly:

‘Who’d have believed it?’

Then he died.

I lay there with him for hours, listening to the great thick silence of the mine. Finally I turned down the lamp and could see the very faint light filtering down the shaft from the entrance chamber. That told me that above ground it was dawn. But I was still too frightened of what might be waiting for me in the main chamber above to dare moving. It was another hour or so after that before I heard voices and shouts from above, and called up to them. The guards who’d presumably found Pyotr had at last thought to look in the mine. I refused to move until they’d taken out Yuri. Then I let them drag me back to town.

16 – Live Bodies

They chucked me in the Isolator for the rest of the day. Then finally they hauled me before the commandant. I remember he was eating his dinner. A day spent prodding my wounds had revealed I was badly bruised, but otherwise intact. The damage to my ankle was just a bad sprain. My eye was swollen up from where I'd gone face-first into the wall. But my biggest discomfort by this time was actually hunger. You can get used to anything except hunger. And I was in danger of getting too hungry to be able to think clearly.

'So it was you all along, was it, Gorobets?' snarled the commandant. 'I might've known. You were the only one it could have been, really, since only you had a pass to move round freely. I'm told you've no alibi for any of the nights in question. And to think I ever let you into my house. What you did to poor Pyotr was disgusting. Too bad about the other zek. His pardon just came through.'

He laughed and tossed me an official chit tersely noting an amnesty for Yuri. It was dated from the previous summer, weeks before the last barge had left for Irkutsk. Holding that back for another season was his idea of a great joke. He turned to hand his secretary the half-eaten plate of tinned beetroot he'd been gobbling. As he did so I folded the sheet and tucked it into my sleeve.

'It wasn't me,' I said, as calmly as I could. I looked forlornly at the wasted food. 'If it was me, how did I do it? And why the hell would I have killed Yuri?'

'It seems your accomplice Yuri Melnik was injured by Pyotr in the struggle,' he said.

'With what weapon? And what weapon did I use on Pyotr? And why would I have stayed with Yuri's body?'

He stared at me stupidly for a few seconds. Then he said, with a certain desperation:

'How should I know? You're the convicted murderer. Anyway, if it wasn't you then who the devil was it?'

'I don't know. It was dark. I couldn't see anything. If you think it was me then lock me up. But I assure you the killings will continue until we get to the bottom of this.'

'Oh believe me, we will lock you up,' he said, uncertainly: 'You'll have a guard just to yourself. If there's no funny business tonight then we'll know it was you. You'll be shot in the morning.'

With that I was dragged away to the hospital. My words must have had some effect, as at least I was spared the cells. If there was another murder that night he needed me fit to resume my duties. So I was allowed to treat my wounds, but then tied down to a bed in the operating room, with a guard posted at the door.

The commandant was certain the culprit was a zek. With twenty three hundred murderers to choose from, why look anywhere else for a killer? But I'd made him doubt it was me. And now he had a guard's death to avenge. He knew that everyone in Ubiichogorsk was waiting for his response. He chose to do the worst thing possible: to encourage the guards to carry out random beatings. They were frightened and very angry anyway, and already taking it out on the rest of us. Official clearance let them off the leash. Soon the camp was in uproar. Teams of guards were ranging through the barracks beating up zeks. From what I later gathered, by late afternoon things were coming to a head. The 'Politicals' were seriously contemplating fighting back. By evening the whole town was at boiling point. One way or another, there was going to be more blood.

Perhaps for this reason, and no doubt after an emergency conference amongst themselves, several barracks bosses came forward and suggested to the authorities that the Kazakhs might be responsible. Most of these Kazakhs had been notorious *basmachi* bandits back in Turkestan. They'd formed their own group in the camp and stood well apart from the others. Denouncing them was technically a breach of the code - even a declaration of war on 'Bandits' barracks. But many people thought the code barely applied to foreigners anyway. And the Kazakhs were unpopular even with the rest of 'Bandits', which was badly divided along language and religious lines.

The commandant was tempted by this suggestion that the Kazakhs were to blame. He was now worried the murders were cover for anti-revolutionary sabotage, or even the prelude to a full-scale prison rising. It was an unusually brutal form of resistance, if it was. But then these Kazakhs were viewed as little better than savages, even by the wild standards of Ubiichogorsk; and they were especially despised by the commandant. They all gave each other alibis. But that only suggested that, if they were in it at all, they were in it together.

Of course, the sabotage theory would soon turn out to be nothing but a 'false Dmitry'. As I was tied up in the sickbay these Kazakhs were locked up in their barracks, with ten guards posted to them at all times. And yet - as you will see - the killings continued.

Determined to stop the killer or killers striking again that night, the commandant had all of the barracks locked, and guards posted to each of them to keep watch. They did head-counts every hour. I was stuck in the annex to the sickbay, tied painfully to the operating table. Even with his resources stretched to breaking and me rendered utterly helpless, the commandant still posted a guard to sit outside the door, keeping one eye on me and the other on the men in their beds in the main ward-room.

The sickbay stood some way apart from the other buildings, away at the far south corner of town. This distancing was deliberate in case of quarantine (thanks to the poor food and hygiene there were regular outbreaks of Typhus and other diseases). The commandant didn't care about survival rates, so 'malingerers' and 'lazy Oblomovs' weren't allowed in. Only cases that were probably incurable were granted the dubious luxury of staying there. That meant that, apart from the dying Nikolayevich and the old engineer, there was no-one else in there at that time. Neither of them were in any fit state to cause any trouble, or even get out of their beds. And with me tied down helplessly next door we'd been left with only one guard. The commandant clearly hadn't expected any attack to come from outside a building rather than inside.

It was shortly after Midnight that we first heard 'The Screaming'. It was more of a cry – a strange voice on the wind. High pitched, insistent, and gloating. It chilled you to the very bone. I immediately recognised it as the noise I'd heard in the mine. It seemed to be coming from the woods, but also to move. To be distant at first, then closer to. It was certainly impossible to get any clear sense of the direction it was coming from. We heard it three times over the next hour or so. After each time the guard and I looked at each other uncertainly.

Then, just after two, we heard it outside the window.

The guard had just sat back down after pacing around the ward. As soon as we heard something outside he leaped up to go and investigate.

'Untie me!' I begged him in a whisper. 'Don't go outside!'

But he left me there helpless and rushed off into the main sickbay. Utterly unable to move except arch my back and strain without hope at the leather straps that held me, I craned my head to the side to try to look through the door. From my position spread-eagled on the operating table I could see nothing of the neighbouring room. But the door was wide open and I could hear everything that happened over the next few dreadful minutes.

As soon as the guard left my sight there was crash and the sound of splintering wood. This was immediately followed by the screams of the three men next door - drowning out the noise of a violent struggle - which were silenced one by one until the despairing sobs of the last man living were finally cut off with a strangulated choke. For a few seconds there was silence. Then, quiet but distinctive, cautious foot-falls on broken glass and – worst of all - the sound of guttural breathing. It was coming towards the open door to my room.

17 – Gorobets and the Master

An odd shadow fell across the open doorway. I tried to stop breathing. I lay there helpless waiting for the end. This struck me as a damned annoying way to die. But just then a warning siren sounded. The shadow disappeared. I heard shouts coming towards me from the main camp. I screamed at the top of my lungs. The deputy commandant burst in with a dozen guards. Evidently now satisfied of my innocence they untied me and I was able to stagger next door and see for myself what had happened.

The doors of the sickbay had been ripped off their hinges. The main ward was like a charnel house. The guard had been caught under the debris and then apparently crushed before he could raise his weapon and get off a shot. The other two had been butchered in their beds. Blood was sprayed all over the floor and walls of the room. Enough body parts were left to account for all three of them. And Nikolayevich - the only other man, remember, who'd survived the killer - was now smeared over the ward in a dozen pieces (with quite a few important bits missing, too).

At least it was now obvious to everyone with a brain that the killer or killers weren't from Ubiichogorsk. Apart from me all the convicts had been locked in their huts and accounted for by the guards. And, since they'd all been keeping watch on the various barracks, all the guards had been accounted for to the satisfaction of the convicts.

This posed a real conundrum. If it wasn't someone from Ubiichogorsk then who the hell was it? Could it be White partisans who had somehow hidden out in the Wilds? But then they'd neither used guns nor taken them from the guards they'd killed. And in any case, there'd been no partisan activity for years. How would they have survived so long, and why strike now?

I was the first to point all this out to the commandant. I also noted the other surprising thing: the tracks in the snow. There weren't any. Or rather the snow was once more disturbed, but not in a way that made sense. As on the very first morning, something had made some marks. But they were hard to see - more like a general scuffing and flattening.

It seemed care had been taken to cover the tracks. But then again not that much care. For with a little patience it was perfectly possible to follow these scuff marks. They led us a crazy dance in circles round the wood. But we were eventually able to follow them all the way. They led to the shore of the lake. There they stopped all together. Standing there on the beach and looking out we noticed that the ice out in the lake was broken up. I stared into the water. Baikal is ice cold, blueish, and clear. But in that winter twilight it was black.

The commandant was also looking out over the lake.

'I doubt anyone could've got over this last night', he said. 'Or at least, if the ice-cracks were recent and they did, they wouldn't be able to get far going back. Which means anyone who's come across the lake to attack us is still nearby. But in that case, why would they've gone down to the water?'

We looked across at Dianda. The ice in the narrow trench between us and it was intact. It looked like it was still possible to get across to the island.

'It's the best lead we have', said the commandant. 'It must be the primitives.'

No, I thought, but I'd bet they know about it.

The Buryat tribesmen were still very superstitious. And now they thought their gods had deserted them, as they were no longer allowed to sacrifice to the lake. I later found out that was an important part of their religion. They had a sprinkling of Buddhism and a Communist veneer, but really at heart their beliefs were still Animist. They thought that the Gods come from the Sky. That unhappiness comes from Moscow. And that evil comes from the lake.

The greatest of all evils they called the Vegohzi. In their language I believe it meant 'devil'. They worshipped the most disgusting gods. Five-headed demons that lived in the wind. Monsters with twenty four arms and a necklace of skulls. The mummified bodies of their own ancestors. But for all that they were afraid of the Vegohzi.

The Vegohzi was a great devil from the deepest of the ninety nine hells. But it came to spawn in the lake for a season, every third year of the rat. [The Buryats had an eleven year cycle - like the Mongols' but with no year of the monkey, which was an animal of which they had no conception.] They'd try to appease it by leaving reindeer tied up to trees as a sacrifice. There were rumours they even sacrificed their children. But it seemed this was more in hope than expectation. So when the Vegohzi was due they'd move their families and herds well away from the shore.

Of course all this was now pagan superstition and strictly forbidden by the Party. And besides, Russia was starting to starve to prove that collectivisation worked. You couldn't just let a whole tribe leave their farm. The government were practising for the Terror Famines. The indigenous peoples felt it before anyone else. As in Ukraine later on, they ate their daughters first.

Anyway, these Buryats wouldn't go near the lake when they thought the Vegohzi was there. Their shamans wouldn't allow it. But now the Party was *forcing* them to stay.

They'd complained to the governor of Irkutsk Oblast, and even sent someone to warn *us* to leave. The commandant revealed all this now, though it was the first I'd heard of it. Five weeks ago one of their shamans had ridden into town and suggested at least lighting fires, for the Vegohzi feared nothing but fire. He'd explained that it was in Baikal that season and that it was hungry.

Of course the commandant had merely laughed all this off at the time, but now it didn't seem quite so funny. It looked to him like some sort of warning to get off their ancestral land – and proved they'd crossed the lake and were attacking us. The only thing he hated more than us zeks were aboriginals. To be fair, the loyalty of these Buryats to the state was highly questionable. And who knows what dying men will do for their savage religions.

The commandant was really frightened now for his own safety. The tribesmen had a fearsome reputation, and it was known that they didn't take prisoners. He was all for fortifying the camp, taking back the tree-line, and digging in until a relief force could get through from Irkutsk in the spring. With all his engineers dead there wouldn't be much more mining that season anyway, and at least now he had a suspect to blame that didn't implicate him in incompetence. He positively leapt at the theory. It's amazing what desperate men will allow themselves to believe, rather than confront anything that would change their World view.

He was much more reluctant, though, to risk more men investigating. I begged him to let me go with half the guards and the dog teams and follow the tracks, strange and disturbed as they were, to see if they continued across the ice to the island. If the killer was hiding on Dianda then it would be better to go over in force and flush him out during daylight than wait to be picked off one by one at night. I felt ready to risk anything to stop the killings.

He refused – he was scared senseless by now, as I say. If there was a war party of Buryat bandits camped out on the island, he feared he might attack them with all his guards and still lose. And there was the prospect of a prisoner uprising to think about too. I argued with him for an hour. Eventually, 'as a favour to an educated man', he agreed to let me go with just two guards. They were the most useless pair he could think of. Men he must've felt were expendable. It wasn't that he thought we'd be able to deal with the Buryats. It was more that, if we didn't come back, at least that would confirm the new theory to his satisfaction, and he would know for sure that he was under siege.

The guards didn't like it much either: being sent to look for killers with a killer for company. They each had one rifle, which they kept trained on me in case I tried anything. Besides that they had a two-man dog-sled with camping equipment, food, and dynamite from the mine. The point of the dynamite was simple: if they were attacked by superior numbers and had to retreat on the sled, they could blow the ice behind them to cut off the island. Naturally, what happened to me in that circumstance wasn't important. I was to go ahead as un-armed bait.

18 – Notes from Underwater

We set out an hour before dawn, which would be about ten by that time of year. We knew we only had four hours of daylight. The idea was to explore the southern half of the island whilst it was light. If we hadn't found what we were looking for we'd camp overnight. And if we were still alive we'd search the northern half next day.

As we stepped out on the ice it was only just thick enough to take our weight. There were worrying fissures and cracks everywhere, and the occasional larger hole – air holes for seals, we thought. The island was really a volcanic mountain that rose out of the lake's deepest trench at the fault line: right above the abyss. Beneath our feet there was a thin crust of creaking ice - and below that a full verst of black water – and under that the earth itself was a fragile crust. At one stage the sled broke through the ice, though with the help of the dogs we were able to get it out. Then we gingerly picked our way across to the island. One of the guards thought he saw something moving under the ice. I explained it was a great air bubble, trapped as the water froze and expanded, and now moving under our weight.

When we got to the island we hurried straight off the beach and into the treeline. The guards made me go ahead of them, unarmed, in case the killers were waiting ahead. I was half expecting them to finish me off themselves there and then, so they could flee back to the safety of the camp and claim an ambush. All day I crept through that forest, imagining myself in the sights of hostile guns from behind and God-only-knows what in front.

We spent the next few hours exploring the southern slopes but finding nothing. There might have been some scuffed markings by the water but if there were they didn't lead inland. Everywhere else the snow was pristine. Towards dusk we reached the top of what seemed the main summit. But now we could see it was a false summit. There was a taller mountain beyond, invisible from Cape Kotelnikovsky, with a sort of low valley between them almost at lake-level. Hence, presumably, 'Devil's saddle'. Or at least, hence 'saddle'.

This saddle was at least somewhat sheltered so we decided to make camp, about fifty yards from the water. It was almost dark now. The rest of the island to the North East would have to wait until the next day.

The guards unloaded the equipment and tied up the dogs. I noticed they were excitable and nervous. I didn't like the idea of camping so close to the lake. I pointed out that here we'd be visible to anyone on the unexplored inner slope of the second mountain. It'd be much better to camp somewhere on higher ground. The guards debated this crossly between themselves. Then they agreed to scout out the further slope before we built a fire.

Of course this involved me once more marching off unarmed into the face of Christ-knows what. To be fair, the first guard came with me to 'keep an eye', whilst the other sat and smoked nervously by the dogs. I crept up the steep wooded slope, trying to be as quiet as possible, and moving awkwardly to keep the weight off my sore ankle. Every few steps I stopped to listen. From time to time snow would fall from the branches of trees under its own weight. Other than that the forest was silent.

When I'd got about half way up I suddenly slipped, and went cursing arse-over-heels back down the slope, eventually coming to rest in a thorn bush. It must've been audible from many versts away. It was dark by now, and not easy to see far in the woods, though a bright moon sometimes emerged from high scudding clouds. I'd slipped perhaps thirty feet past the guard who'd once been behind me. Trying to catch up with him, I scrambled up a scree of loose rocks and onto a sort of clearer shoulder of ridge, from which I had a good view of the scene.

The dogs had started up, presumably at the sound of my fall – at least, that's what I thought at first. And it's clearly what the second guard thought too. I could see that, down below in the clearing, he'd cocked his gun, advanced a few paces, and was crouched staring up in my direction. I thought about calling out to reassure him, but I confess I decided: 'bugger it – let him stew'.

I could see the first guard above me to the left, on a spur of a clear plateau. I was waving at him to reassure him I was alright, and that I wasn't trying to get away. But instead of waving back, he was standing stock still as if frozen with horror. And he wasn't looking in the direction I'd gone, or ahead of him up the slope, but staring in disbelief back down at the saddle. Following the direction of his gaze I suddenly saw what he'd seen and the guard below hadn't. About twenty yards out from the shore there was a dark shape that must've been a hole in the ice. But it seemed to be getting larger and more irregular.

Then the moon came out and showed it properly. I can barely describe the horror of what I could see. It was a creature – an appalling creature - hauling itself out of the lake, clambering through the ice-hole. It was black and wet and bigger than a man. Its slimy hair glistened in the moonlight. But from that distance I could make out little else. It now set off silently on a crouching run over the ice.

In seconds it had reached the shore-line and was galloping silently over the snow towards the back of the second guard below. The dogs were really going mad now, but the more they barked the more intently the man peered up the slope towards us, not realising what was closing with him from behind. The first guard shouted a warning, but of course that merely distracted his colleague even more from the direction of danger.

The unspeakable thing was on him now – without breaking its crouching stride it arrived right behind him. It drew itself up to its full height just as he sensed it and turned round and looked up at it. Then it pounced. I could hear an 'Ugh!' of surprise as he was buried under it. Then I saw what looked like his arms being torn off and flung many yards through the air.

Once it had done this, though, it put down the wreckage of the guard and looked around. The dogs were howling but it wasn't interested in them. Instead it was looking up the slope towards where the first guard had shouted his warning. He saw this too, and turned up the slope and ran. But the awful creature was after him at a pace he could never beat. As I lost it in the trees I thought for a second about burying myself in the snow where I was, and hoping it hadn't seen or heard me. But then I thought it was bound to *smell* me – after all, I hadn't had a bath for twelve years. And I remembered how it had hunted me and Yuri down, even into the mine.

There was just one chance and I seized it by instinct. There was no point trying to run away uphill, that much was clear – besides, with my swollen ankle I wouldn't make it far. It would take a good minute to catch the first guard up the steep slope of the mountain. So while it was chasing him, I charged *down*-hill towards it, sliding straight down the slope back to the saddle. I was counting on it's taking us one at a time. Sure enough I tumbled out of the forest onto the flat to find myself alone. My plan had been to make a dash for the dead man's gun. But I could see at once his mangled corpse was too far from where I'd come out. It's a funny thing, but that moment I lost all hope of my own survival and I felt a great sense of liberation. There was only one thing left to do. I went for the dynamite.

I'd got as far as the sled before I heard the second guard's shots, then his screams. He went on screaming for a while - the thing seemed to be deliberately taking its time with him. But in taking so long to die, he did me a favour. I had time to rip open the box with the dynamite. Not time to fix the detonators, mind. But time to find Yuri's lighter. And since survival looked impossible I determined on a different plan. If I stood and let it come for me and waited til it was right on top of me, I might be able to blow us both sky high. At least I'd spare any more victims and rid the World of its evil.

The worst of it was getting the damned tapers to light, and then just standing there, watching them burn down one by one, then pinching them out and lighting another one. I guess it took it no more than a minute for the awful creature to get back down the slope, but it seemed longer than all the time I'd served. Now there was nowhere for me to go, and nothing left to do except to die.

When it finally appeared it wasn't from the direction I expected. In fact it came out of the trees nearest to me – it had stalked me to get the quickest line for the kill. Then when it broke from cover it was on me so fast I could barely get my next taper lit, let alone get a good look at it. I even fluffed my last words again. This time, to be fair, I couldn't think of anything heroic. I just shouted 'bugger!' as I got the stub of fuse I was holding lit and tossed it into the box with the rest of the dynamite.

For the second time I made an explosion I expected to kill me and for a second time I somehow survived. This time, though, it did really hurt me. It must have blown me twenty feet in the air. I landed very painfully, and would've been seriously injured if the deep snow hadn't broken my fall. I still have splinters from that box in my face after all these years. They ache like hell in the cold.

For a moment I was blinded by the blast. I tried to stand and force my eyes to work but they wouldn't. The thing was screaming a scream that practically shattered my ears. But the scream was moving away from me not towards me. By the time I could make anything out it had loped back off to the edge of the lake. It crashed straight through the ice and swam off – as fast in the water as on land. I don't know how badly I wounded it, but I certainly gave it the shock of its life.'

Gorobets paused to shake his head in wonder. The Englishman scoffed. I said:

'And that was the Vegohzi?'

'No. That's when I *saw* the Vegohzi.

19 – Never Rehabilitated

There was a great disturbance out on the lake. The whole island seemed to shake – at first it was like one of the Baikal earthquakes, from the grinding of the tectonic wound that forms the lake. But then water started pouring out through the fissures and holes and then there was a great splintering of the ice. The surface bubbled and swelled. What I saw next was…'

Then he shook his head and swore and turned away.

'Go on!' we both begged him.

'What I saw was – the top of a huge black shape - writhing… coming up from the depths - smashing its way up through the ice. There were... I realised that what I'd fought wasn't the beast itself but some sort of monstrous parasite that lived on it. Or one of its many offspring. For they seethed all over its smooth grey-black skin, crawling in and out of crevasses along its flank. It was impossible to make out its shape - they were in a different form from it – but as for the thing itself, I could get no clear sense of its anatomy. Its size was incredible. It was inconceivable. A blasphemy. Most of it was under water, and what I could see was swarming with creatures like the one that now joined it. Hell is a beast with other beasts inside it. After a moment it sank and disappeared again under the ice.'

Here he stopped talking. There was a stunned silence in the carriage. He looked as if he was going to cry, either with wonder or relief. Eventually I asked him:

'What happened next?'

'Oh, well I'd reconciled myself with death. And then I found myself somehow alive; truly alive – for the first time in years. It suddenly occurred to me there was nobody on Earth who knew that. 'For all they know I'm dead', I kept saying to myself. I'd had enough of their justice. I had the dogs. I had the sled. I had camping equipment and food for three men. I even had a gun. I'd never get a chance like this again. And now I felt ready to take it. I think it was only when I let my last hope go that I felt free to risk living, and worthy of being free.

So I decided to make a break for the South.

If the Vegohzi let me off the island there was no reason to return to Ubiichogorsk. Clambering back up the slope I found the body of the first guard. He'd been stabbed through and bloodied. But the creature – doubtless eager to get me – hadn't had time to do much more than devour his face. Even more than his colleague, he was unrecognisable. Beating myself against the cold, I stripped and swapped my clothes for his. Now if the authorities at Ubiichogorsk ever found him they'd assume he was me, and that he'd been killed or taken away elsewhere. They had no reason to look for either of us alive. In the pockets of his coat I found his papers, a wallet with a few roubles, and (the real lifesaver) a packet of cigarettes.

I un-tethered the dogs and we picked our way out onto the ice. Then I climbed in the sled and was away. The dogs ran like the wind when I gave them their head. They were as anxious to get away from that place as I was. We flew south on the ice all night and all the next day. Then I camped and rested the dogs, then did the same the next day and the day after that. Four or five days later, I think it was - just as the food was giving out - I rounded Listvyanka point into Port Baikal.

At the very outskirts of town I found a sort of tavern. A mad joy seized me and I went in for a drink. My first in thirteen years. It was worth another 'tenner' on its own. The whole Red Army couldn't have stopped me having that drink, though I half assumed they'd pick me up as soon as I'd finished it. But to my amazement nobody paid me any attention.

I'd had several days to think of a plan. My first thought was that Irkutsk was the murder capital of Russia. That'd been true before the War, anyway, when there were hundreds of murders a month. A man of my profession could do well here.

‘What profession is that?’ asked the Englishman: ‘Murderer?’

‘I meant an expert on murders. But I was still too close to Ubiichogorsk and Baikal. I longed to get as far away as possible, to somewhere where the sun shone and the ground wasn’t frozen. And anyway I needed a secure new identity. Fortunately my only friend had given me more than one gift that might save my life.

Here Gorobets took an old battered lighter out of the pocket of his coat and placed it on the seat beside him. Next he took out a yellowed paper that was headed ‘Notice of Pardon’. Then he felt inside an inner pocket and brought out a tiny black and white photograph, badly creased.

‘This is Mariya. I knew what she looked like. And I knew she lived in Yuri’s village outside Petersburg. I sold the dogs and caught the train back West. In a week I was walking up the path to Yuri’s old house. Look! – there was even the fir tree with the ribbons tied into it he’d so often told me of. Here was the little green wooden door. When I hammered on it it was opened by a woman. Her sad face was etched with anger and uncertainty. But I recognised her at once – she was if anything more beautiful than the photograph. My throat choked up with tears and all my words failed me, but I was able to hand over this lighter and this paper.

That was enough for her to let me in and listen to my story – the very story I’ve just told you. It was enough to have her take me in - first to hide me. And then, after we’d moved far away, to guarantee my new identity as her ‘pardoned’ husband. It was enough, eventually, when she’d finished grieving for Yuri, for her to become my wife in deed as well as name. From then on the World knew me as Yuri Melnik and I tried to live the life that had been taken from him. The name Gorobets I left behind on that island. And with it I left everything I had been. It was only my old skin I couldn’t shed, and these marks I have on it that are the stamp of the gulag. There is nothing I can do to get rid of those.

The year after my rebirth we went to Petersburg (it was called ‘Leningrad’ now, after that old zombie they keep on display) and laid a wreath at the graves of my parents, a wreath at the tomb of Count Varovsky, and a wreath where they’d buried the Countess. At each place I, Gorobets, murderer by profession and training, who had seen and endured enough horror to harden the heart of any man, broke down and sobbed like a baby.

I think it was only then it finally hit me. I was free.

20 – Unquiet Flows the Yenisei

'Every natural system has a top predator. The taiga and the steppes and the oceans all have theirs. A city must have a top predator - even a city of murderers. And the same is true of a nation. The more brutal the nation, the more monstrous that predator must be. It is to slander Nature to pretend She is benign. Abomination takes many forms, in beasts as in men. And that is true of *human* nature too. Any system that denies that is doomed to catastrophe.

My health was half-broken by Ubiichogorsk. So how have I survived so long? Well I had something else beyond happiness and hope to sustain me: I knew something that was known by no other man alive. And I knew I somehow had to live for thirty three years to prove it. I owed it to the World. I owed it to science. I owed it to all those who'd been killed.

Ubiichogorsk had gone. Where it once stood there was nothing but a wide area of strangely flattened trees that had died long ago. Needless to say I could not find it on any official record. It had simply disappeared from History.

And to my despair, before the third next year of the rat, they'd put in the dam across the Yenisei at Angara, where it drains from Lake Baikal towards the Northern Sea. There were no sightings of the Vegohzi around Baikal in '59. The lake was full of pollution now. I began to think the creature was extinct, and any remains hidden forever at the bottom of the lake, or deep under the arctic ice.

But elsewhere in Russia that year there was a strange rumour. You may have heard of that incident at the Dyatalov Pass in Sverdlovsk Oblast. Those nine skiers who were killed near lake Syakhl in the far North. The greatest un-punished mass-murder in Russian History. Well, the second greatest, I suppose. They never did find the culprit. But *I* know what happened. Because I went there too. As soon as the newspapers said the police had called off their investigation I travelled up to Syakhl. It took me two months to find it. But at last I caught what I was looking for...'

Here with trembling hands he reached into the other pocket of his coat and brought out a battered envelope, which he handed to the Englishman. In it were two dozen black and white photographs of a lake. They showed a great black shape out in the water. Sure enough, as you looked at them, grimy and well-thumbed as they were, your eye began to reconcile them with the vast monster Gorobets had described. I'm not a gullible woman, but I've never been impressed by any such things as I was impressed by these. It still makes me sick to remember it.

The Englishman, needless to say, wasn't having it. He scoffed at poor Gorobets and called him a hoaxer or a madman or an idiot.

Gorobets just shook his head sadly, and said:

'We mustn't cling to what we hope and believe against all new evidence.'

'You *claim* this is evidence', answered the Englishman, 'but it could've been fabricated, or… exaggerated… or distorted. That such a thing should continue into this century, and shouldn't be known to everyone in Russia – to everyone on Earth… that it shouldn't have mobilised humanity to defeat it as surely we should… you must take me for a fool.'

'A fool, yes', replied Gorobets, sadly: 'and the worst type of fool. Those who refuse to believe in evil are as dangerous as evil itself. You could stare it in the face and not recognise it. There's no evidence that could convince you, except being fed to the Vegohzi yourself. People believe what they want to believe. You don't want to believe that this ancient evil walks. I've only told you of twelve deaths. But I could tell you of another monster in Russia that, in our lifetime, has consumed twelve million men. Twelve million souls: catalogued, witnessed, widely reported – the evidence all there to been seen by anyone who wants to look at it. That I myself have seen it in its awful majesty. That I bear its fatal mark upon my skin. But that no-one talks of it and no-one thinks of it and there is no reckoning. And of course you wouldn't believe that either. The Vegohzi was real. I believe it lives to this day, hiding just out of sight. It will continue to live as long as the World denies it.'

At this point Gorobets got up and pushed the photographs into the Englishman's reluctant hands.

'Go on! Take them! Take them back to the West. Publish them! Make the World know what happened here.'

And with that Gorobets shrugged and walked out of the carriage.

As soon as he was gone the Englishman laughed joylessly and said:

'At first I thought the man was a drunk. Now I realise he was a lunatic.'

And with that he picked up the photos, went over to the window, and – before I could stop him - threw them out. The wind surging past the train whipped them out of his hand and back along the outside of the carriage and into the dark vastness beyond. There was nothing else to say. I stood up and left.

At this Polina stopped talking. Our compartment was still for a minute, and there was no sound except the snow thudding softly against the window. The Americans stared at each other wide-eyed. Then suddenly the carriage gave a lurch - the track ahead was at last cleared - and the train pulled slowly away into the night.

'What about you?' I asked our Russian room-mate. 'What did you think of... what Gorobets said?'

'Me?' Polina smiled her sad smile. 'I thought then what I still think today. That there has been real evil in the World. And if we are not careful it will return.'

'I've heard your story', I said. 'I will remember it.'

The City of Dreadful Night

East of Suez, some hold, the direct control of Providence ceases;
Man being there handed over to the power of the Gods and Devils of Asia'

The Mark of the Beast

'This is the full story I told on the train. I was in India at an academic conference, when I was told it by a clever and charismatic tour-guide. He had just showed us round the sights of Old Delhi. He was a gifted story-teller, and he made the tourist sights of that ancient city come alive. Later we bought him dinner in the old dining room at the Imperial. We were joking about how boring it must be to tour the same sights over and over, with demanding and ignorant Westerners. He laughed and gave a professional lie about how much he enjoyed meeting his clients.

'And', he added, 'I am always learning something new. Sometimes their stories are even better than mine.'

We pressed him for an example.

'Well,' he said, 'Just last month I heard something ghastly and bamboozling from a proper English lady on my tour. *She* had heard it from the horse's mouth, so to speak. I remember every word with no embellishmentations.'

Naturally, we took the bait. We pressed him for more.

'If you insist. Are you ready? This is what that nice English lady said:

''I have a story for *you* now, since you have told me so many on your tour. I heard it at night, at the old Jantar Mantar observatory of the Emperor Muhammad Shah, where I got talking to another Englishman. We were trying to work out how best to use the observatory to look at the moon. It was very atmospheric. He was eager to talk to me, and to tell me about somewhere he thought I would love, as it was even more atmospheric. He asked if I had been to India before and I told him I had many times. I asked if *he'd* been there before. He said he'd once been in Calcutta, and that something strange and awful had happened. Sensing he wanted to tell me, and always game for a good story, I made some polite noises - and soon it all came out. This is what he said:

'''I met James McFarlane in the bar of the Oberoi Grand Hotel in Calcutta. Kolkata, I should say, since that is what we should call that great and dreadful city. I was on holiday there with my wife, but she had succumbed to the inevitable: we suspected the culprit was a daal she had eaten – in an enthusiastic lapse of caution – whilst we waited for the over-night express from Lucknow . The Oberoi was a splurge. But she needed a luxury bathroom, and she didn't care how much it cost. She had spent the previous night in the toilet of a standard class Indian train carriage. I took it that she had seen horrors there that were too awful for words. She would never speak of it afterwards.

I had never stayed in a place like the Oberoi. The contrast between its gleaming luxury and the squalor of the city beyond – which seemed extreme even by Indian standards – was unsettling. My discomfort was only increased by the demeanour of the staff, whose impeccable service and absurd deference was guaranteed to embarrass an Englishman.

They didn't embarrass McFarlane, though:

'You shouldn't be like that with them', he said, as I apologised desperately to a waiter who had brought the wrong drink, and who looked just about ready to slit his wrists in atonement.

'Distant, polite, but firm – that's the way they like it', McFarlane continued. 'They may not get paid much by our standards, but where *they* come from it's a small fortune. Anyway, they prefer it that way, like back in the old days: they don't want you to be friends with them – it makes them uncomfortable.'

The waiter returned with a complementary Gin and Tonic. This time I merely thanked him with a nod. Sure enough he seemed happier this time, his honour partially restored (though he still gave off the impression that he would have preferred to be horse-whipped). Not that I could get the hang of it when McFarlane wasn't about.

I had been sent down by my wife to explore the hotel facilities, having run out of sympathetic noises to make through the locked door to our bathroom. After a lonely but glorious meal I had gone for a night-cap in the 'Chowringhee Bar and Billiards Room'. Even more than the rest of the hotel, this was a bizarre hangover from the days of the Raj. There were old prints of Englishmen in khakis hunting tigers, and sepia photos with titles like 'Inspection of the 35th Pathan Horse'. Fat businessmen smoked cigars in studded leather seats. I couldn't work out if it was wonderful or grotesque. McFarlane, who was the man sitting nearest to me at the bar, knew his opinion on the matter:

'You get a real sense of what India was here,' he said, after a few opening pleasantries. 'And of what she can be again.'

'What do you mean?' I asked.

'I mean that this country is rising fast. In another thirty years they'll have caught up with China. Good job too: since the Wars knocked *us* off top perch we've had to rely on the Americans, but it looks like they can't hack it much longer. Time to turn from one former colony to another. Why not? They're wonderful people. They speak English and they've got English laws and there are more than a billion of them.'

I muttered how poor the city seemed compared to the new India I'd seen in Mumbai: the slums and the families on the streets, the horror stories of homes burrowed into the rubbish tips.

'Terrible, isn't it? They've had decades of corrupt local government here, which of course has made things much worse. Would you believe it?! - my taxi driver said things were much better when *we* were still running the show.'

'Really? My taxi driver tried to tell us the entire story of the Ramayana and the Mahabharata, which he said were books which give you long life if you read them (though with their stories within stories within stories, they certainly seemed to make for an unnecessarily long ride).'

'That's the point: all these people will work for peanuts. No-one else will be able to compete. They'll be the biggest industrial economy on Earth. And eventually that'll make them rich.'

'You mean by people slaving for a dollar a day in Victorian-style conditions?' I said.

'Oh yes, but not for long. Look at China. Look at *us*. How do you think *we* got so wealthy? The poorest worker in Britain would live like a prince out here. Not that anyone back home does much work these days. Anyway, what else do you propose to do about it?'

I muttered something vague about multi-national corporations getting too big. With a friendly chuckle McFarlane interrupted me:

'They're nothing – absolutely nothing. Didn't you know that the whole of this country - and all that money and all those people - were all once owned by a single company? A single company that carried half the World's trade. The biggest empire the sub-continent's ever seen. Conquered and held by a private army. And the whole damn thing run from a small office in Leadenhall Street! Who do you think built this city in the first place? The 'Honourable East India Company', that's who. In those days we knew how to do business. They don't teach it in schools anymore: the government don't want our kids working out what they're doing wrong. That's what I'm writing my book about. That's why I'm here in Calcutta.'

He rocked back on his stool and drained his whisky and soda, before beckoning the chastened barman over for a refill. Then he told me the following.

It seemed he had been a businessman in the City for many years, but had 'given all that up' (which I took to mean he'd been sacked). These days he wrote history books instead, in between bouts of serious ill health. He'd already had some success with a military history of the Zulu Wars. Now he was working on 'John Company' – a history of British India. Calcutta was an obvious place for research: the Company's capital in the sub-continent. He was particularly interested in someone called 'Hindu Hawkins'. Hawkins was an eccentric figure from the early days of the colony, when Warren Hastings was Governor-General. McFarlane fancied him as a hero of the Anglo-Indian fusion that he was cheering for. He was an Englishman (or, at least, a Scotsman). But his nickname had come from his conversion to some esoteric forms of Indian religion. He had even dressed like a native. And he had been notorious for bathing every day in the Hoogly. He was apparently quite unmoved by either the filth, or by those monstrous catfish that live in it, and get the taste for human flesh from the corpses washed down from the Ganges ghats upstream.

'Hawkins was impervious to disease', McFarlane told me. 'In those days the average lifespan of a European in Bengal was one or two monsoons at the most. Some died fighting, some were murdered, and some shot themselves - when the prickly heat and the boredom got too much. Some died of drink in their bungalows in hill-stations miles from anywhere, with no-one but embittered native servants to bury them. But most died of fever. One day they'd get off the boat, the next day they'd get sick, and the day after that they'd be dead. Those that survived tended to cling to Fort William and hide in their mosquito nets. I don't blame them – thank God we now have Lariam. But Hawkins exposed himself much more to native life, and he was as hardy as anything. He spent half his time at his duties in Calcutta and the other half on private expeditions. He used to go off up-country, looking for ancient scriptures, for which he had an infatuation. Indeed he was quite an important figure in the study of Indian literature. Hindu stuff mostly, but he wasn't particular: he would take Zoroastrian, Sikh, and Jain texts too, if they were obscure enough to appeal to his tastes.

'There was one text in particular that obsessed him. He had picked it up at Patna from a 'fakir', who said he'd found it in the ruins of the great library of Nalanda.'

'Nalanda?' I asked.

'Nalanda was an ancient university so vast that it burned for three months when the Muslim armies sacked it. This text was the rare Pala recension of a version of the story of King Vikram and the vampire. Do you know it?'

I confessed that I did not.

'It would be a good thing for you to read. Hawkins certainly knew it – I think he believed it was true.

'In the story a necromancer living in a cemetery tells King Vikram that he can acquire a great power. All he has to do is bring the body of a merchant that is hanging in a nearby tree to a certain cursed spot in the graveyard – and to do so without speaking. The King agrees. But when he fetches the body he finds it's possessed by a *vetala* – a sort of demon that inhabits corpses and practises a kind of vampirism.

'The *vetala* asks him a series of riddles, to which he must give a correct honest answer on pain of death. But each time he answers he breaks the necromancer's injunction not to speak, and the body returns to where it was in the tree. In the end it asks him a moral riddle without a solution. He can't give an answer, so he stays silent. He's now finally able to take the body to the cemetery. But from his answers the *vetala* has discovered that the King is a good man, so it warns him the necromancer really plans to kill him. Forewarned, Vikram kills the necromancer first, and gains the great power for himself.'

'A passable summary, but you have made a mistake.' The voice was that of a well-spoken Indian man who was sitting further along the bar. It was clear he had been listening intently. 'There are many different versions of the story, as you know,' he continued, in impeccable English, rubbing his spectacles on his sleeve. 'But the Pala recension is quite different. In that version the vetala *is* the evil spirit of the necromancer, inhabiting the body of the merchant, since the necromancer's body has died. And it does not help Vikram, but entices him to go to the cursed spot and kills him there, so it can swap hosts, leaving the merchant's body as an empty vessel, then inhabit *Vikram's* body at the moment he dies, and so become the King himself. He then goes round telling garbled versions of the tale, to gloat and to cover his tracks. Some believe the story is true, and that he has been doing the same trick ever since, whenever the body he's in gets old or sick or in trouble.'

Flustered and somewhat annoyed, McFarlane turned to the older man, who apologised for the intrusion and introduced himself as Doctor Ghosh.

'Pleased to meet you,' I said, and we all shook hands. 'I do hope we have not said anything that has offended you?'

'Not at all, not at all - a very interesting conversation. I had not heard of 'Hindoo Hawkins'. Tell me: what became of him?'

'Well,' McFarlane continued, somewhat more cautiously, 'That was the time of the Great Bengal Famine...'

'Ah, now that I have heard of', Ghosh said, quietly.

'You'll have to enlighten me', I said.

'This great Company of yours had been granted the *diwani* tax rights' said the Doctor. 'Its officers had a certain discretion. Some used it to ease the burden on their districts. I'm afraid others used it for personal enrichment-'

'Yes,' interrupted McFarlane, regaining the initiative, 'But Hawkins didn't do either. He enforced the maximum rice tax, which he doubled and doubled again at the very worst point of the famine. The disaster affected all British India and took with it a third of the population, but his districts suffered the most. Desperate locals begged him to relent, and made him all sorts of offers, but he insisted that free trade must prevail. Some said he abused his power, though I think that unfair, and of course he was something of a pariah for his unconventional habits. Now even close colleagues thought he'd disgraced himself as an Englishman. He got into serious trouble, and was cast out from Calcutta society. They later found him hanged from a tree in the Maidan.'

'He killed himself?' Ghosh said, surprised.

'He did. And he must have been planning it for a while, because he had already designed his monument and left instructions for the man who found him. He's buried in the Old Cemetery on Burial Ground Road, which I believe grew up around his tomb. I'm going to be there tomorrow afternoon if you would care to join me. I've been transcribing the names and inscriptions as part of my research, and it's quite a big job. Hawkins' mausoleum is a famous example of East-West architectural fusion, and there are all sorts of interesting stories about it. Well don't you worry about them: the cemetery as a whole is well worth a look, though it's always had a rather grisly reputation.'

The next day my wife, mortified, sent me out to see the city. But unlike Delhi the sights of central Calcutta turned out to be mostly British. Of course, rather than an ancient capital full of Indian temples and mosques, this had been just a Company trading post that had grown into a mega-city of millions. Now that I looked at the Writers' Building and Dalhousie Square, the Victoria Monument, and the cathedral, and so on, I started to see what McFarlane had been going on about. Even, if I'm honest, to find it slightly thrilling. Here were magnificent European buildings, thrown up in a jungle half way round the World. There *was* something incredible about it, which no one back home would ever speak of, and which even the guidebooks skirted around in embarrassment. I reminded myself of the appalling stains on our record, and there were so many things that I could never be proud of. But in spite of myself I started to see things McFarlane's way, about the architecture at any rate. And it seemed a shame that all these magnificent buildings were crumbling away.

The modern city, crouched under a blackened monsoon sky, was a weird mix of these grand European constructions - dilapidated and festooned with Indian signs - and brutal post-war buildings grimmer than anything back home: run-down, filthy, and ravaged by the climate. The old town was crammed to the point of chaos, every entrance packed with cheap goods, rip-off clothes, and food that was fast turning putrid. Rats darted in and out of restaurants along the streets. The heat beat down oppressively despite the rain. A soup of sweaty, faecal atmosphere choked alleyways that smelled of plague.

I decided to make my way over to the Old Cemetery as Macfarlane had suggested. It was the 14th day of *Pitri Paksha* and the streets were full of people celebrating. Cars packed beyond sanity drove past hooting. The crowds were overwhelming, even in the rain. My route took me through some of the narrow poorer streets of the old town. A couple of aggressive beggars tried their luck, but eventually they gave up and left me alone. Once I was pawed at by a man badly disfigured with what looked like leprosy – his hideous hands twisted up into bizarre and horrid claws. I fled, feeling guilty, upset, and a little frightened, and was relieved when I eventually emerged to find myself in Cemetery Street.

The entrance to the old cemetery was a dilapidated modern building. It stank of turmeric and was guarded by a suspicious and rather charmless old man. He was eager to sell me postcards, but strangely reluctant to allow me entry. Stuffing a wad of notes into his tray seemed to overcome his scruples. He agreed with me when I asked if another Englishman was inside, though 'yes' seemed to be the only word he'd say.

Once inside the walls I could catch my breath. I found myself in a large overgrown complex. The whole place seemed to be more or less empty. It was completely walled-off from the noise and colour and chaos of the city beyond. In here great trees dripping with water were filtering out the light into greens and greys. Scattered amongst them, tangled with jungly undergrowth, loomed the tombs.

They were much larger than I had expected – many were very grand indeed. Or, at least, they had been once, before the monsoons had waged war on their stonework and the vines had clambered all over their eroded inscriptions. There were rectangular plinths and high obelisks, pyramids and domed cenotaphs, even temples with Grecian urns and classical porticos in which you could shelter from the incessant rain. They would have seemed absurdly grand in an English graveyard, but out here I suppose labour was always cheap.

As I walked down the central path away from the entrance, there did not seem to be anyone about. In a sort of trance I wondered from tomb to tomb, reading off the inscriptions where I could. They said things like:

'This monument was built for Cptn Havelock James Fitzwilliam, of Her Majesty's First Punjab Rifles, missing beyond the Khyber; Also his beloved wife Harriette, departed this World of grief, November 6th 1842, still waiting for his return, with their daughters Emma and Anne-Marie, dead of fever, The Lord Giveth and the Lord Taketh Away…'

There was a good story there, I thought to myself. It was strange, these English characters with their cosy Jane Austen names, ending up here in a ghastly place like this.

Hypnotised by the tombs, and relieved to have got in from the street, I found I had wondered off the paths. I was walking between different plots, which in places seemed quite easy, because they stood apart from one other. I soon realised that this was an illusion. The most badly damaged monuments had been removed – the dead were underneath me where I walked.

It was then I saw a curious tomb that stood on its own beneath an Ashoka tree - a great dark twisted specimen covered with parasitic vines which wound themselves out over the ground and around the tomb. The tomb was not built in the clean western lines of its neighbours. Instead it was a large square mausoleum in what I had learned to call the 'Indo-Saracenic' style. It had pointed eastern arches supporting a stupa-like dome, with steps up to an open entrance on one side. Both its outside and – presumably – its inside were covered in a baroque profusion of carvings and statues. It looked like there were eight Eastern deities on each side. The stonework was different in colour from that of the other monuments. It was darker, and stained a curious browny-red. At first this was rather a startling effect. Then you realised it must be some sort of rust patina leaching out from the joins, either from the iron rivets that held the stones together, or perhaps from the masonry itself.

'The 'Bloody Tomb'', said a voice. 'Isn't it magnificent?'

It was McFarlane, who was standing behind me. I had not seen him because the tree was between us as I approached. Somewhat startled I said something like:

'Yes, it is rather impressive, isn't it? 'Hindoo Hawkins', I take it.'

'That's right,' he continued – he seemed strangely tense. 'The inside's worth a look too. It has a curious inscription, though I'm not sure I fully understand it. Dreadful poetry, but you get used to that in old cemeteries. Let me show you – see what you make of it.'

Walking up the crumbling steps, we entered the dank black void underneath the mausoleum's rotunda. Inside the air was gross. From the sweet rotting stench it seemed some animal had been living there, or at least using it for its business. It looked like there was filth and bones and other detritus on the floor. McFarlane shone a torch around the stonework. With the weather and the dirt it was somewhat hard to read. But as my eyes adjusted I could indeed see a strange inscription that went round the inner frieze beneath the cupola:

'Whether the Cruelty of the East be best,
or rather yet the Rapine of the West;
Whether Europa's Wisdom wisely pricked
the ancient Conscience of the Asiatick,
And whether the Love of Orient
Excused the Tyranny of we who went,
Speak the proper Answer, ye who read
Or else thy Heart may crack and ye may bleed.'

I wasn't sure what to say, so I said nothing. McFarlane, munching on a mango picked from a nearby tree, said as follows:

'When I first came here a couple of days ago my answer would have been: 'Yes, Yes, Yes'. But now I can't work out what Hawkins himself thought, at least by the end of his life. It's an odd sort of riddle, isn't it?'

'Is it a riddle,' I said, 'or a curse?'

'Sorry old man - don't know what you mean.'

'Should you really be eating those?' I asked, suddenly realising the source of his mango. 'I mean: this is a graveyard, after all.'

'*Well…* it's not been used for over a century. And besides, they're delicious. Have one -'

Just then we heard a moaning sound outside. Startled, we stepped out of the mausoleum. Some way off down the avenue of tombs we could see a strange figure. She was an Indian girl in jeans and a cheap *choli*, hunched over awkwardly and clearly in distress. There was something - well - not quite right about her. She was stumbling forwards somehow through the rain, though her feet were twisted so far in that it was a miracle she could walk at all. Her arms were curled inwards too, and she was making strange guttural noises. She had seen us too. She gurned at us with a troubling and salivary wide-mouthed grin. I couldn't tell if she was simple, or suffering from hydrophobia, or God alone knows what. You see all sorts of strange beggars in Calcutta, and the range of their complaints would baffle any doctor. I feared, for a guilty and horrifying moment, that McFarlane would feel duty-bound to see if she needed help. Back home I would have done myself, but somehow out here it was different. I was very reluctant to get any closer.

'Come on,' said McFarlane, to my relief, 'I'm done for the day anyway. Let's get back and see about that dinner.'

We turned and picked our way back to the entrance as fast as was decent. On our way back, after a few minutes of awkward small talk, McFarlane said:

'Funny thing that – I doubt *she* had paid her admission. Last night the chap on the gate insisted on turfing me out early. He said it wasn't safe after dark. Seems there have been a couple of deaths around here over the years. Tramps found dead in the graveyard, and no-one sure why. The cemetery caretakers are supposed to have evicted the poor families who used to live in the tombs. They get some money from a British charity and they're meant to look after the place. But there still are plenty of wild dogs and vagrants who gather there at night. It's probably best to be on the safe side anyway. The public health provision round here is still shocking.'

That night we had another drink in the Chowringhee. We were joined briefly by Dr Ghosh and by my wife, who had rallied for a moment (though soon she retreated with a relapse). She said later that she been impressed with the Doctor but had found McFarlane a bore, and didn't like the way he leered at the waitresses, though increasingly I found him excellent company. She also said that he looked more ill than *she* felt. But whatever the truth of this, I agreed to meet him at the cemetery again next day. (The way things were apparently still going in our bathroom, I gathered I'd otherwise be spending the evening alone).

The next morning I walked around the Maidan and took some indifferent photos. Then I visited the Temple of Kali - the goddess of time, death, and change. The temple was full of officiants, and their faces expressed imminent and rapturous belief. As I looked at the strange idols of the black goddess with her necklace of skulls, I thought for a moment about the journey of 'Hindoo Hawkins'. It all seemed like a very long way from the reassuring tedium and token religiosity of the Church of England services of my childhood. I could see how a man could find or lose himself in this great and mysterious country, amongst its throbbing multitudes of men and gods.

I was a bit late back, and hadn't had time for my second shower of the day before I was due to pick up McFarlane from the cemetery as we'd agreed. It was both hotter and wetter today, but that meant that the streets were a little clearer. I made it through the old town in no time at all.

But when I arrived at the cemetery the grumpy old porter at the desk tried to turn me away. According to the official opening time it should have been no problem, but the man insisted they were closed for a festival. I asked him if he'd seen the other Englishman. I gathered he had - and that so far as he knew he was still inside - but he still tried to claim they were closed. At first I stood there stupidly, unsure of what to do. I still didn't know whether I should wait for McFarlane to join me for dinner. And it seemed too ridiculous to go all the way back to the hotel, especially given that he might be waiting for me just a few yards away over the wall. Calling the old man back I explained I had a message for my friend, but wouldn't stay. Eventually the offer of a generous pile of rupees gained me admittance. These were accepted grudgingly, along with a comment that I could please myself. But it was made clear that it was on my head and I'd better be no more than a few minutes in there. Then he pulled down the shutter at his window with a definitive clatter.

Inside the cemetery seemed completely deserted. It was raining heavily onto saturated ground and the paths were like a quagmire. My footprints were easily visible in the mud. Clouds of mosquitos, exploiting the arrival of a tasty snack, started to trouble my neck. At first I beat them off. But after a while it was easier just to let them suck my blood. The bites would give me hell by the morning. As I made my way deeper into the graveyard I started to wish I'd stayed in the hotel. There was no sign of McFarlane on any of the main paths. I left the paths and started to make my way to where I reckoned I had met him the previous day. I thought about calling out his name, but somehow I couldn't bring myself to do it.

I was about to give the whole thing up as a bad job, and to beat a hasty retreat to the Oberoi to dry off. But just then I noticed what I instantly recognised as McFarlane's satchel. It was lying on the step of what I now saw was the reverse side of Hawkins' tomb. Looking around me I started to walk outwards in a concentric spiral from the tomb, peering from side to side to see where he might be. The vegetation here was quite thick, and slimy wet leaves were slapping me on the arms and face. Finding myself stalking through jungly shrubs, with my feet slipping around beneath me in the mud, I felt distinctly unwelcome and unhappy. Pausing from time to time to listen, I became aware of my loud short breaths. Moving on again I somehow got tangled up with some vines, and I started to thrash around myself to get free of them. With mounting panic I broke through into a clearer spot, right underneath the branches of the great Ashoka tree. There right in front of me was McFarlane.

He was in a terrible state. He was lying on his back with his legs splayed out awkwardly and his arms crossed in front of him - as if in defence. His eyes were wide open and unblinking and his skin was white. There seemed to be flecks of blood around his mouth and throat as I dragged him out from under the foliage.

Suddenly he opened his mouth and started to speak, in a foaming, guttural voice.

'Ah, it's you. Be a good chap and carry me to the tomb. No don't argue – it is imperative that you do it. I was working on the inscriptions. I heard a noise and I thought it was that beggar from yesterday coming up the path. I decided to step into the tomb so she wouldn't see me. But the shape of the thing must have thrown the noise. When I got in there I found myself suddenly face to face with her. The bitch bit me! It's bloody painful I can tell you. No I don't want water – take it away. I now understand how it's done. It's the most incredible thing. I'll show you…'

He was rambling now – it was clear he was delirious. I tried to help him up so we could stagger away from that awful place. I muttered something to soothe him but he carried on:

'No listen! You must take me to the tomb. Read out the riddle again, for Christ's sake. I'll make you understand it -'

Just then I heard a moaning from the tomb. I confess I dropped McFarlane, shouted that I'd go and get help, and ran for it. The gatehouse was now shut up and empty. I climbed over the gate and didn't stop running until I got back to the Oberoi.

Without any knowledge of Bengali, and badly shaken, I could do no more than retreat to the hotel to alert the concierge. Fortunately Dr Ghosh was in reception and agreed to come back with me to the cemetery. Twenty minutes later we were at the tomb. McFarlane was back under the tree, where I had originally found him. Dr Ghosh kneeled over him. He asked me over his shoulder to tell him again what had happened.

'Ask Macfarlane!' I replied.

'What you say is impossible', said Ghosh. 'I believe this man has been dead for several hours.'

Eventually some policemen arrived and trampled all over the area some more, they said there was nothing else they could do, and he was taken away to a mortuary. The rain got heavier and I went with them to the police station, where I spent many hours filling out forms and repeating my story.

Two days later my wife and I flew back to England. After a month or so we got an official report in the post. It noted that Mr McFarlane had disappeared from the Oberoi hotel, and had last been seen at an 'unconfirmed' time in the Old Cemetery, having had some sort of heart attack or seizure (it emerged he had been mortally ill for some time) and suffered a bad fall, from which he had subsequently died. In the absence of any other evidence, any report of criminal activities, or any contact from family members, the Kolkata Municipal Police indefinitely suspended the case, and his death was recorded as unsuspicious, 'resulting from long-standing serious ill-health brought on by excessive historical research'.

I have often wondered what would have happened to me if I had answered Hawkins' riddle. Or what I should have said.'

We stood in silence in the moonlight of the Jantar Mantar, surrounded by the monuments of the Mughals and the British, and the roar of the great Indian city beyond. If the Pala recension is as Mr Ghosh described it, I realised, then there were troubling implications to this obscure account. Mr

MacFarlane may not have been quite what he seemed, at least by the time of his death, and at any rate his motives might have been as murky as those of 'Hindoo Hawkins' himself.'

'Why do you British always assume it is all about you?! Did it occur to you that perhaps even *Hawkins* had not always been quite who he seemed?'

'Ha! No it did not. But now you say that and now that I think about it, I might I have been right to be frightened – even frightened of the man I was now talking to. After all, I only had his version of the story. Indeed, he gave me the most peculiar look, and asked me what I thought about ancient curses. I didn't know what to say, so I started to walk away, out of the observatory. He came with me all the way back to my hotel, before I could get rid of him. And to distract him I told him a curse story of my own, about an ancient Hittite figurine, that I was once told by a friend at Oxford. Then he disappeared. I never saw him again.'

You see? I told you what that nice lady said was really ghastly. And I believed her every word I can tell you.'

My colleagues and I were delighted with the tour-guide's story, and fell about to telling others of our own. One said it put him in mind of some papers in his possession, that told of a real Chinese ghost story. Another, to everyone's entertainment and my utter bafflement, told us a long, gory tale he had heard on a train in Russia, which itself contained yet more improbable stories. The Devil alone knows what to make of it all.'

The Black Sands

"A man's greatest pleasure is to destroy his enemies,
to take their possessions,
to see those they loved in tears,
and to hold their wives and daughters in his arms"

The Secret History

This report is translated from elegant medieval Persian. The original is annotated with the following introduction in English, which was written some time in the late 1830's. It was found in a hidden niche in a ruined mosque, in the remotest quarter of Turkmenistan. The other awful contents of the niche will be guessed from the pages below, which speak for themselves:

The Tournament of Shadows

I, Captain Havelock James Fitzwilliam, of Her Majesty's First Punjab Rifles, write these words in the hope that one day these papers may be found. It is ten nights since I rode out from Khiva, disguised as a Pashtoo. I knew by then that it was but a matter of time before the mad Khan's patience ended and his famous 'hospitality' began. Whether his whim would have had me sold in the slave markets, or beheaded in the square, or treated to heaven knows what infernal tortures, I am now at a loss to know. But messages had been passed to me that I was no longer safe, emissary though I was of the Governor-General. The Khan's ear bends to Lieutenant Lazaroff and Petersburg. And though he no longer believes, as when I arrived, that the British are 'a sub-tribe of Russians, addicted to beef and deceit', he swears he will never ally with us now he knows that our King is a woman. No doubt his men are also out to kill me, but I wager it is Lazaroff who is half a day's ride behind me, with his bloodthirsty Cossack scouts. I have played my part as a piece in the great game; he will do all that he can in his power to remove me from the board.

That is why I rode South, straight into the desert, rather than follow the Oxus the way I had come. I fear this was not enough to throw my pursuers from the scent. For a week I was lost in the vast desert of Khorezm – the 'Black Sands' - hoping to get to the ruins of Merve and to water, before my own gave out. From here I planned to strike toward Herat; and thence to India, and to safety, and to her. Such, at any rate, was my intent.

Though I did not know it at the time, my mission had already failed before it had begun. I was granted 'shooting leave' from my regiment after the strange affair of the teeth (about which much has been written elsewhere). I was tasked by the Governor-General with this perilous journey into Tartary, there to discover, if I could, the military strength of the secret kingdom of Khiva and to turn the Khan, if *he* would, to wage war against the Tsar. It would be a war that he would lose but we might win; a war in which he and his Khanate would be used and thrown away, or else eaten up as our protectorate, once our forces had settled with the Afghans. I was to get to Khiva before the Russians. The journey there was perilous enough: three months hard trek across unmapped wastes. But when I arrived I found that Lazaroff had beaten me to the prize. He was already there, poisoning the mind of the Khan against us. He has ever been our chief opponent in this tournament of shadows. [I swear it was he that had a hand in that murky business at Kandahar.]

The Khan, it must now be assumed, will side with the Tsar (if he will side with anyone), or at least he will listen to none of my words and will fall to the designs of Petersburg. Our forces in Cabool will be imperilled and the way to India from the North will lie wide open. No doubt London has not grasped this hazard to our interests. It need hardly be said how vital this intelligence must be for us. If anyone finds these pages I urge them in the name of God to get them to Calcutta or to London poste-haste. And yet how absurd a delusion that is. As absurd as the hope I could find a safe hiding place in the Mosque of the Labyrinth in Merve.

I had read of the mosque in Mollasadra's commentary on Sohrevardi's *Illumination of the Seventh Way* and in Zahirridin Aufi's *History of the Lords of Turkestan* and in other venerable Persian scholars, as I studied the Mahommedan languages in the Writers' building in Calcutta. They were agreed it was the finest work of that most brilliant genius, Al-Shirazi, whose exquisite Minaret of Heaven I had seen outside Balkh. Each of his buildings, I have read, has its hidden meanings and hermetic secrets. He was a dark Sufi, from a sect that worshipped Iblis – the Devil – whose love of God was purer than his fear of Him (for he chose to live in Hell rather than bow before Adam, and selflessly devoted his existence to creating tempting amusements to divert and test men's will; he was thus the only angel who understood the corrupt nature of Man and why it is necessary for his salvation – and who saw that true principals emanate from the self, and must be obeyed, over any external injunction and whatever the cost). Al-Shirazi's Mosque of the Labyrinth was the subject of several poems of mystical rumination by Ibn Husayn Al-Amili and other wise men of the East. The different interpretations of its mysteries were, alas, too subtle for my imperfect Persian, and none of them satisfied me that their authors, learned men though they were, had truly discovered the Labyrinth's secret. Nor had any Westerner penetrated the Kingdom of Khiva nor the vast Khorezm Dessert to gaze upon its ruins or illustrate its glories. Indeed no European had been through here since Alexander of Macedon, and even he had the wisdom to turn back when he set eyes upon the Black Sands. Perhaps in part, then, it was curiosity that drove me into this burning waste. And how dearly I have paid for that I now see all too well.

For three thirsty days I rode across this trackless and forbidding wilderness, until at last my horse smelled water and the barren ground gave way to a large tract of poppy-strewn grass and scrub. After a mile or two I beheld, rising before me, the ruins of ancient Merve. They are like something from a fantasy of the Thousand and One Nights. Remnants of her vast city walls lie for many miles about. Inside their enormous circuit, where once stood glittering gardens and seraglios, I saw huge hills of mud. These cursed mounds of eroded walls and towers were all that remained of the great city of the Khorezm-Shahs. One steep volcano of obliterated masonry I realise is no less than the carcass of the great university of Tekesh, to which scholars had once travelled from across the known World. Another must have been the palace quarter of the Shahs (for they had built seven palaces, it is said: one for each of the forbidden pleasures). On a third, somewhat lower and apart from the rest, a single building still stands out proud against the sky, the building I had dared not hope to find: the Mosque of the Labyrinth.

The great mosque, though not so large as I had thought, is exquisite in every part. The setting sun glints from the green and lapis tiles that still adorn its dome, and casts elaborate shadows from the brickwork of its many-faced exterior. That it alone has survived whilst the city was destroyed is testament to its construction, its location, or its function - or perhaps to its singular beauty, which is enough to temper the wrath of any vandal. Standing apart as it does from the mud-brick structures of the city, which have long-since returned to their elemental form, its sturdy masonry alone stands proud but mournful over a landscape of unparalleled desolation.

The building, as I have said, I found to be much smaller than my expectation, and my relief at catching sight of it was tempered by the thought that its size afforded but little opportunity to hide. Indeed, as the only structure in the city that still stands, it is the natural place for anyone to stop for shelter, as such it were bound to bring the Cossacks straight to me.

The edifice had been designed to stand apart from other structures on the summit of a man-made terrace. My curiosity mixed with concern for my own fate as I tethered my horse and scrambled up the mound to inspect the mosque. There must, I thought, be some fearful tight corridors within for it to justify its famous appellation. But my confusion was complete when I stepped through the ruined doorway and into the interior. 'Tis but a single room! The great white vault spans the entire space within, its drum resting on tiered squinches, its circle ingeniously rising from the seven walls: a soaring miracle of construction. Swallows had made nests in the corners of the stuccoed ceiling, and several, disturbed by my presence, flew about the mosque. The tile and plasterwork is marked with smoke, no doubt from the fires of passing nomads, yet the designs themselves survive in a masterpiece of interlocking arabesques.

Was it this that was the Labyrinth? The words of the Prophet, barely legible against the convolution of their settings, are endlessly repeated inside an intricate multiplicity of lines, which radiate their exquisite patterns to infinity. True, many men have lost themselves in following that path. Yet, magnificent as they are, they would hardly mark this out so far from other buildings of the age as to justify its name and reputation. No, the secret of the mosque must lie elsewhere.

One curious feature is the decorative bronze plates at the centre of each wall, below the windows, with the tile-work running around them, (save only the furthest wall, opposite the entrance, into which is set the mihrab). These metal plates are themselves adorned with starburst decorations, but otherwise their function is obscure.

The windows of the building, with intricate carved latticework, are also very strange. They are set at varied angles in the walls, themselves of uncommon thickness, so that the window openings slope from inside to out (though this is disguised by clever perspectives in the tile-work patterns that runs into them). Furthermore, the windows in the walls before one as one enters are matched by false windows in the tile-work on the walls behind, beside the door, so the illusion of symmetry is preserved.

Puzzled, I stepped outside again and walked around the building, trying to see what prospect the windows afforded from without (would to God I had not done so!). This availed me nothing, since the windows were set too high in the walls to look through, and in any case their latticework blocks the view.

Yet here is another mystery: outside there is one window to each wall, excepting the wall that houses the entrance door. But on the inside there are no windows in each of the walls immediately flanking the entrance. I started to count the windows to make some sense of this and, as I did so, I naturally counted the walls. It took me a couple of circumperambulations, both inside and out, before it hit me, with the force of a revelation. There are only seven walls inside the mosque. On the outside, with the entrance, there are eight.

I knew this was impossible. The mosque lives up to its name. Inside, two interior walls meet at the door. Outside, the door is set into a full wide wall of its own. I paced out the internal and external circumferences of the mosque. As was to be expected, the outside perimeter is larger – quite substantially so, given the depth of the walls, necessary no doubt to support the great weight of the dome.

But they are not, it now turned out, of uniform thickness. For there was a very great deal of additional support on either side of the entrance. Additional support or, I now supposed, additional space. And it is into this space that the extra windows must open. For how else could there be more windows without than within? Nor were these windows blank, though they were too high to look through from outside. From the inside there was no sign of them, excepting the pair of false windows in the tiles.

I quickly turned my attention to the metal plates beneath these false windows. Close examination of that on the right revealed nothing – it was possible to prise it away from the virgin brickwork behind. It was only when I came to that on the left that I knew at last the secret of the mosque. For here was no decorative panel. It was a hidden door.

Exhausted though I was, I put my shoulder to the metal and pushed as hard as I was able. A cloud of dust kicked up from the floor and the panel began to give backwards, gratingly at first and then with surprising ease, closing gently behind me as I squeezed through the opening it revealed. As my eyes adjusted to the gloaming, I saw I was in a niche, very tight but tall, lit from the high window without. The tiny, airless room was carved from the extra space afforded by the difference in shape between the inside and the outside of the mosque. Now, at last, were revealed the genius of Al-Shiraz and the mystery of his labyrinth.

But the exclamation of triumph died on my lips when I beheld what filled me with dread. For there, slumped against the wall, part-skeletal yet still clothed, there lay what had once been a man. On the floor next to it, beside some rusted bowls and saucers and other effects, I found these sheets, covered in black calligraphy, into whose margins I have scrawled my own words. They are written in the most elegant hand, though they read like a nightmare from Vathek. You may well imagine my despair as I read them.

A Tale of the Marvellous With News of the Strange

'To create perfection you must destroy yourself. How well I now understand the bitter laugh of Ibn Athari, who, when he laid the final brick on top of the Minaret of the Moon, was seized by his own apprentices and hurled out to his death. He must have guessed the subtle intent of the Sultan – a cruel and learned man who had blinded his favourite painter, torn off the ears of his court composer, removed the hands and tongue of his best poet, so that they could never mar by repetition the mighty works he had commissioned.

Did Ibn Athari laugh because he already knew his fate – even welcomed it, as proof of the perfection of what he had built? Or did he laugh because in that instant he understood the intense betrayal that every apprentice harbours for his teacher? Or did he laugh at the terrible triumph of becoming immortal with his masterpiece at the moment of its creation and the summit of his powers?

How well do I, Khawaja Muhammad Mas'ud Al-Shirazi, member of the secret Brotherhood of the Chosen Brethren, astronomer, poet, philosopher, and the greatest architect since Athari, know all those thoughts at this moment, the forty-fifth day of my death. Of course I would never have been so mad as to accept a commission from that Sultan. My own master, Al-Nasir li-Din Allah, thirty-fourth Caliph of the Empire, is a man of very different temper.

It was he who summoned me from the House of Wisdom in Baghdad. I had just completed my investigations of the secrets of the temple of the Frankish knights, and was in need of another project. The Caliph's instruction was simple: to build this, the most beautiful edifice on Earth. And to build it not for him, but for his enemy the Khorezm-Shah. The war between the Caliph and the Shah had raged for years when I was dispatched east to Merv. I would be a token of the forgiveness and love that the Caliph felt for the Shah. I would build a monument to the eternal peace between them. I would transform the walls and palaces of his capital and build the Mosque of the Labyrinth at its heart. The Caliph sent with me gold enough to build a city and a peace that would last forever. The peace will last forever, but not for the reason the Shah thought. For the Caliph's true design was the opposite of what he purported. The Mosque of the Labyrinth would be a trap, in which the Shah and his whole people would lose themselves forever.

Merv is the greatest city of the East, a rival to Baghdad herself, and nearly as ancient. Under the Khorezm-Shahs it has grown in stature, size and beauty and been adorned with monuments designed by the greatest masters of the Shah's domains. Its markets, baths, palaces and gardens are unsurpassed in beauty. Chief among its splendours are the Library and Madrassah of Tekesh, which has lured scholars of five religions and of none from across the World. They have even come from the House of Wisdom itself. The books in its collection, they say, would take a hundred men a hundred years to copy. Many are unique. This rich library is one of twelve in Merv, including (a perverse and dangerous innovation) one that is reserved for women. Elsewhere, aqueducts and wells bring water for the million subjects of the Shah that live within the walls. This was the city I had been sent to transform. And transform it I did.

Caravans from the East had already brought news that the great wall of Alexander had been breached, and the cursed tribes of Gog and Magog had finally broken through. Temujin, Khan of all the northern nomads, had brought his army south of the wall - and laid to unutterable ruin and destruction the lands of the pagan emperors. Now no more caravans came from Cathay, and that spoke louder than any rumours. They say Temujin worshipped a demon called Tengri, but he was not a man distracted by philosophical nuance. His guiding principle was total war – a war of annihilation - until the whole World, from ocean to ocean, was his. His law code was beautiful in its simplicity. It allowed and encouraged the most dreadful of crimes. But it decreed death for tilling the land, water pollution, horse-murder, and spitting. His soldiers were the greatest horsemen on Earth and could survive any hardship. They dressed in rat-skins, ate lice and ticks, and drank the blood of their horses as they rode. Before such a force, none could stand. My master had despatched messengers to the Khan to stir up his hatred against the Shah. But none had returned. And none dared repeat the attempt. Instead he had me send silver to Inalchuq, who governed Otrar for the Shah, to pay him to commit the crime that condemned millions to death and turned great cities forever into desert.

It was a year since the last caravan had come safely through from Kashgar that 100 horsemen rode out of the desert to Otrar. They came from Temujin with a message for the Shah: 'I am master of the lands of the rising sun. You rule the lands of the setting sun. Let us make a treaty of friendship.' The Shah would have had them loaded with gifts and sent safely back to the Khan. But before the Shah knew of the emissaries, Inalchuq, corrupted by silver, chose a very different path.

Thirty three of them he impaled on stakes outside his palace.

Thirty three he had cast into 'Pits of Despair' beneath it – round dungeons filled with vermin which, starving, you eat as they eat you.

Thirty three he condemned to the terrible death of 'the boats' – tied down in the sun and force-fed milk and honey, until their bowels loosened and their innards were crawling with maggots, so they died slow in their own filth.

The hundredth he made to watch all this. Then he sent him back to Temujin, by way of answer to his embassy from the Shah.

After that another year passed with no firm news from the East. My work on the mosque surpassed anything I had achieved in my career. By spring the dome had been completed and by summer the tile-work was finished. The Shah, delighted, now asked me to repair the city walls, to prepare them for a siege if Temujin came. So it was that I constructed bastions, barbicans, false gates and moats enough to break a thousand armies. And, in a corner of the seventh Eastern tower, I made the door that would let an army in.

The Shah was not a clever man. His limited mind was unable to discriminate the difference between size and beauty. 'If you doubt our power, behold our buildings', that was his adage. Yet it only takes a single weakness of construction for the greatest of buildings to fail. My four sally ports were of course in the plans – I had discussed them in person with the

Shah. He himself had tested the ingenuity of my secret doors: doors impenetrable from one side, but which opened easily from the other.

These doors were stoutly constructed and plated with solid bronze. They were chamfered so that their outside was a sheet of patterned metal, quite flat against the wall in which they stood. Their mechanisms were controlled by hinges of my own creation, subtle devices whose secret I carry with me to my death. They present no lip to prise open from without. Besides, even if there were one, the more pressure applied against the door, the more solidly the hinges lock it in place. From inside, however, a single man can push them open. A raiding party could issue out of them to attack their enemies' siege works at their will.

It was only after my first three secret doors had been constructed, and their operations demonstrated, that I installed the fourth. But this time I reversed the mechanism. The door would not open from within like the others (for which I found some excuse about materials that I lacked). A simple experiment would have shown how easily, once unlocked, this door could be opened from without. The experiment was never made, and by the time it was complete the Shah had other things upon his mind.

Of course the workmen had no understanding of what they were making for me. The only one who guessed my plan was my apprentice, Biruni, whom I had brought with me to oversee the work, and to finish the mosque that now was all but complete, along with its secret. How can you have a labyrinth in one room, from which all points are visible from all other points? This was the greatest of my inventions. This is also the cause of my death. It only takes a single weakness of construction for the greatest of buildings to fail. The weakness of the Mosque of the Labyrinth was my trusting its final stages to Biruni – may men shit on his beard - whilst I concentrated all my efforts on the city walls. When we had done I sent Biruni back to Baghdad, with a message for the Caliph that his plan was working.

At the end of the forbidden month, Temujin came out of the desert like a whirlwind and the horizon was black with his horsemen. He had brought with him an army of two hundred thousand. His dreadful son Ogedei crossed the Mountains of Heaven with a hundred thousand more, and a siege train filled with devious machines, that threw giant stones, rotting corpses, whole palm trees, and balls of burning human fat, manned by the captured Chinese craftsmen who had devised them. They were at Otrar before the Shah had even mustered his men. A faction in the town took up arms against the garrison, declaring that they should surrender. But once they opened the gates the Tartars killed them all anyway, saying such traitors could not be trusted. When they found Inalchuq they made him drink molten silver. They say Ogedei uses his silvered skull as a wine-cup.

The Shah sent a great army against them but it was swallowed up. One by one his other cities fell before the Khan's wrath. Their whole populations were put to slaughter and their buildings demolished and burned. Trusting to his walls, the Shah gathered his men in Merv, behind its unconquerable fortifications. Even with the devilish weapons of the Chinese, the invaders would not breach my defences. Iblis himself could not have broken into the city. Not without a traitor within. And even if there had been a traitor, surely none would dare let in the Mongols, knowing as they did that they would kill everything that lived, search every hiding place, destroy all the buildings - except the mosques and mausolea (for Temujin, though a pagan, was a superstitious man).

Supplies for the siege were barely brought in when we first smelled the enemy's army. For the stench of the great horde arrived a full day before the vast clouds of dust were seen. It was a sweet odour of leather, sweat, shit, and putrefying meat. At the head of the horde was Ogedei, who had sworn to show his father through feats of blood and slaughter that – of the thousand of Temujin's sons by a thousand wives – he alone was worthy to be his heir. Ogedei's men marched up to the moats, with Muslim prisoners as shields, and filled the moats in with their bodies. Elsewhere they started tunnels to undermine the walls' foundations. Against its towers their mangonels hurled endless streams of stone and fire. Nothing was of any use against my defences.

On the third night of the siege I shone a lantern from the seventh Eastern tower, at the point on the walls above the sally port. Then I unlocked it and hurried up to the mosque, to hide in my secret room. It wasn't long before I could hear, through the grilled windows high in the walls, the screams coming up from that quarter of the town. Then I sat here, pressed in but safely hidden, as the greatest city of the East was put to the sword.

In the morning Ogedei himself entered my mosque and addressed the city elders and their families that sought refuge in it. Climbing to the pulpit his dog-like voice proclaimed, through an interpreter, the awful sentence: 'I am the scourge of God. If you had not committed great sins, God would not have sent me as a punishment'. He then ordered each man in his army to decapitate two dozen captives. He had with him 40,000 soldiers. They finished their task in two days and piled the people's heads in pyramids around the city. The town was then erased from the Earth and salt was sown in its fields. The irrigation systems were destroyed and the country returned to steppe. A city of a million men, women and children and I was the only one to survive. They even killed all the cats and the dogs. The Khan's soldiers tripped on streets slippery with human fat. From my high grilled window I saw the river run red with blood. Then – which was worse – it ran black with ink. All the books of the dozen great libraries - irreplaceable ancient learning - were thrown into the water. Then finally the river itself was diverted so that it ran through the town, where it washed away those of the mud-brick buildings that had survived the worst of the fires. And all the while I watched from safety this terrible thing I had done.

But I had been right about the mosque. Set on a hill by the high citadel and apart from the other buildings, it alone was untouched by fire or flood. I knew it was too sturdily-built to be easily demolished, even had the barbarians wished to do so. It was to be left, immaculate and alone, its prospects unsullied by lesser architecture, in the ruins that had been this great city. Nor of course did anyone think to question its shape, nor come close to discovering its secret. When the invaders finally went (and I had stored enough food and water for a month, which was ten days more than I needed), I would emerge from my tiny cell into a desert in which nothing was left alive. Then I would be picked up by a squadron of Turkmen riders in the pay of the Caliph, who would smuggle me to the border, to safety, and my reward: as much gold as I could carry on a camel. Payment enough for sitting in a cavity in the walls, enduring the stench of a million rotting corpses. It was only on the thirty third day – four days after the last invaders had left – that I thought to try the door.

Biruni, my loyal apprentice, could not have made a mistake. It must have been as a wilful act that he had reversed the mechanism. The door (propped open, of course, behind some scaffolding before I entered, waiting for the moment I needed it) would open easily from outside, from the interior of the mosque. But from inside even a battering ram could not shift it, even if there had been room enough to wield one. Perhaps Biruni hoped to secure my reward for himself. Or perhaps he was sickened by my actions. Most likely he wished to punish me for making a building he could never surpass.

It only took me a minute to understand that I was a dead man. The next twelve days and nights I spent in desperate attempts to find some way to prise or dig or claw my way out of the tiny room. I knew from the start that such attempts would be futile (for had I not designed and built this mosque myself?). Now thirst has put an end to my attempts. My last hope died when the day passed for the arrival of the Turkmen. If they ever came, they went nowhere near the mosque. I wonder now if the Caliph ever sent them, or perhaps he thought he'd save himself a camel-load of gold. Now I sit here waiting for death and writing down this account, for the first man who thinks to open my door. I hope he sees the genius of my design. I hope he is a man of the book. Finally, I hope for his sake that he does not let the door close behind him.'

Book for the Dead – The Mummy Returns

'*I was alone with the dead men of a dead civilisation*'

The Ring of Thoth

''Neither rotted nor putrefied nor become worms, nor fallen into decay, and possessing all the members of his body, he lives who lieth within me'.'

Salma Kanawati ran her fingers over the hieroglyphs, with a mixture of reverence and triumph.

'Except it is empty', said Khamis.

'Except it is empty', agreed Salma.

The two of them crouched beside the object with the silent patience of children who, having unwrapped a long-desired gift, luxuriate in a moment of contemplation.

'Too bad old Massri couldn't be here,' said Khamis. 'Whatever you think of him, he would have wept with joy to see it here.'

Khamis Hussan was a sentimentalist, even about his boss the under-curator. Or rather his ex-boss. Because for now he had to get used to the idea of deferring to the woman beside him. Salma answered him curtly:

'Not enough to see it installed. Massri showed his true colours in London. He was a fool and a traitor. The museum is a better place with him gone.'

'I agree of course. And I know he was only promoted because he was one of the Brothers. But he did care about the museum. For him to disappear like that is strange. I just wish I knew what had happened. I'm sure you're right that he went to ground in England, or maybe re-located to Qatar. But then why didn't he take his family?'

'Good riddance, either way', said Salma: 'He only got the job from his connections – and he must have known his time was up. I don't think he even realised what an amazing thing this is.'

The object was indeed unique, even by the standards of the collection of the National Museum of Egyptian Antiquities, into which it had just been unloaded. The long campaign for its return had been just a foretaste of the difficulty of transporting it to Cairo. For they had been forced to agree to transport it in one piece. Now it was installed in an alcove behind the Late Period Funerary Monuments room, off the end of the main ground floor gallery. There, if you stepped behind the huge legs of the two seated statues, there was a cramped and seldom-visited space, with a jumble of crates and disorganised artefacts. With the bulk of the packaging removed they could at last examine it up close.

None of the photographs had done it justice: it was unlike anything they had seen in all their careers as Egyptologists. Taken together the object was somewhat taller than a man. It was topped off by a pyramidion of Egyptian alabaster, covered all over with symbols. The square base of this capstone sat in a groove at the centre of the black granite lid. Beneath this lid was the great sarcophagus itself, built for Pharaoh Shepseskare the First, which the edifice around it was supposed to show off. The sarcophagus rested in turn on a large marble plinth, with a square base but carved sloping sides which continued the line of the pyramid above. Three porphyry cannopic vases stood at three corners of the plinth, their lids carved respectively with the heads of the Gods Duamutef, Qubhsenuef, and Hapy. (The fourth vase, with the head of Imsety, had been removed from the monument decades earlier, and was in the possession of the British Museum, which refused to return it). At the centre of one face of the plinth, above a typical carved 'false door', the monument was completed by an absurd statue of its creator. He was dressed in a Victorian Englishman's conception of a Ptolemaic toga. Underneath this, with barbaric impudence, were carved over the ancient inscriptions the words: 'Sir Galfridus Bellingham'. Bellingham. A ludicrous name for a ludicrous man. At Salma's instigation the monument had been placed so that this side of it faced the back wall. The less attention drawn to him the better. Spotlights had been positioned to pick out the best of the sarcophagus carvings.

'It's wonderful,' said Salma.

'It's odd,' said Khamis, sniffing. 'And it smells odd too.'

'That's probably from the packaging. Look at all this dust and polystyrene. Let's have one of the men clean it off overnight, then tomorrow we can get a proper look at the hieroglyphs. This sarcophagus is one of the finest I've seen. Too bad about the contents.'

The mummiform inner coffin had had to travel separately, along with the mummy inside it, whose leathery, nut-brown head protruded through its damaged cartonnage. It had been unloaded for now along the wall at the other side of the room. It hadn't originally belonged with the sarcophagus anyway. It had only been put inside it two hundred years earlier, on the whim of the eccentric English collector. Besides, even if this one was undistinguished by their standards, in Salma's view it was always worth having mummies out on display. Everyone likes a good mummy.

'We should get it into an atmosphere-controlled cabinet in one of the mummy rooms.'

'I agree,' said Khamis. 'It doesn't do to keep mummies exposed. They don't like the air.'

At this point a third person came into the room. An Englishman.

'Hello, how is it?'

'Everything's ok, Mr Stewart.'

'Trevor, please – call me Trevor.'

To Salma, Trevor Stewart had proved to be a great disappointment. There was something awkward and furtive about him, perhaps even a little craven. The man was clearly an oddity, even for that eccentric nation. Or maybe he had just spent too long hanging around with mummies. Salma would be the first to say that could affect people in funny ways. Still, in her new position of authority she hoped to enjoy the respect of a fellow curator, even one of a minor collection like the 'Sir Galfridus Bellingham Museum' in Cambridge.

Khamis, however, seemed as oblivious as ever:

‘How is England. I have always wished to see England. Do you know Mr Dan Cruikshank? I know Mr Dan Cruikshank! He has visited us several times.’

‘Err, no …’. Trevor looked somewhat bewildered. There were large sweat-marks over the armpits and the lower back of his shirt.

‘Oh, Mr Dan Cruikshank: a great scholar-’

‘Thank you Khamis,’ Salma interrupted. ‘As you can see, Mr Stewart, we have installed it in one piece, as agreed.’

‘That is something,’ said Trevor, ‘and you have not had to deconstruct it? I heard there were some difficulties getting it here. I did try to warn your predecessor…’

‘There were some unfortunate things during transport, but nothing serious. We Egyptians still know how to move stone. And it is put here in one piece, as we agreed. But still I don’t understand why? It is made of stonework of different ages. The base is 31st Dynasty – you would say ‘Ptolemaic’ - except this very stupid English graffiti - we will remove it. But the sarcophagus is 5th Dynasty: as old before the 31st Dynasty as they were before us. Really it should be taken off and put in the Old Kingdom gallery…’

‘Oh no!’ cried Trevor, at a somewhat inappropriate pitch. Lowering his voice, he continued: ‘Whatever you do you mustn’t touch the shrine! This piece has stood undisturbed in England for almost two hundred years. And anyway the records are clear: Sir Galfridus acquired the sarcophagus in Alexandria from the French after the surrender of the Army of the Nile – they had taken it from a Fatimid mosque where it had been used as an ablution tank. Before that it was an altar in a Byzantine church built from stones plundered from the Memphite necropolis. Even before that it was re-used by a High Priest of Atum sometime in the 21st Dynasty: you can see where he had the Pharaoh’s name chiselled off. It’s been thousands of years since it was emptied of its Pharaoh and re-used. We can’t just ignore all that time – that’s part of history too. You have plenty of sarcophagi, but only one with a monument like this built around it. Don’t disturb it! The Bellingham Museum only agreed to return it on those terms. I still think it was a terrible thing to move it, but our funding...’

‘I know what we agreed, Mr Stewart, I just don’t see why-’

'Galfridus was one of the most important Egyptologists. Without men like him so many things would not have survived. His name must be preserved.'

The man had been a discredited amateur, a ruthless plunderer, and eventually a madman, thought Salma. With his theories about the racial origins of the ancient Egyptians he was the first Caucasian Supremacist in the field - though by no means the last. He'd constructed this absurd 'monument', which had formed the centrepiece of his collection, from pieces of completely different eras, and not even in an ensemble that matched any known ancient precursor. He'd added insult to injury by fixing the statue of himself to it: its stern and jowly features had glared out ever since.

That Trevor Stewart was loyal to such a creation just confirmed Salma's views. What a terrible thing it was that men like Bellingham had been able to come over and steal her country's history. What an insult that she and the National Museum of Egyptian Antiquities had had to deal so diplomatically with this ridiculous organisation. Thank God the days of Egypt fawning to the British were over. Salma was confident that the arguments used to get the Bellingham monument were the first step towards the return of many other looted treasures that now sat in dusty old museums in Europe. As finance director of the museum, her husband had already been involved in approaches to the Louvre and the Egyptian Museum in Turin.

Salma did not say any of this. Instead she asked:

'I haven't yet had a close look at the hieroglyphs…'

'They're from the Book of the Dead. The secrets of resurrection revealed by Thoth, scribe of the Gods. A guidebook and passport to the underworld-'

'Actually it should be translated: 'Book *for* the Dead'', Salma interrupted, offended by his patronising tone. 'The words are meant to be read out by the dead themselves. That is why they used hieroglyphs rather than demotic: these words are supposed to work magic. They protect the dead from being gobbled up by the 'Eater of Hearts'.'

'And he,' added Khamis, unhelpfully, 'was a difficult fellow to please.'

Salma left the museum by the side exit. Beyond the main gate, out in the Square, she could hear the noise of the camp that had been re-formed once again in recent weeks. Of course it was nothing like the size of the protests that had caused the revolutions of the last few years. She still remembered the atmosphere of those days: the vast crowds, the stench of tear-gas, the rapture and the terror. Now things looked like turning violent yet again. She was no blind supporter of the army, but beside the security worry it was putting people off visiting the museum – *her* museum. Sighing, she went out through the gate to where her husband was waiting for her. He rushed forward and hugged her close.

'Salma, something terrible: I think Bastet is dead.'

'Bastet' was the name they had given to the stray kitten they used to feed in the grounds. The two of them liked to play with it as they waited for each other after work. Salma felt slightly sickened at the news.

'What happened?'

'It was this dog. The gardener said it came into the grounds from somewhere and mauled her. Then it disappeared.'

'What dog?'

'It was a horrid filthy, mangy thing. Not a breed he recognised. Certainly not one of the local dogs. It must have come in from the camp.'

Salma was surprised how much the news upset her. In some unspoken way the kitten had been a part of their new life together. And although there were plenty of other cats that hung around the museum grounds, Bastet's elegant classical features had been unique.

They consoled each other for a while. Then, as they turned to walk out into Tahrir, he asked her if she was looking forward to her family coming the following week. This did not fill him with the same quite dread it once would have done, and he even allowed himself to say:

'I'm surprised they agreed to come. Two years ago your father would barely talk to me.'

'That was before your promotion. And anyway, things haven't turned out as badly as he thought. Just be grateful we're not living in the days of the pharaohs – forget about the wedding: you'd have had to pay a bride-price.'

'You're the one who should be grateful: in those days you might have had to marry one of your brothers…'

'Oh you're so disgusting!' she laughed.

'But what about the new piece from England? Are you happy with it?'

'Very happy: it's a great day for the museum. We were vindicated.'

And with that Salma Kanawati walked off with her husband, with the satisfaction of a woman who feels things are running her way.

That night, though, her sleep was fitful and disturbed. She dreamed that she was walking through the museum. She felt or knew that some terrible shadow was stalking her. There was a dreadful sound of metal beating on stone. To her shock she saw that the mummies in the cabinets on each side were wriggling desperately inside their bandages. As she approached the end of the gallery the beating sound got louder. She felt the floor beneath her feet begin to quake.

She was woken by her husband shaking her. It was not yet light - it must still be very early. It seemed Nasri Douma, the museum's night watchman, was on the phone. He was clearly distressed and shouting:

'Come quickly! Come quickly!'

'What is it?' she asked him, after her husband passed her the phone.

'There's a dead man in the museum.'

'There are plenty of dead men in the museum', said Salma. 'We've got Ramesses III himself in there.'

'*No!* A *fresh* dead man!'

'What?! I'll be there in ten minutes.'

And when they had both dressed and hurried over to the museum they discovered that Nasri was right. It was the worker she had asked to stay late and clean up the monument. It seemed that Nasri – who had worked at the museum for years and was as trustworthy as he was ineffectual – had last seen him alive and well around midnight. He had seen and heard nothing unusual after that until the moment he had found the body on his rounds. It was laid out in the Late Funerary Monuments Room. There was nothing missing and no sign of a break-in. The body had a bloody nose and blackened, staring eyes. Other than that it looked normal, almost peaceful.

'Here's a good-looking fellow,' said the police captain, peering down over the figure. 'How long's he been dead?'

'About four thousand years,' said Khamis. They were standing over the case with the new mummy in it. 'And 'he' is a 'she': that's Nubkhas. She was unwrapped by Drovetti in the eighteen twenties, but she's in pretty good shape considering.'

'A real stunner, I'm sure. What's that?'

'It's her ear.'

'Ugh.'

It was fair to say that time had done little for Nubkhas' looks. Her puckered brown skin wrinkled itself over her distorted shrivelled face and strangely flattened breasts.

'What's happened to her mouth?' asked the policeman.

'After the embalming they'd perform the ritual of 'the opening of the mouth'. So the mummies could eat.'

'So they could *eat?!* Why?'

'Same reason they mummified them in the first place,' said Khamis: 'they thought the body had to be saved to help the sahu – that's the spirit that survives after death.'

'And what are these?'

'They're shabtis – little helpers – they're supposed to come alive when you speak the right words. To work for the dead. At first they buried alive real slaves. But I guess that was too expensive. The main thing was to have the right words. And for the name to survive. If your name survives then so do you.'

'It's a bit pathetic and childish if you ask me', said the police captain. 'I mean just think: they could build all those amazing things to try and live forever. But isn't it a bit pointless if you end up looking like her? They must have been really scared of death to have made up all that rubbish.'

'Well, we still know her name, so in that sense it worked.'

The policeman shrugged. Salma called over to them from the other side of the room:

'I'm sorry to interrupt, Captain, but what are your thoughts?

The police captain retreated from the display case where he had been standing with Khamis and looked at Salma. Salma continued:

'Presumably he had some kind of seizure?'

'A funny sort of seizure, Mrs Kanawati. His brain was physically destroyed.'

It was now many hours since Salma had followed the caretaker to his body, and twenty minutes since they had returned from the police station to the museum. The captain was a man easily distracted, and he wore an air of harassed amusement. Now he stepped forward, took something from his deputy and held it up for Salma:

'We found this on the floor by the body. Do you know what it is?'

It was a swivelled bronze rod some Twenty centimetres long. Salma inspected it. It seemed to be caked in fat.

'It's an embalming hook,' she said, automatically. 'It looks like one of ours from the case in room twelve, though of course I'd have to check. They used it before mummification for extracting the brains. They'd insert it through the left nostril, scrape through the ethmoid bone, then scramble up the brain so they could scoop it out through the nose...'

She tailed off and Khamis muttered:

'My God, surely not -'

'I'm afraid so', said the policeman, with a certain grim relish. 'According to the boys at the hospital they examined him to find the cause of death and found his brain was liquefied. There were no other significant injuries. We'll have to wait for the post-mortem, but it looks like that was what killed him. So he would have been alive as it happened –'

'No!' whispered Khamis behind them.

'That's right', the policeman continued, watching them sideways for their reactions. 'I guess the killer was disturbed when the night watchman unlocked the galleries. We still don't know how he got in or out. Have you any idea who would do something like this?'

'No', said Salma. 'The galleries and the whole museum were locked and only a few of us have keys, though I suppose more than usual at the moment because we've been bringing in this new monument. We have had a few break-ins over the last couple of years. Protestors, or people using them as cover, come in to steal the antiquities -'

'Bloody protestors', muttered the policeman.

'We lost quite a bit in 2011, though we've got most of it back now. All except a couple of mummies that were destroyed. We've tried to tighten security but there's a limit to what we can do - you know how it is. We'll have a closer look but we can't see anything missing. Perhaps he disturbed an intruder? But it seems a bit brutal for a thief.'

'There's no end to human brutality,' said the Captain, with the certainty of a man who knew what he was talking about. 'Call me if you find anything unusual – anything at all.'

It was another couple of hours before they could at last return to their work.

'Why hasn't all this packaging been cleared away?' asked Salma.

'The workmen will have nothing more to do with it', said Khamis. 'First Massri goes missing and now this. They think our new display is cursed.'

'Ludicrous – half the stuff in this museum is 'cursed'.'

'Sure. But one of them said he heard whispering in the side galleries. They want you to get Imam Al-Ja'fari to come and perform a *ruqya*.'

'Idiots! We're going to have to do everything ourselves.'

Still, it seemed Nasri had cleaned the monument before he was killed. Looking at it now you could examine its carvings more clearly. The hieroglyphs on the sarcophagus were mostly late Old Kingdom originals, dating from the end of the Third Millennium BC. But most of the name cartouches had been changed over a thousand years later at some time in the 'Third Intermediate', when the sarcophagus had apparently been re-used for one of the High Priests of Amun. The Cannopic Jars were Middle Kingdom. As for the marble base, it looked 31st Dynasty. And although the carvings were hieroglyphs, the way the stone was cut betrayed the Greek influence.

The pyramidion on top was more curious still. As well as the Eye of Horus there was a masonic set and compass and several other symbols she did not recognise. Also the texts were different on each face. In fact now that she looked at them they were a mess of extracts from the Amduat Book of the Underworld and the Pyramid and Coffin Texts, as well as from the Book for the Dead itself. In other words they contained quotes from many different eras. And they looked very cleanly cut. Salma walked round to the back of the monument to see the fourth face of the pyramidion. A closer look at the Ogdoadic symbols here showed something extraordinary: here was an unmistakeable influence of Basilides of Alexandria and perhaps other late pagan scholars. The implications were inescapable.

'How strange - this carving must be nineteenth century.'

'You mean it's – what? - Twelfth Dynasty?' asked Khamis.

'No, I mean nineteenth century, common era. It's modern! This awful man Bellingham must have had it carved himself - on a blank ancient capstone. Why would he do that?'

She started a rough translation under her breath:

''Osiris, Lord of the Underworld… Set, Cutter off of Heads… Apep, Serpent of Chaos and Eater of the Dead… grant power to pass beyond the secret gates… the stars that never set… spheres of powers and principalities… to those who interfere with this tomb...' It's ludicrous. Some of this incantation isn't proper Egyptian at all – this line here is straight out of Plotinus.'

'Why go to the effort of making a fake top for a real sarcophagus?' asked Khamis.

'I don't know', said Salma: 'It's ridiculous.'

'What do you know about him?'

'Only that he perfected Dr Lepsius's system for translating hieroglyphics. And that he had a reputation as an eccentric. You know he wrote an obituary for his dog? It was actually published in the London press! They said he had an unhealthy obsession with mummies: he had one of the biggest private collections in Europe. I suppose old ideas are simpler than thinking for yourself. But I wish I could make sense of his inscriptions.'

'Maybe he hoped this monument would preserve his name? A man might do anything to live forever.'

A while later Trevor Stewart arrived. He looked distinctly the worse for wear. Challenged as to where he had been he touched his forehead and said:

'Turns out the bar in my hotel serves Egyptian Stella. Had five big bottles last night and I must say I'm feeling it this morning. God knows why the Ancient Egyptians invented beer: *they* couldn't even chill it. And it's lethal in this climate.'

He seemed to know nothing of the events of earlier, and appeared to be devastated when they told him the news:

'Well I did warn you!' he blurted.

'What do you mean?'

'Perhaps this wouldn't have happened if the monument had stayed in London. By now you must have read the inscription.'

'Mr Stewart! If we hadn't learned to ignore tomb curses there'd be no Egyptology.'

Outside a great cheer went up from the protestors' camp, followed by a random outbreak of the usual chanting. Trevor flinched.

'It was tricky getting in here today', he muttered.

'Don't worry yourself about them, the police keep it peaceful.'

'It didn't look that way to me!'

'Well perhaps we're more used to revolutions than you are.'

'Oh, so this wasn't your first then?'

'In Egypt nothing ever happens for the first time. I'm sure you've heard of 1952? Or 1919? No? I'm surprised. After all, it was you we were trying to get rid of.'

'*Me*?'

'You do know that the British occupied us for decades?'

'Oh really? You as well? I suppose we did… err, yes - sorry about that.'

Salma looked out of the window into the square and sighed. Yes, she thought, if it isn't the pharaohs it's the priests. It's been like this for 5,000 years now. The old gods might be chucked out, but in the end nothing changes. All those names chiselled off monuments. And no wonder the dead need books, when the living re-write History for themselves. So much for Cairo, 'Mother of the World', modern offspring of ancient Memphis - the oldest city on earth. Where things recur forever and the past lies on the future like an impossible weight. A city where the dead outnumber the living.

It was well after midnight that Salma and Khamis emerged from the office on the top floor of the Museum. They had spent an exhausting evening dealing with the fall-out of the day's events. Trevor had left sometime earlier, and the rest of the staff had all gone. The public parts of the museum had long since been closed up and the lights had been switched off. They walked in silence through the great atrium on their way to the night-watchman's kiosk, where Nasri Douma spent most of his shifts dozing, or watching football on a small television in the corner. They had keys to let themselves out, of course. But it would be a courtesy to tell him they had done for the day.

To their surprise the kiosk was empty.

'He must be off on his rounds', shrugged Khamis.

'Sure,' said Salma. She turned and shouted out that they were going home.

Her voice echoed off in the darkness. There was no sound in reply.

She and Khamis exchanged glances and he tried shouting too. But in answer to their calls they heard nothing but silence.

'Do you think he's left the place un-guarded?' said Salma. 'I'll have him sacked for this.'

'No,' said Khamis, distressed at the thought. 'He probably just couldn't hear us. We shouldn't take any chances, though.'

He reached behind the desk. There he pressed the button that triggered the silent police alarm. Reassured by their imminent arrival, Khamis grabbed a torch that was lying on the desk and the two of them walked out into the great open atrium that formed the centre of the museum. All the lights were off. The darkness was broken only by a dim glow that filtered through the windows. The blacker shapes of Gods and pharaohs loomed everywhere in the darkness.

They started to walk further into the museum, making as much noise they could. Khamis was as worried for Nasri's job prospects as for his own safety. Salma followed him, not wanting to be left behind. He shone the torch around them as they went. There was no sign of anything - or anyone – that shouldn't be there. As they walked through the main central space, towards the alcove with the new acquisition, Salma began to relax. There was certainly no-one there. She looked around the alcove and at the new edifice that occupied the back half of it. She could see the outline of the case with the new mummy in it, with the dark mass of the monument beyond. For a moment she admired the pyramid: its perfect, brutal elegance as a shape. There seemed to be nothing untoward.

But just as they were turning to leave she saw something strange. The lid of one of the cannopic jars on the Bellingham monument was awry. Instinctively she went over to put it back on. It was the one in the shape of jackal-headed Duamutef. As she picked up the lid she noticed a dark stain on its underside. She looked into it. It should have been empty, but there was an irregular black mass inside. She reached in to pick it up, but her fingers recoiled in disgust at the touch, which was wet and warm. An internal organ.

'It looks like something's stomach', said Khamis, when she had finished screaming. 'And I bet I know what's in the other jars.'

Sure enough he confirmed, on closer inspection with his torch, that there were more guts in Qubhsenuef, what looked like lungs in Hapy, and, in the groove on the far corner where the vase of Imsety had once stood, there was part of a liver.

'How disgusting,' she gasped, 'but the man who did this knew what he was doing.'

'Yes,' agreed Khamis, 'and look over there!'

It was in one of the cabinets along the wall, which had been broken open. A heart, with some of the tubes that came off it. It was lying on one half of some Middle Kingdom weighing scales. The cabinet also contained valuable papyri and gold amulets, funerary masks and heart scarabs, but none of them had been taken. This was clearly not a robbery. It was only then it occurred to Salma to wonder who or what these organs belonged to. She did not have to wonder for long, for it was now that she saw it – the dark mass on the floor in the corner.

The head of Nasri Douma was lying in one of the bronze bowls from the 'cult objects of Set' display, which had been placed on the floor by the Bellingham monument. His eyes had been removed and replaced with pieces of glass. With a shock she realised she had almost stepped over it in the dark.

'Oh God no!' cried Khamis: 'poor Nasri! I'm going to get the lights on. Stay here just in case – it's safer until the police get here. I promise I won't go far. I'm surprised they're not here already.'

Whoever had done this was gone, at least from this room, but it must have only just happened. Nor could it have been random. It had to be a ritual killing, by someone who knew their Egyptology. There was certainly a logic to the placement of the organs, which accorded with the ancient rules. True, the head made less sense – the bowl on the floor wasn't related to funerary or mummification rites, but was for food offerings left for the dead.

She walked around the case with the new mummy. It was lying undisturbed in its coffin. Then she walked to the monument again. It was then that she saw something else that was odd. There was an unusual amount of dust or sand on the floor. This was curious – she and Khamis had cleaned up the room themselves the previous day. She crouched down on all fours to try and make it out in the darkness. There seemed to be a trail of it that got thicker as she crawled round the side of the monument. Then she half-thought there was a noise and she froze. She listened but there was nothing: it must have been her shoes against the floor as she moved. She made herself count to ten and then started to crawl forwards again, along the back of the monument.

It was then that a hand grabbed her foot.

Gasping, she tried to rise, but the hand twisted her leg and dragged her backwards. She kicked out, freed herself, and scrambled up – turning. But as she staggered back she tripped over something and fell, landing hard on the marble floor. Dazed, she looked up, only to feel the terrible weight of another body crawl quickly on top of her and pin her down. In the near-pitch black of the gallery she could make out only the deeper blackness of the figure and smell the stench of it. It was much stronger than her, and had pinned her arms at her sides with its legs as it sat astride her. Then a sinewy hand gripped her about the neck and squeezed so hard that she gasped for breath and could not cry out. Bit by bit it pushed her head back with an irresistible strength. The figure's other hand drew close. There was a pause for a second and then Salma felt metal against her nose. It was an embalming hook.

Slowly but with steady, remorseless force, it was driven into her left nostril and up her nose. The pain was more intense than any Salma had ever felt. Within seconds blood was pouring down the back of her throat where the hook was tearing through the soft tissue inside her face. But - with the figure's hand around her throat and her head already forced back as far as it would go – there was no way she could cry out or move her head. She became aware of a deafening rasping sound that at first she could not interpret. She realised in panic through the pain that it was the sound of the hook scraping against the bone, where the top of her nasal cavity met the inside of her skull. There was nothing she could do except utter a strangulated choking cry and know that within seconds the instrument would be deep inside her head and into her brain. She tried to pass out but the pain was too immense.

Then at last she heard a hum in the distance, that signalled that the lights were turning on. The figure slipped off her. The hook was still stuck in place. She tried to roll sideways, hand on the end of the scraper but not daring to move it. Blood was pouring out of her mouth and down her throat, choking her so she could not speak. She stood up and stumbled blindly backwards, the embalming hook still wedged up her nose. Then, screaming, she ran back into the gallery and round the corner, towards where Khamis would be. One by one in the rooms ahead of her the lights were coming on.

She had no idea if her attacker was following behind her or not. She got about half way before colliding with a figure that rose suddenly rose up beside her. But it was not Khamis. As the lights there flickered on she saw it was Trevor Stewart.

'Stop!' he said, in English.

'Mr Stewart! Thank God!'

Trevor caught Salma in his arms and manoeuvred her forcefully onto the padded bench in the centre of the room: 'Lie down here!'

Salma heard herself sobbing incoherently. Trevor bent over her as she lay prone on the bench and reached out for the hook. That moment there was a noise behind Trevor, who let go and started to straighten up to look round. Then there was a dull crunch. He said 'ugh' and sank to the floor.

Salma screamed again.

'It's ok – it's me!' - it was Khamis. He was standing in front of her holding a small granite bust of Thutmose IV, which he had just brought down very hard on Trevor's head. He shone the light of his torch around the room. Trevor was lying brained on the floor, stone dead. There was blood all over him – his own and probably a good deal of Salma's as well. Khamis put down the bust.

'What have you done?!'

'My God, don't you know what was he doing to you? Look at your face! I'll ring for an ambulance. Don't move.'

'Don't leave me!' begged Salma: 'it wasn't just him! There was… there was *something else*'

'Don't be crazy – of course it was him. I just found the rest of Nasri in one of the side galleries. I was just coming back and I saw him leaning over you as I came into the room. Thank God I got here in time.'

'You're wrong… someone else...' she was sobbing now, blood pouring from her nose, as she managed to get the hook free and threw it across the room. Khamis rushed into the galleries she had run from.

But there was no one else there. They were alone.

Needless to say the police captain was only too happy with the way things worked out. Not only had they a clear culprit, but he was a foreigner too. And one, it seemed, who would not be much missed back in England. Even better, he was dead, so there was no question of jurisdictional difficulties.

It was only the next evening, after she had been released from the hospital and the police had finished their questioning, that Salma was able to return to the museum and look around it in daylight. Even in daylight, it was all she could do to make herself walk through its galleries. And, when she reached the alcove where she'd been attacked, she felt sweaty and sick to her stomach.

It was here that she remembered her discovery of the previous night. Sure enough, along with a smear of her blood, there was a trail of sand round the back of the monument. Following it, she saw that it had come from a hole on the reverse face of the plinth.

Running her hands along below the statue of Bellingham, she noticed for the first time a crack in the stone façade where the false door was carved into it. Now, with a little manipulation, a section of it fell forward and came away entirely in her hands. The stench that greeted her was overwhelming and unbearable. Along with the smell came more clouds of dust and what looked like natron. Behind this broken panel she could now see there was a large hollow cavity inside the plinth. Then, getting down on her belly and shuffling forward, she was able to squeeze her head and torso into the hole. She reached out her hands in front of her. It was impossible to see inside - but it did feel like there was something in there. She crawled further forward and stretched out as far as she could.

As she squeezed her whole body forwards into the space, its weight - or perhaps her pushing - must have disturbed something within the plinth, for there suddenly seemed to be some movement inside the cavity. Twisting round as much as she could she thought she felt something loose to her right giving a little. Sure enough she felt to that side and realised there was a mass up against and behind her. In the dark she felt awkwardly along it with the back of her half-freed right hand. It was something course like a fabric and then something smooth. It had tufts of wiry hair. Then she felt its arms close around her.

Gasping and twisting herself free, she scrabbled back out of the space as fast as she could and fled.

'I told you it wasn't Mr Stewart – or not only him.'

'What are you saying?' asked Khamis, as she dragged him back to the gallery, with a couple of other members of staff in tow.

'No!' she cried, 'the monument – I opened it. It's a tomb!'

'What are you talking about? Of course it's a tomb.'

'You don't understand – go and *look!*'

Khamis followed her back into the alcove. He gasped when he saw the excavations she had made at the back of the Bellingham plinth. He bent down and shone his torch into the hole.

'Be careful – don't get too close!'

'*You* should've been careful. Old tombs that are suddenly opened can release all sorts of dangerous chemicals and gases…' He broke off with a disgusted gasp.

'Do you see him?'

'I see something…'

'For God's sake be careful!'

There was a pause as he rummaged in the far corner of the dark space within.

'There's nothing to worry about in here, just this old thing.'

He brought out a rancid object. It was the remains of what looked like a dog that had been mummified, with only partial success.

'But what else – *what else?!*'

'There is nothing else. See for yourself.'

Bending over gingerly, Salma looked into the plinth.

'Impossible!'

It was quite empty.

The unpleasant disturbances at the Cairo Museum were soon forgotten amidst the wider bloodshed of another violent summer. But they remain a cause for debate and scandal in Egyptological circles. The city police concluded that Trevor Stewart was alone responsible. It seemed that, unhinged by the breaking up of the collection that it had been his life's work to preserve, he had gone mad and committed two murders and an attempted murder.

But Salma Kanawati, who moved to Alexandria with her husband shortly after recovering from her lucky escape, came to a different and stranger conclusion. A conclusion which was only strengthened when she found this entry in the Encyclopaedia of Egyptology:

Sir Galfridus Lee Bellingham b. 1778, Engl. Amateur antiquarian and collector, who brought many artefacts back from Egypt. Highly suspicious of the later generation of professional archaeologists. His methods, now discredited, influenced Plongeon and Bligh-Bond, but came to be viewed as eccentric, even un-natural. Deep interest in the Gnostics and Neo-Pythagoreans. Expelled from Royal Oriental Society after delivering controversial paper on physical resurrection. Mental breakdown in final years. D. 1853. Final resting place unknown.'

The Cleansing of the Temple

'I will take the unknown road
to the land of the Cedar forest,
where no man's name is written,
and I will see the evil that lives in that land,
the watcher of the forest
who never sleeps,
and whose name is Oblivion.'

Gilgamesh, Tablet 2

This story was told to me by a friend, who teaches philosophy at Oxford. It's a nasty one, and as you'd expect it does make you think. He told it one winter's night in the Senior Common Room, where we had retired after dinner, to drink port in front of the fire:

'It happened to a former student of mine. Reshma Nasherwani is one of the most impressive people I've taught. She'd have done even better academically, if it hadn't been for her illness.

Not that she thinks it's an illness, then or now. 'Don't medicalise my beliefs', she says. And she has a point. If the History of Philosophy has shown us anything, it's that those who look most deeply into the heart of human nature - who see themselves most clearly - are also the most susceptible to despair. We argued it out for weeks in her third year before she let me get her help. We changed her mind that time, with Lithium and Prozac.

She is one of those people with a thirst for knowledge, but also an anxious hunger for affection. Both traits can be dangerous. She took her degree, and would have stayed on for the Doctorate. But it seems her father had other plans for her. Metaphysics was not a respectable career choice. So she went off to London to train for the Bar. She landed a prestigious ‘pupillage’ at 1 Coke Court Chambers, specialising in Equity and Trusts.

She’d been pupil there just a few weeks when I got her email. She was coming up to Oxford that evening. Could she drop round to Old College? I agreed right away. For some reason I told my wife I had a college meeting.

When she knocked on my study door, I saw at once there was something wrong. She was pretty as ever. I noticed she’d changed the way she wore her hair. But her usual spark was gone. She looked tired and anxious. Underneath her make-up there were stress spots round her mouth. She came in - hugged me - and burst into tears.

I can picture her exactly, sitting there on my sofa, laughing away the last of her sobs, wiping her little nose with my hanky. She took a trembly sip from a glass of water I’d thrust at her. I told her to start at the beginning. This is what she said:

‘Oh Doctor – no I just can’t get used to using your first name - I don’t know who else to talk to. It all started at Halloween, when the clocks went back. I’ve always had a thing about the clocks going back – a silly superstition, you’d say. You know it’s very bad luck to forget. My Gran used to tell us when we were kids: ‘Reshma, don’t forget to put the clocks back, or one of the whispering djinn might get you. Well I’d run out of time with some drafting for Richard. He’s my pupil master – basically my boss. I was working through the weekend to catch up. I was exhausted. I’d been in Chambers all that Saturday. And when I got home Alex was out. He had his phone off again. He didn’t come back that night. What? Yes. Alex and I are still together-’

She sounded a little defensive. She’d been going out with Alex Bradbury since her Freshers’ week at College. He was a bright kid - and was something in the City now. I don’t know how well he treated her.

She continued:

‘I was worried and I couldn’t sleep. I wanted everything to be right for him when he came home. And I managed to get myself into a real state. I still don’t know exactly how I did it, but I think I must’ve put the clocks back an hour – before I got to bed that night I mean - and anyway when I woke up, what with everything else, I'd forgotten I'd done it and I put them back again. That was it. I lost an hour. I'd do anything to get it back.'

'Well,' I said, 'it's easily done.'

'On Monday morning I was supposed to meet Richard in Court. But all my clocks were wrong – I was an hour late! He was furious. 'Really unprofessional', he said. I'd lost my hour. It's been the same story ever since – I can't catch up.

'I was trying to remember your tutorial on Time: the link between the Past and the Present - Parmenides calling Time an illusion - Kant saying it's just the way we rationalise Sequence. Then Einstein shows everyone's wrong: it's really a form of *space* - it bends – it appears to change depending on your relative speed. So clocks on an object moving quickly away from you seem to slow down. Perhaps Time's stopped for me because I've stopped - stopped moving forward, I mean - and the World is speeding away from me. It's like I've been left behind. Like I'm a mile after where everyone else is - one hour outside the life others are living. I can't see anything much to look forward to.

'At work I get convinced I can't do it. And then I'm so frightened that I'm useless. It's one of those fears that fulfils itself. I stay as late as I can, 'til Richard sends me home. Then I go and work in the library. But I can't seem to get anything right, or finish anything fast enough for him. I wish he knew how hard I'm trying!

'My father [here her voice caught again] – he died last year. No I'm fine - thank you. I don't think he ever really got over Mum's suicide. I was too young to be told the truth about her drowning – I was only seven when it happened. After that I was everything to him. And he so wanted me to be a barrister. He was really proud of me. But now I worry that I'll never be kept on in Chambers. I feel I'm letting them both down. So I want to know: what's wrong with me? Why am I so completely useless? How do I get my lost hour back?'

Here, finally, she paused. It seemed clear her old condition had returned. With the same over-intellectualised paranoias. No doubt brought on, like last time, by exhaustion and stress. She always did push herself too hard.

I thought for a moment and said:

'Err… well, you could start by re-setting your clocks.'

'No you don't understand! I do that every day. That's just it - the disturbing thing. When I do they start to slow down again. And next time I look: they've all stopped. Every clock in my flat. And always at the same time: 00:38.'

She fell silent again. I became suddenly conscious – in that way that we cannot hold on to, and that would drive us mad if we did – of the furious four-beats-a-second ticking of the clock on my desk.

'But ironically,' she added, 'if I hadn't screwed up my clocks I'd never have seen it.'

'Seen what?'

'Oh sorry! I hadn't got to that, had I? I'd never have seen Ichabod.'

'Ichabod?'

'Yes – that's what I call him. You know, like in those Logic lectures: 'Socrates is a man. All men are mortal. Therefore Socrates is mortal. Ichabod is immortal. Therefore Ichabod is not a man' - or whatever!'

'Oh OK, 'Ichabod'...'

'It was that first morning. In the hour I'd lost - before I realised I'd lost it. I thought I'd pop into Lincoln's Inn Library to pick up some books. There's a display case in the hall outside the library. It's full of bits and pieces of stuff they've dug up from the Inns over the years. All sorts of funny old things. I must've looked at them before. But somehow I'd never seen Ichabod and - oh my God – look at him!'

On her phone she showed me a series of magnified photos. The photos were of a dark object in a rather forlorn display case. Her own blurred reflection could be seen in the glass.

The object was a small metal statuette, maybe nine inches tall. It was of a curious thin figure, cut about and very worn; primitive and ugly. It was warped out of all proportion - its fingers, for example, were absurdly long. And it was strangely scored all over its body, as if it had been hacked at repeatedly with a blade. The thing's face – if you could call it a face - was unpleasantly distorted. Its mouth was twisted and open. Its hollow eyes had presumably once held inlays.

'So what do you think?' She asked. 'Richard couldn't see why I'd have wanted a photo of something like that.'

'To be honest,' I laughed 'I agree!'

'I thought you'd be interested! Or that anyway Professor Jarvis would be.'

Jarvis certainly would be, I conceded. Besides she sounded a little hurt. And I'd learned that any enthusiasm when she was like this had to be nurtured. How could I have known the danger?

'Come on then,' I sighed, 'let's see if the old man's in.'

'Really?' she said, 'For my Aristotle paper I used to go to his lectures on Ancient Athens: 'New College was being besieged by Balliol and Magdalen, funded by the Great King of Cambridge'! And the way he used to talk about the Trojan War and the old gods - as if he half believed it all. We all loved him.'

'Yes I'm sure,' I said, 'and no doubt one of these days we'll be inspected, and he'll get us into all sorts of trouble.'

We went straight round to the Warden's lodge. Jarvis flung open the door and his hound exploded out at us. 'Down boy!'

I introduced Reshma. She flinched from the dog and said:

'Ooh Professor Jarvis – I'm so pleased to see you!'

'Ignore the beast, he's over-excited – down boy! Do come in.'

I told Reshma to show Jarvis her photos and glumly she passed him her phone. It seemed her joy was gone again and she withdrew into melancholy silence. I'd seen this look of hers before. I knew the despair was back with her then, heavy and black as ever. She was looking uneasily at Jarvis's dog. It was making unpleasant growling and yelping sounds at her. Perhaps it could sense her fear.

Jarvis, however, was fascinated:

He angled the phone and held it up to the light: 'It looks pre-classical - maybe Assyrian. Where did you see it?'

She told him the story.

'What an ugly fellow! I've never been a fan of archaic sculpture – look how much they've buggered up the proportions. Not much to celebrate from an aesthetic perspective… except perhaps that power objects get from being very old. But to find something like this in Lincoln's Inn! I wonder if they know what they've got… You must show these to Clovis Finlayson. He's a queer fish of course, but this is just his bag. Knows more about the Ancient Near East than any man living. Clovis used to be at Sparta,' [by which he meant Balliol] 'but now he's at the Brit. Mus.. It was a shame to lose him from the University to a museum. But he enjoys it - he's like a good man who's accidentally found himself working in a brothel.'

He couldn't say much more about it. But he seemed to think that, if genuine, it might be an important find.

'Yes' Reshma murmured as we left, 'poor old Ichabod is rather horrid to look at, isn't he?'

That night, after saying goodbye to her, I looked up 'djinn' in the dictionary. The entry read:

'Supernatural creatures of Islamic folklore. Often described as beings of smokeless fire. Possessing free will. Frequently evil. They are treated by scholars as cultural survivals; memories of the pre-Islamic gods and demons of the Ancient Near East.'

And so a week later I found myself breaking my usual rule and taking the coach up to London. It was just as I remembered it: the pollution, the noise, the impatient haste of passers-by. In the sky above the City hung a greasy and malignant gibbous moon, circled by a sickly yellow aura.

I came up out of the tube at Chancery Lane, arms folded against a bitter wind that blew down the steps and into the station. Ragged pages of the Evening Standard whipped past me as I emerged beneath the over-hang of a crouched half-timbered building. Reshma was waiting for me outside the entrance to Gray's Inn. Leaning forward to kiss her cheek I noticed her eyes were puffy and ringed with black. She looked as subdued as before.

'I'm pleased you're here', she said, but her thin smile died as she said it. Then her voice dropped, and she told me she still had 'trouble with her clocks':

'Since I lost my hour everything's been going wrong,' she said. 'Alex and I… I think I'm losing him. He turned round one night and said he didn't love me anymore. He's met someone else, I'm sure of it. There's this girl at his office… We had a massive row… He's always out now. It doesn't matter how much I beg him not to go. I'm trying to arrange to spend more time with him. But he says to give him more space...'

'I'm sorry to hear that', I said.

'I can't sleep. I keep having the most appalling dreams. Dreams about someone… some*thing*… unspeakable. Following me. I think I know the things it wants to do.'

'Normal anxiety dreams,' I interrupted, 'we all have them. They're only a problem if we pay attention to them. Too much introspection can be dangerous- '

'But these – these are *not* normal dreams. And I'm finding it hard to concentrate at work. Richard gave me this opinion to write. And I just couldn't get my head round it. So I asked Benjamin – he's the other pupil – for help. Pupils are usually at war with each other – stabbing each other in the back. After all we're basically both going for the same job at the end of the year. But Ben's really nice. He told me to look for a case he said had the answer.'

'That's good then isn't it?'

'Yes but after work I went to Lincoln's Inn library. I spent hours looking for it, but it didn't seem to exist. I stayed at the library too late. Can you believe it: I fell asleep. I was at my usual desk up in the high gallery. I guess the librarians can't see you up there. I don't know what woke me – I don't like to think – but when I opened my eyes all the lights were off. They'd closed up for the weekend. I was locked in!'

'What did you do?'

'I hammered on the door, and shouted at the top of my voice. But the whole building was completely dark and the noises just echoed off into nowhere. I called Alex but his phone was off, so I left a message telling him to come and rescue me. Eventually I thought of ringing the lodge and finally got someone to let me out. But then as I was leaving the Inn someone jumped out and scared me.'

'Who was it?'

'I've no idea. There's a soup kitchen in Lincoln's Inn Fields and lots of tramps gather there. They're famished I suppose. I feel sorry for them, of course. But there's something scary about them, isn't there? I often wonder what they've seen - what they're thinking. Do you think they hate us?'

'I don't know. Maybe.'

'Perhaps one of them wandered into the Inn afterwards, looking for somewhere to sleep. There was a gross musty smell about him, too. Fortunately Alex arrived just in time. At first I thought he'd been playing a trick on me. But he said he'd only just got there. I shouted at him anyway. I'm such a crap person, I really am.'

'I don't think you're a crap person.'

'Thanks Doctor.'

We arrived at the British Museum just as the last visitors were leaving. Professor Finlayson met us in the lobby and walked us through the galleries to his office. He was a rather extraordinary man. He looked as if he'd just been dug up by Tony Robinson. He wore a crumpled leather suit jacket of almost Neolithic antiquity, complete with proper lapels and pockets. He was balding above a froth of frizzy white hair. He sported a magnificently unkempt beard. His sallow face was creased with lines of amused intelligence.

He asked after 'Young' Jarvis, about whom he spoke indulgently, as though he were a mere intellectual infant. Apart from that he made no concessions at all to the normal laws of conversation. Instead he kept up a verbal deluge of bewildering learnedness on a wide range of subjects – regardless of whether or not we were following it. As we descended the steps from the public galleries, for instance, there were several comments made quite unapologetically in Latin and Greek. Even at one stage, I believe, in Sanskrit. To illustrate some philological point he actually started singing an ancient Sumerian hymn, to the tune of 'British Grenadiers'. I caught Reshma's eye, and for the first time in ages she grinned. We reached his cramped study and she showed him her photos.

'It's very scratched, I'm afraid,' she said, frowning, 'Do you think it's interesting? Jarvis – Professor Jarvis – seemed to think it might be.'

Finlayson peered at the images, muttering to himself delightedly.

'Did he now? Well well well', he mumbled, 'And now I can see why. What luck! You are quite a find, aren't you Sir? Old. Yes so old. Of course these 'scratches' on you are not scratches at all. No no no - that would never do. They are indeed writing - 'σήματα λυγρα'. Fairly late Akkadian cuneiform, by the look of it. I wonder what you have to say to me, eh, after all this time? Mirabile dictu!'

Here he turned to us again. He spoke with the exasperated patience of a teacher addressing children:

'You must remember that for half our history we wrote without alphabets - using wedges scratched on clay. Though admittedly it's rather rarer to see cuneiform on metal like this. I fear from these photos it is no simple matter to read it all…' (he peered over it again more closely and groaned) 'But I can just make out the beginning of the inscription.'

'What does it say?'

'It says: 'Behold! I belong to Jové Wot, that Hatti men call Yové-Watna.'

'Errr…?'

‘This could be a very important find indeed. It’s – my goodness – it’s tantalising, isn’t it?’

‘Why?’ asked Reshma.

‘Eh? Oh well, let us not get ahead of ourselves until I translate the rest of it – no no that would never do - this is pure speculation, pure speculation, you understand, but I think this figurine might just be a very important part of the history of the Hittites, and – who knows?! – perhaps of the Middle Ages too.’

‘The Hittites?’ I said.

He tutted in mock exasperation.

‘Umm… remind me?!’

‘Oh dear dear dear! The Hittites were a major Bronze Age civilisation who ruled Turkey and Syria in biblical times. Every bit as advanced as the Egyptians. Then at the very end of the Bronze Age – paff! – they disappear. The end was sudden, complete, and final. After about 1200BC we have – nothing. Silence. Every city and town in their Empire was destroyed by fire. We’re talking about massive depopulation, lasting hundreds of years. The towns and cities deserted. Social organisation forgotten. The complete obliteration of their society.’

‘I guess we easily forget’, I said, ‘how precarious Civilisation is.’

‘Quite so, quite so,’ he said. ‘It was a traumatic shift from the Age of Bronze, which they possessed, to the Age of Iron, which they did not. Some Egyptian sources talk of overwhelming incursions of ‘Sea Peoples’ across the frontiers. But whether these barbarians were the cause of the apocalypse, or were just displaced by something else – climate change, perhaps, or a natural disaster – that’s the real question. We just don’t know. It was a true Dark Age. Even literacy was lost.’

‘What?’ asked Reshma, ‘You mean people forgot writing?!’

‘Yes yes, very careless of them! Because of course as a result there are no records. We don’t know what really happened to them. I always think we take writing rather for granted. We forget how old are the meanings lying dormant in even the most mundane words. Err, let me see…' he grabbed at the nearest modern object to hand – a Kit Kat on his desk, 'Look at this for example. Even this - our Latin letter 'a', which comes of course from the Greek 'alpha', is a corruption - via Phoenician - of the Proto-Canaanite 'aleph', which was itself originally a pictogram of an ox – a distant memory of our pastoral roots. And of course I could tell a similar story about the other letters. We ignore all these echoes of the truly ancient at our peril…'

'But how could they just forget something like writing?' asked Reshma, bringing the Professor back to the point.

'Eh? Oh, well back then writing was much more vulnerable. Only a small class of scribes knew its secret. You might say it was more like a form of sorcery. Just stop for a moment and consider its power. With writing you can make an idea move through Space, or Time. Even outlast your death. In fact you can send a thought across Millennia. A thought that could influence anyone who reads it. A message, of hope or fear, or love or… hate. A prayer. Or a warning.'

Reshma leaned forward with fascinated excitement.

'In any case', he went on, 'for three thousand years no-one even remembered who the Hittites were. Then, in 1906, Winckler's expedition for the German Oriental Society was excavating near the village of Boghazköy in Turkey and they dug up Hattusas – the great Hittite capital. In its destruction layer they found something truly astonishing: a lost literature. The great royal archives of the Hittites. Thousands of texts on clay tablets. Set hard by the fire that wasted the city that made them. Unread for 3,000 years. And in a language no-one now knew how to read. But we did eventually manage to decipher them. Hittite turns out to be an Indo-European language, quite similar to our own. But we've translated only a tiny portion of the texts. There aren't many Hittite speakers around, you see, what with all the funding cutbacks. A few at Ankara University, a small department in Berlin, and there's the odd person at Oxbridge with a smattering…'

‘And then there’s you?’ I asked.

‘Yes, I speak most of the main written Indo-European languages, although my Old Church Slavonic’s pretty rusty….’

‘But what do they say?’ asked Reshma, now laughing with impatience.

‘Oh - they’re mostly dull administrative documents that just happened to be preserved. Legal and religious paperwork, you might say - or rather ‘clay-work’ I suppose. It’s infuriating, but none of the surviving tablets give much clue as to what happened. It must’ve been sudden and violent though – they found unburied bodies everywhere, even abandoned meals. And all the texts pre-date the end. Or rather – all but one…

‘You see Winkler did find some very damaged tablets in a kiln in a temple near the Sphinx Gate – they were still being baked when the city was sacked. It’s the fragments of a letter to a client King in Carchemish - never sent of course - and it seems to refer to the coming cataclysm. Tantalising. But frankly it poses as many questions as it solves.

‘The point is it mentions this Yové-Watna. He may have been a rival claimant to the throne, or perhaps a foreign chief or king. It could just be a co-incidence, but we’ve found no other cases of the name. So you see your figurine might just be of this man. I have the translation of the letter somewhere, if you want to read it. Yes – erm - here it is.’

He took down a stuffed cardboard folder, flicked through it, and passed us a typewritten sheet. It read as follows:

‘I, Suppiluliumas, Great King, King of Hatti, Lukka, Kizzuwatna, and all the lands as far as the [Euphrates?], do beseech you, Talmi-Teshub, King of Kargamiš, that before it is too late you urgently send us help.
[LINE MISSING]
Wilusa was destroyed by the men of Ahhiyawa. The Kaska horde thought it a sign of our failing strength. They

ravaged Anziliya and despoiled the temples and slew the men and raped the women and took away the children.
[BROKEN]
In wrath I mustered the chariots and the armies and all the might of Hatti, and I smote the Kaska people and slew prodigious multitudes.

I pressed on in triumph even unto Azzi-Hayasa, the far land, the cursed land, where no man's name is written, and the Gods tread not.
[3 LINES MISSING]
beyond the crossing-place of a mighty river, where the chariots could not follow, to the great forest that is in that land. For seven days I trod the paths of the forest, that many fear to tread, but the Goddess, my Lady Arinna, held me by the hand, and I conquered my fear.
[LINE MISSING]
and found out what was secret and uncovered what was hidden
[   ] came again to the spring
[   ] in the place where three paths meet
[   ] the guardian of the place, the silent one
[   ] he took twelve
[   ] performed the cleansing of the temple
[   ] could hear them still screaming
[   ] and those that then lived turned back, but I would not turn back, and I seized great Yové-Watna, whom the people of that accursed land call
[   ] and I brought him back in triumph to Hattusas.

But then I lay down with my head on my arms and dark sleep came over me, and I dreamed I was back in the forest and was again in the place by the water,
and I saw the Evil that lives there, and it stirred
[   ]
And my commander of a thousand that was slain in that place came to me in my dream, with bloody visage and fearful lamentations. He said that I and all our people would die, and all the Gods would die, and words(?)

themselves would die, and our cities would be destroyed by fire and utterly accursed. For Death was coming to the land of Hatti, and the very name of Hatti would be lost. I awoke and asked my servant, 'Did you call me? Then why am I awake? Did you touch me? Then why am I afraid? Did a God pass by? Then why is my flesh so cold? For I have had a most disturbing vision.'

Then the lands sickened, and the crops failed, and the people grew sick, and everywhere the barbarians made conspiracy against us, and Death came in black ships from over the Sea. Every mouth turned to me and asked 'Why, Great Lord, have these horrors befallen us'? But I could answer them not. I turned my mouth to my Lord the Thunder-God and asked 'Why, Great Lord Teshub, have these horrors befallen us?' But the Thunder-God answered me not. In despair we performed the dread sacrifices(?) from the ancient days of my ancestor Labarnas, that Hattusilis forbad, and we wept many tears as we each slew our (youngest?)
[ ] but still Death walked abroad in the land, and in the temple they heard Yové-Watna laugh.

But Ammunas, once high priest of my brother, the false King Arnuwandas, came unto the palace and smiled, and turned his lying mouth to me, and said: 'Great King, I know why these horrors have befallen us. You have brought them hither. For you have let in a great Evil to the Land of Hatti. Send Yové-Watna back, beyond the crossing-place of the river, to the land of the great forest. And then take the chief of the overseers of a thousand and divide into two
[ ] that the land may know safety, as it did in the days of your father, Tudhaliyas, when the Hatti people prospered and the World was at peace.

So I sent Yové-Watna back, beyond the crossing-place of the river, to the land of the great forest. And I took the chief of the overseers of a thousand, and I divided into two his (goods?), and his sons and daughters, and his wife, and

finally himself, and the two halves I set up on each side of the crossing place of the river [Halys], that Yové-Watna would not return and cross it in his wrath. But Yové-Watna, beloved of Illuyankas, did cross, and the Evil is returned, and all the scribes give themselves to the Gods, and we know not why they do it.
[9 LINES MISSING]
Truwisa is burned, and Arzawa is burned, and Alasiya is burned, and all the cities are taken and made a wilderness. And the men are slain, and the women raped, and the children taken, and the land declared accursed. And all our chariots are away in Lukka fighting, and yet more evil men come in black ships from over the Sea, and none can stand before their arms. Brother, behold! - I beseech in the name of Kubaba that you send us help before it is too late
[MISSING TO END]'

'That's all we have of the inscription,' said the Professor, pointing, 'but then there's this bizarre colophon':

'The End. Third tablet. Hand of Alluwamnas, master scribe. Alluwamnas knows why the scribes give themselves to the Gods. It is an awful thing, an evil we shall none of us escape.'

We were silent for a moment. A neon strip light flickered loudly in the corner. Then Reshma asked:

'What does it mean?'

'We've absolutely no idea', he said, 'I think it defies interpretation. And remember this text is the *best* written source we have for the Bronze Age Collapse in Ancient Anatolia.'

'So no-one knows what happened to- ?'

'To poor old King Suppiluliumas, or his loyal scribe Alluwamnas? Sadly not, but I somehow doubt it was pleasant. Whether this 'Yové-Watna' allied with barbarians to revenge himself on the Hittites – or who exactly he was in the first place – we just don't know. The gruesome description of what sounds like human sacrifice is certainly not what we'd expect from the Hittites at this era. No no no. But then we're talking about a society right on the edge.

'And as for that business with the river-crossings, many so-called 'primitive' cultures treat liminal areas like that as places of, well, sinister or supernatural power. It's a bit like the way the parish boundaries here don't extend across the Thames. Half way across and you're beyond the limits of the respective ecclesiastical authorities. Religiously speaking, you're in no-man's land. That's why you get so many folktales of the monster at the ford or the revenant on the bridge. The Devil lives always at the edge of things – at the boundary. Anyway,' he added, 'how did you find him?'

'I work near Inner Temple - I'm a lawyer there.'

'Oh that's right, Jarvis said: you're the *advocatus diaboli*.'

'So what on Earth is it doing there?' I asked.

'Ah. Well I did make some progress on that. That's to say – it's not my area, but I do have a really rather sexy theory. Talking of boundaries, you'll know of course why Inner and Middle Temple are where they are? No? Tut tut! The Inns of Court are ancient Liberties, just outside the old walls of London Town, 'without' the boundaries of her City parishes. In other words they're just beyond the border of the Corporation, so neither the writ of the Guildhall nor the Bishop of London runs there. Spiritually dead ground. Perfect for lawyers, eh?! But that's just a coincidence. The connection with lawyers is only six centuries old – I believe the first Black Books of the Inns start in 1422. The Masters of the Bench took the place over from a very different crowd: the Knights of the Temple. Hence the name of course. And that, I believe, is where our friend here may come in.'

'How do you mean?' asked Reshma.

'Well it isn't featured in the Chronicle of Albert of Aix,' said the Professor, 'so I suppose there's no reason you'd know it. But there's an intriguing story in the

Annals of Pseudo-Psellus, preserved in summary in the *Byzantine Compendium*.

'In the year 1101 a young man called Odo of Speyer joined the crusade of Raymond IV. They crossed the river Halys in good order and marched into the unknown East. Three days later they passed beneath great heathen images carved onto the face of a cliff. Now those reliefs must've been Hittite - their route took them right through what had once been the ancient Hittite heartlands. But they were marching into a trap. A vast army of Saracens was in the hills around them. There was no way out. They were massacred almost to a man.'

'I still don't see-' Reshma started to say.

'Now our Odo and one retainer managed to find a horse and cut their way out. They fled East into the mountains. They were lost for weeks in deserted country. Eventually, thinking they were followed, they took refuge in a forest, where they wandered for seven days without food or water. Finally, they started to hallucinate from thirst and had terrifying visions 'from God.' They found a spring, and by the spring they found a figurine. They took it as a sign of deliverance. They recovered their strength and left the forest, somehow finding their way through the Cilician Gates to the safety of Christian lands. They reached Antioch on Good Friday 1102.

'Odo went on to become a founding knight of the Temple at Jerusalem, though there is no mention of him after that. I think it's possible he took the statue with him. When the Kingdom of Jerusalem was destroyed, and the Temple Mount cleansed of Christian worship, the Templars disbursed to their sites all across Europe. Including of course our Temple Church here in London.

'In 1312 the Templars themselves were suppressed and purged from the Temple and burnt. They were accused of sodomy, heresy, and sacrilege. Under torture many confessed to spitting on Christ's cross, and worshiping a graven image they called 'Baphomet.' It was a slander of course, for the show-trials – men will confess to anything to avoid castration and disembowelment. But the common story suggests the Order did possess an important object of that name. Now it strikes me that 'Baphomet' sounds very much like a corruption of 'Bavemot' or 'Bovemot' in Old Armenian. And that - if we follow the usual labio-dental changes, and other philological rules – does sound deliciously close to 'Jove wot.' That could just be our Yové-Watna. Perhaps this fellow here eh?

'Too bad we'll never know for sure. There haven't been any Templars since the land was turned over to the lawyers – an even more sinister bunch in my view! And the archaeology of the area, even if it could be attempted, would be quite hopeless. After the Temple was purged of the Knights, the Inns were destroyed by Wat Tyler. The revolting peasants burnt all the books, tore down the buildings, even slew one another in their drunken fury. The Wars of the Roses brought yet more destruction – they're said to have started in Temple gardens. Then the Great Fire obliterated the area again, and later of course the Blitz.'

'It sounds like over the years they've had a lot of bad luck', said Reshma.

'Yes I suppose they have', said the Professor, 'Anyway, if you're happy to come back next week, I'll contact the Inn and see what more I can find out.'

A week later Reshma met me off the tube at Embankment (for Temple station was closed) and, rather stiffly, she hugged me. I said that she looked thin and I was worried for her.

'Did I used to be fat?'

She laughed at my discomfort, but I could see things were no better with her. If anything they were worse. She looked run-down and had a heavy cold. Still, she was excited to see me. Or, at any rate, relieved.

'Shall we drop into Chambers on the way?' she asked, 'I can show you where I work.'

We walked along the Embankment, past Cleopatra's needle with its biscuit-base hieroglyphs. The river churned black and silent to our right. To the left were the lawns of the Temple where they slope down to the river, under a phalanx of trees that guard old London's legal quarter from the layman. It was already dark. A tentative rain that had been floating down all evening was gaining confidence. There were no lights on in the red-brick row of Georgian offices that Reshma told me was King's Bench Walk. She fobbed us through a gate and we turned in under a rusticated archway. Carved figures stared out at us blankly from thc stonework. Our shoes clipped along a cobbled street. It led up to a courtyard flanked by ancient buildings. In the centre was a fountain - still green water and dead leaves. A huge Mulberry tree stood sentinel above it. The skeleton of its branches was framed by clouds lit an angry orange by the glare of the City. Electrified gaslights threw out halos in the sodden air. It was my first time in the Inns of Court. Who knew that at the centre of the modern capital there beat this decrepit medieval heart?

'You can't say it isn't beautiful here', I ventured, tentatively.

'Ever since I got here', said Reshma, 'I've thought two things. That it is achingly beautiful. And that there is something indefinably wrong with it. Or perhaps something's wrong with me – maybe this place isn't ready yet for, well, people like me. When I'm here I feel… haunted. I don't mean by the funny sort of things that people are supposed to see here: like the disembodied head of Oliver Goldsmith, laughing at lone passers-by. Or Hawkins, the Hanging Judge – wigged and robed - marching off towards the Courts and disappearing through a wall. No nothing so silly. What I mean is just - oh I don't know - that here when other people are around you still feel alone. But when they aren't, well, you don't. Perhaps the Professor is right – the statue brings bad luck.'

Reshma led us through a labyrinth of passages and courtyards. Set into the facade of one old building was an iron sun-dial, dated 1686. Looking to break an awkward silence, I said something like:

'That's what you need – you'd have a job stopping that clock.'

Reshma read out the engraving underneath it:

'Shadows we are and like shadows depart.'

I tried to say something jolly but it sounded forced and lame. The silence of the gloomy old offices looming over us seemed to suck frivolity away.

'Anyway don't joke about it', she said 'I still can't get my stupid clocks to work. Every time I get them going, they stop at thirty eight minutes past midnight.'

We emerged under a sort of cloistered portico, our footsteps echoing around us. There rising up in front was what I knew must be the Temple church. It's a curious building, more military than ecclesiastical - round at one end, and sunk below the level of the modern ground. A few raised tombs were scattered randomly across the court: low, weather-beaten, odd. Coke Court stood nearby: a mute cluster of Victorian buildings just to the north of the church. When we reached the Chambers annexe at number 5, she swiped a card and let us in. I felt like an impostor.

Reshma worked in the dark high-ceilinged room of her Pupil Master, Richard Lavery. Of his personality there was little evidence, except a bland work of modern art hanging above the fireplace, somewhat incongruous amidst the grand Victorian mouldings. I wondered if he knew how hard he was working her, or how close she already was to breaking point.

The room was filled with hundreds of files of legal papers. They were stacked in cardboard boxes across the floor, and up into a ziggurat by the window. They constituted, it seemed, a refuse-heap of millions of administrative words. I tried to imagine how an archaeologist of the future would judge our society in three thousand years, if they were all that was left of us. The bookshelves were lined with old leather-bound law books. One remaining shelf was Reshma's. It held a few fearsome legal textbooks, some primary-coloured student guides, and (I was pleased to see) her battered copy of Heidegger. Good for her.

She worked in the corner, facing the wall. On her old desk were a profusion of highlighted documents, her laptop, and a scattering of hairclips.

'So how have you been getting on?' I asked.

‘Oh you know. Good days and bad days…’ she said, blowing her nose, ‘Actually mostly bad ones lately.’

‘You can tell me.’ I said ‘That is - if you think it’d help.’

With that she let loose another torrent: personal, forceful, incoherent:

‘Oh God! I’m finding it so hard to work. I can’t get this thing last Friday out of my head. Horrible. It was the night before I came up to College to see you. I was working late in Lincoln’s Inn, looking for this case. And I got locked into the library.’

‘Yes’, I said, ‘you told me.’

‘Anyway the night-porter came to let me out. I thought he was really creepy. So instead of walking with him to the main gate, I went into Old Square to go out through the back. There was a thick fog that night. ‘A good chancery fog’ Richard called it. It was hard to see anything distinctly. All the old buildings seemed only half there. It was so spooky. There were these straight shadows that cut through the fog whenever a car went past in the distance. I suppose I was a little frightened.

‘As I went through the passage under the chapel, I could swear there was someone following me. At first I thought it was the porter. I didn’t want to speak to him again. So I hurried on. But of course I didn’t realise that they lock that gate at the weekend. So suddenly I was cornered. I looked around but I couldn’t see anyone.

‘Why is it that whenever you suddenly realise you’re alone you try not to make any noise? Is it in case something hears you? But you know you’re alone. Or is it because you’re straining to listen? For something disturbing - that you know can’t be true and desperately don’t want to hear. Is it wrong to listen like that? Once it’s in your head you won’t get it out. Perhaps by fearing it you may make it true. I started to listen for strange sounds in the fog and then I *knew* something was there.

‘Just then I got this text. I assumed it was from Alex – when I was in the library I’d called him to come get me. It just said ‘I am coming.’ I texted back: ‘where are you?.’ But then I realised it wasn’t from his normal number, but from one I didn't know. By this time I was back in the under-croft beneath the chapel. Then I got another text from the same number. It said 'I can see you'.'

She shuddered, then continued:

'That was when it happened. It seemed to come out of nowhere. It was dark, of course, and - as I said - foggy. Anyway I was concentrating on the texts. Usually your eyes pick up peripheral movement. So I always think it's unrealistic in films, when horrid things creep up on people. But at that moment I was concentrating on the texts, and the brightness of the screen in the dark. So I couldn't see anything. The light on my phone died and I suddenly realised there it was - completely still - standing right next to me… this *figure*.

'I don't know what he wanted. Maybe to touch me. I almost think he reached out to grab me. I screamed and ran for it. I ran to the main gate (there was no sign of the porter) and out into Lincoln's Inn Fields. By the time I stopped running there was nobody there. Just then Alex came round the corner after me. Thank God! I was just so frightened.'

'I'm not surprised', I said.

'Since then I've found it really hard to sleep. I'm always – you know – on edge. I don't think it was the porter. Although of course he had my number from when I rang the lodge for help. Anyway I just can't stop thinking about it.'

'You should try to', I said.

The story seemed to have changed somewhat since the last time I'd heard it. I guess that's normal with things like this.

'I was so stressed that weekend that I took it out on Alex' she continued, 'I sort of accused him of cheating on me and he said he didn't know why he hadn't, with me being like this all the time, and then he stormed out. Now he says he 'wants to take things easy for a while'… Well what the hell does that mean? I don't know. I'm trying to do as much for him as possible, but the more I try and talk to him the more annoyed he gets.'

'That doesn't seem very fair' I suggested, helplessly.

‘What with all that and without the case I got really screwed up about the opinion and of course I didn’t finish it and on Monday Richard was really cross. Everything I do now at work I have this gnawing fear in my stomach. I can’t wait for it to be time to go home, but then I’m frightened of being followed. I sometimes feel like… like I’m always being watched. Dogs keep going crazy at me when I walk past. And tramps keep shouting at me.’

‘Shouting what?’

‘How should I know? Nothing I can understand.’

‘Like what?’

‘Well – like yesterday this tramp jumped up and stared at me, at least I think it was at me – I couldn’t see anyone else. He called out – ‘who’s that there?’ and then said ‘Watch yourself, Love!’ and started laughing. I’m sure that statue’s bad luck. I feel there is something, you know - nasty - about it.’

We were soon walking through the galleries of the British Museum to Finlayson’s office. Huge granite faces, stern and uncomprehending, stared down from the monuments on every side. The Professor greeted us warmly. He looked more crumpled and fragile than ever. He seemed a little on edge. He glanced over our shoulders as we went into his office. And he quickly shut the door behind him.

‘Come in come in come in. That’s it. Well, one of the joys of antiquarianism is the journeys of ancient objects. Many of the relics in this museum have very long and tangled histories. That’s what happens when precious objects last for a very long time. People use them for different purposes. And they come to have all sorts of stories connected to them. When you’ve existed for millennia you tend to acquire a past.’

‘What do you mean?’ I asked.

‘Well – take that marble stele you passed in the hall on the way in. It’s been part of a Roman sarcophagus and a barbarian altar. We think it was presented to Napoleon III and we know it was stolen by the Nazis. And there are two full centuries where we have absolutely no idea where it was. Or what about this cannopic vase with the porphyry head of Imsety? There is a great story to this vase, or what it was once attached to, which I have just written a paper about. I had to dress it up as work of fiction for them to publish it in the Egyptology Journal. But in fact, though you wouldn't believe it, the whole thing was entirely true – I looked into it, you know. People in my profession must learn to keep an open mind. Speaking of which, let's have a look at you...'

At this he lent over his desk to reach for a shoe-box. He slid it towards himself and took off the lid. The box was full of tissue paper. He rummaged inside and lifted out an object. It was the statue.

''*Exegi monumentum aere perennius*'...', he added, as he handed it to Reshma with an expectant expression.

She ran her fingers over it, shuddered, and passed it to me. It was surprisingly heavy. To hold it was to be confronted with its incredible age.

'And -', he continued, taking it back and turning it in his hands as he spoke, 'as I thought – it is a fascinating object. Very rare indeed. Odd too. I contacted the Inn and they've let me borrow it to run some tests. At first I thought I'd dated it wrong. You see it's made of iron.'

'I thought you said the Hittites were Bronze Age?' I said.

'That's the odd thing. They were. This is meteoric. We know because I had them analyse it and it's made of Kamacite. That's an alloy of iron and nickel that doesn't occur naturally on Earth. Indeed as a material it's older than the formation of the planets. It's only found on asteroids and meteorites.'

'You mean it's-' Reshma gasped.

'Yes. It doesn't belong here. It fell to Earth from somewhere else. Of course the ancients really valued such materials. Especially before they knew how to smelt terrestrial iron from its ores. Though there was a strong iron taboo. No doubt that's why - after it fell - they made the metal into this religious figurine.'

'Religious?' asked Reshma.

'Yes, you see it turns out our friend Yové-Watna wasn't a King after all. He was a god. With his own cult site somewhere in North-Eastern Turkey. Back then people believed that gods and demons literally accompanied their statues. If you defeated an enemy you might steal their gods. That way you'd divert the gods' protection. Although of course you might also call down their wrath. So this is a real deus ex machina: *'And I will send an Angel before thee; and I will drive out the Canaanite, the Amorite, and the Hittite.'* But I'm afraid King Suppiluliumas's letter now makes even less sense than before....'

'How can you be so sure it's a god?' Reshma was struggling to hide her impatience.

'Because of what's written on him. You can't really read it unless you turn it in your hands. Now I've managed to translate it in full. The text is late cuneiform script, as I thought. But the inscription itself is bi-lingual. One half in Hittite with a few Sumerograms. The other written syllabically in a totally unknown language. It *may* have some affinities with Hurrian, but not enough for me to read it. That itself makes it very significant. I hope I may live to get to the bottom of it. It doesn't matter for your purposes, though. For presumably it says the same thing in both languages.'

'Which is what?' cried Reshma.

'I've written out a rough translation – here have a look.' With that, and a curious expression of relief, he handed her a crumpled piece of paper.

Trembling, she read it. Then she gasped and for a long minute stared out of the window. Her reflection in the pane showed her face a mask of fear. At last, with apparent resolution, she turned. And - blank with disgust - she passed it to me.

It read as follows:

'Behold! I belong to Jové Wot
That Hatti men call Yové-Watna
The Cruel One, the Silent One, the Destroyer
You who read this are utterly accursed
He can see you
You will not see him until the end
Give yourself to the Gods to save yourself

Lest he meet you in the place you most fear.'

Beyond the Museum's iron railings, ponderous and pneumatic, a bus was driving past. In the distance we could hear a siren, traffic noises, office workers laughing outside a pub. Reshma looked wretched and wouldn't catch my eye. There was in the room an unspoken mutual apprehension of embarrassment, awkwardness, and unease. After a moment the Professor started to speak:

''Baleful signs' indeed. A sort of primitive curse. No doubt to protect the God from theft. Belief in dark magic was universal back then. I've seen lots of curse documents, though none I'll admit with as much pure malice as this one.

The Hittites were extremely superstitious. I think they would have taken this very seriously indeed. Perhaps too seriously…

'We should be careful not to judge them. They were as clever as we are, even if their scholarship was less advanced. And after all they were facing apocalypse. The fact is that societies threatened with catastrophe can often behave in ways that seem bizarre. Pre-scientific cultures seek religious rationalisations, usually with disastrous results. Fear can lead to perverse and self-destructive behaviour. And self-doubt, like a virus, can enter a civilisation that was strong and bring it to its knees.

'If the latest Hittite scholarship is right, there were only a few dozen literate scribes at any one time. That is a very tenuous chain. It seems this class of scribes was abruptly and totally wiped out. I don't need to tell you what bad news it is, for a complex and organised society, to lose all its literate members. It's bad enough what's happening to ours.'

'What do you mean?' I asked.

'Oh ignore me – I'm turning into a grumpy old man. But I don't think you need much historical perspective to see it. We stand on the very threshold between the Age of the Book and the Age of the Internet. Soon the only people to read books will be fusty old antiquarians like me. Societies, cultures, and civilisations have gone down to changes that were much less profound – an improvement in sailing technology, perhaps, or the invention of the stirrup. Now we can all send messages to each other all over the World. But before you get too excited about that, you'd better ask yourself this: what do you call a place where all the murderers, rapists, paedophiles, killers, and psychopaths on Earth hide out undetected? You call it the Internet. Next time you get a message from out of the ether,' (and here he glanced anxiously at his desk-top) 'ask yourself who sent it. And why. If the Devil exists, he'll be online.'

'If the Devil exists', I said, 'I'll have to re-write my book on Truth and Logic.'

'At least we don't have to worry about this' Reshma said, suddenly brightening, 'After all, if this curse actually worked, this thing would have been killing people for hundreds of years and we would know about it.'

'No no not at all' said Finlayson 'That's one of the great pleasures of Hittitology. Nobody's been able to read this for thirty two centuries. Ha ha!' The Professor slowly tailed off, drumming his fingers on his desk. 'We are the first… Ah. I see what you mean. Well – now there's a thing…'

You'll have already guessed what happened next. And of course it proves nothing. Because, if it hadn't happened, I wouldn't be telling you this story. One morning twelve days later they found Clovis Finlayson. He was lying on the floor of the museum, between the great winged Assyrian bulls. The cause of his death was unknown. But the police 'weren't treating the matter as suspicious.' It seemed that those who knew him were unsurprised. He had an inoperable stomach cancer and severe anaemia. He had been given just months to live. It was not thought necessary to open the body.

Unfortunately Jarvis, who told me the news, also passed it on to Reshma. You can imagine the results on her psyche. That night I got four increasingly hysterical emails. Their subject heading was: 'that place that we fear most.' It was hard to make much sense of them. As if she were unable or unwilling to express herself coherently in print. I won't set out her private correspondence. But their flavour can be summed up by the final message. It simply said: 'I'm scared.'

So next day I arranged to make a third trip up to town and ride to the rescue. Walking along the Mall and through Trafalgar Square in the dusk, I was suddenly struck by the statues. I hadn't really noticed them before. But as I now trudged through Central London I started to see them everywhere. I realised how few I recognised. We seem to have forgotten our gods and heroes. Perhaps we too live in the ruins of a civilisation we no longer understand.

The place names resonated differently to me as well. With repetition the familiar syllables sounded foreign, odd. Filled with strange ancient echoes. 'Fleet street' – there was a river here once, was there not, or rather it *still* flows here, underground, hidden, forgotten. And didn't they used to put up the heads of traitors on Temple Bar? Odd thought - the cruel history of these roads we tread so carelessly. Ludgate Hill: the gate of King Lud – who was he again? St Clement Danes, Old Jewry, Cripplegate. What have they to do with us? And then of course the Temple Church itself. Crouched here in our present, an unwanted relic of our cruel past, before the arts and sciences sailed us out of the dark. Do we stop to think about it? Doesn't anyone else feel it's just a little sinister? What barbaric oddness was there here? In this same familiar space of ground. At a different point in time.

I met Reshma on Fleet Street, under the gnarled Tudor building that acts as the gateway to Inner Temple. This time she was fighting back tears before she even got to me. I took her over the road to a really old pub - a dungeon of warped and blackened wood and ancient stone. We circled down through several levels of cellar, the walls decorated with rusting metal tools. In the deepest level we found a discreet booth. There, with despairing resignation, she unburdened herself, and the words tumbled out of her in a torrent.

'I'm cursed, I know it. I feel these waves of grief and fear. 'Grief gets away from you and you reach out to hold onto it, but you haven't the strength. But Fear follows you. You see it over your shoulder. And when you finally think you've left it behind: it comes round the corner, staring, and you realise it was there with you all along.'

'But what's happened Reshma?' I held my hand up, trying to slow her down.

'Alex's left me. I… I… There's no use pretending any more. I found this other phone he had. Went through the sent messages. To that *bitch.* 'What do you expect?' he said – 'you know we've been coming to this for months.' He left… I begged him not to… I humiliated myself... Followed him in bare feet to Bankside. He shouted at me to 'leave him alone.'

'So that's it: I'm all on my own now. All these years I've trusted him completely. And I thought I knew everything about him. But I didn't know him at all. He was my most fundamental truth. But turns out it was a lie. All my future, and all my past, just seems gone. Everything I'd thought and felt. It was just an illusion.

'Suddenly I feel there's *nothing* I can be certain of anymore. Except that Schopenhauer was right: 'Human existence is a kind of error', he said, 'it is bad today and every day it will get worse, until the worst of all happens'. How is it that we're made to crave love above all, but we always act to destroy it? The truth is that evil wins, and no-one lives happily ever after, and every one of us will choke out our last breath somewhere, in pain and fear. We live and die alone and it means nothing.'

'You're only saying that', I said, 'because you've lost someone you love.'

'*'Love'* – that's also a sort of ancient curse, I see that now' (she was really working herself up, wringing her hands as she spoke. She was like a crazed over-charged version of herself as the words rushed out of her) 'When you love someone you give them total power – to hurt you in your soul. You basically say 'do with me as you want'. They'll either reject you for someone else or they'll never feel for you the way you feel for them - you'll always be their slave, waiting for them to leave.

'And if by a miracle they do love you back - and that doesn't kill *your* love – you'll both have power over the person you need. And you won't resist using that power - to get control - because you're scared. You'll both be so frightened you'll end up destroying each other. Love is abusive because it gives power and power corrupts. The best you can hope for in life is unloved loneliness. Or just affection that falls, if we're honest, a long way short of love. Which of course is really the same thing in the end.'

'Thinking is dangerous' I said. 'You should try not to do so much of it.'

'There's something else that was a total lie', she added: 'Richard was never on my side. Yesterday I came back to the room for something and as I did I could hear him on the phone. He was joking about me and he said – I can't tell you what he said. It was so disgusting. I won't forget his sleazy laugh. After all those months of effort to impress him.

'I should have known they didn't really want someone like me. Benjamin will be fine. He fits in all right. Can you believe it - the case he told me about never even existed! He was lying all along, just to screw me over.

'I feel like *everything* I thought was true was a lie. You taught me to question it all. But how can you live if you can't take certain things on trust? Like your friends aren't betraying you behind your back. Well I doubt everything now. Even the laws of Nature… I don't think I even believe in them anymore…

'Anyway', she added, in a low voice that was slightly ashamed, as if she were testing me, 'I don't expect it will be long now. The World would be better off without me anyway. They say water is the gentlest way – like Mum.'

'What do you mean by that?' As she'd intended, she'd got my attention.

'You know – what happened to the Professor. I'll be next. Unless I take matters in my own hands. I've already seen him.'

'Who have you seen?'
'You know who I mean.'

'No Reshma.'

'He came for the Professor and next he'll come for me. He already tried, that night they locked me in the library. When I was walking through the under-croft in the fog, and I stopped to look at those horrid texts. When I looked up *it* was there. I knew at once it was implacable, malignant. It put an arm out and touched me – I remember its dirty fingers clawing through my hair. It was him. The djinn. Ichabod. The same as the statue.'

'But Reshma, that's not what you told me-.'

'I know what I saw! He's always following me. I glimpse him. In my
blind spot.'

'Your mind fills in what you see there.'

'Then it must have got in my mind, mustn't it! Yes, it got in there alright. Waking or sleeping, he's there. I think I see him more and more. I know I'll never be rid of him.'

'You're ill. You need help.'

'That's what Alex said, weeks ago. That's why I went to see Dr Bruckner again.'

'What did he say?'

'The same as you. That I was ill. But I'm not ill! He prescribed me lots of pills…' [she listed them]

'You know those drugs have side-effects? Visual disturbances, hallucinations -.'

'Yes, horrible, that's why I stopped taking them. And why I took photos of it on my phone.'

She handed it over. I scrolled through a series of blurred pictures of the legal quarter, and a couple of one of the Thames bridges. There was nothing to see and I said so.

'But look! In the distance. And there! Don't you see: the curse is real.'

A shimmer? A smudge? In one photo of the bridge there clearly was a figure. It was standing far away behind the painted cast-iron parapet. But, at that distance, you couldn't say it wasn't just a commuter in a suit. No it was ludicrous.

‘Reshma, you’ve got to stop this. Ancient curses don’t work - unless you make them work by believing in them. Be -’

‘Be what?’ she interrupted, ‘be totally phlegmatic, like you?’

‘I was going to say: be realistic’, I said, somewhat hurt – it was a criticism that had been levelled at me before by my wife.

‘I thought you’d spent the last ten years of your career disproving Realism.’

‘Yes’ I said, ‘but that’s just-’

‘‘Just’ Philosophy?! It usually stops following me when I leave the Inns. You step out into the roar of London, and it’s all bill-boards and… traffic and… people everywhere. Steel and glass and light. It seems impossible to believe in anything that isn’t material. But then three nights ago it got out, and followed me onto the Embankment. I just somehow knew it was there. Well I tried to do what Dr Bruckner said – to drive away the bad thoughts. The chapel bell rang just as I was leaving. ‘Ask not for whom it tolls…’ I started singing a nursery rhyme my Mum taught me, under my breath. ‘Oranges and lemons, Say the bells of St. Clement’s. You owe me five farthings, Say the bells of St. Martin’s. When will you pay me? Say the bells of Old Bailey. Here comes the candle to light you to bed, here comes...’.’ She tailed off.

Yes, I thought, I know how that one ends.

‘I was crossing the road onto Blackfriars’ Bridge, and there was no-one around. It was raining heavily – it seems to have been raining for weeks. I thought it was gone. I was humming a different song now: ‘London Bridge.’ ‘Iron and steel will bend and bow, bend and bow, bend and bow.’ That was when I saw it at last. Fair and square. It was standing on the central span of the bridge. You know that’s a famously unlucky spot. Lots of cab drivers won’t cross it. And there it was. A dark figure, quite still – he was waiting for me. I had to get a bus all round by Waterloo instead. It’s been there the last two nights. Waiting. I remember what the Professor said about the river. That's the place I fear most. I know we all have one.'

'Don't be daft', I said. Though - thinking about it later - I realised that if pushed to it we do.

'What's he going to do to me when he comes for me?' she asked.

She laid her head on my shoulder. I suppose I put an arm round her. Her hair felt soft in the crook of my neck.

'Reshma. I can't believe I'm having this conversation with you. These dark thoughts are just rationalisations… manifestations of chemical states in your brain. Low levels of seratonin, perhaps. High levels of dopamine and cortisone. I thought you of all people would know that. You've had work stress and - relationship problems and - of course that causes anxiety, depression, paranoia… obsessive ruminations… it's obvious. You're depressed, so you can only think and remember bad things. I think we all end up living in the World as we fear it to be. But give it a year and you'll look back at this and laugh. You can't seriously believe in – whatever you call it – this djinn, this curse, this *thing*? It's nonsense. Remember your philosophy. 'To conquer fear is the beginning of wisdom.' And Nothing can come from Nothing - *Ex nihilo nihil fit*.'

'I wonder, if you were going through this, whether you would still be philosophical? Anyway I do remember my philosophy. It taught me enough to know there are problems with our 'rational' view of the World. Profound problems. And I remember something else. *Esse est percipi*. To be is to be perceived. Well I *have* perceived. Whether you believe me or not. And I know what I saw – the thing that killed the Professor. Face to face - that night - in the fog. The most unspeakable sight.'

I couldn't help noticing again how much the story had changed. I suppose that's how these things usually get started.

'But *Reshma*-'

'And don't forget what Science says about the random nature of the World. Things aren't really where they seem to be until we observe them. We fix them into place, into reality, by the very act of perceiving them. Time and space are really one, and they warp and bend. Anyway, why won't you believe me? You've held it too. You've been part of this since the start. Since it called to me to see the statue.'

'Now you really sound crazy.'

She took her head off my shoulder.

'I thought at least you'd understand but you don't', she said.

'I do understand. Frankly you've erected a huge architecture of paranoia on some pretty flimsy foundations. Please, Reshma, you've got to see how insane this all sounds. Ok you're right – not insane. I shouldn't have said that. But *use* that great brain of yours. Stopped clocks don't bring bad luck. That's what superstition is. We notice the correlation between two things. And we assume an invalid causal link between them. In fact the truth is far scarier: the universe is disordered - as you say random. And we can do whatever we want in it. And we have to take responsibility for that. And for the way we feel about it.'

'No,' she said. 'The World is meaningless and the things we do in it absurd. There's no such thing as true love. I'm alone and I'll die alone. Intellectually we secretly know this. But we get distracted by the day-to-day – our work, our relationships, the little lies we tell ourselves to make it all bearable. It's when those are stripped away we really see it. How pointless it all is - how meaningless. And then what argument can there be that Nothingness isn't better?'

We went on like that for hours. But there's no point arguing with the mentally ill. You'll never change their minds. Eventually it was closing time, and I had to get back to Oxford (all these trips of mine to London were increasingly unpopular with my wife). So we pretended to reach a positive conclusion, and parted on a false note of reassurance and gratitude that neither of us believed. I was sure it wasn't the end of it. I watched her disappear through a low door from Fleet Street into the Temple. I somehow knew it would be the last time I saw her.

Perhaps I could have done more. But I'm not sure what. It was her bad luck that something lurked malignantly in the shadows of her mind. I couldn't get at it. It was beyond reason, at the very edge of madness. Like the dark thoughts that come to us at the threshold of sleep, when the door to the subconscious opens and nightmares pour out. She is – was – someone who deserved better from life. Perhaps she could've found happiness, if her fears hadn't consumed her. But she ran out of time.

I was sitting in the far room of the College SCR, staring out of the window, when a colleague came in to ask me if I'd heard the news. When I asked him 'what news?' he would say nothing. He just looked over his shoulder, towards the main room. Irritation mingling with foreboding, I rose, and stumbled along the direction of his gaze, into the inner room where they were standing. Their murmured discussion stopped when I came in. Another colleague stepped forward and took my hand and said:

'Come on, there's a television in the JCR.'

She made a sympathetic face, and led me there. And though she wouldn't tell me herself, I already knew what it would be.

Reshma's youth, her looks, her background, these apparently made it worthy of prurient press attention. The smiling photo of her at a College Ball. The helicopter footage of the team taking her weirdly stiffened body from the river below London Bridge, where the tide had carried her from Blackfriars. The fatuous debate about working conditions at the Bar. That awful hand-washing interview with her hag-like head clerk, as she sang her praises. Such is the World we live in.

Alex Bradbury was not as resistant as I'd feared to my approach. He cautiously consented to meet me for a coffee.

'I'd been telling her for weeks that it was over between us', he said. 'But I'd never have believed it would've made her… do what she did. No we broke up way back in October. You could say if you like that I was insecure, or afraid of commitment. But you've got to understand she'd been impossible for months. So paranoid she wouldn't let me see anyone – wouldn't even let me out. So jealous about me all the time that it was impossible to love her. I suppose fear made her make the thing she feared most come true.

'I need you to know that living with her had become impossible. I don't see how I could have done it any more gently. I still cared about her. But I should never have agreed to what she asked. She begged me to do it slowly. Said she couldn't cope at work otherwise. I agreed, because I felt sorry for her. Maybe that was the wrong thing to do. But I know the problems she's had in the past – you know how she was at College - and how vulnerable she is. She made wild talk about killing herself. But that was nothing new. I never thought she meant it.

'But maybe suicide is the only sure cure for Depression. She went completely nuts. She just wouldn't believe or accept that it was over. Would blame anything and everything – a horoscope, a djinn – but never herself. I think she kept re-setting the clocks - though she denied it - to the time I first told her I no longer loved her. I'm so sorry this happened, believe me. I still care for her, and this is the worst thing. I blame myself. But I also blame her – I can't help thinking it was selfish thing to do.'

But I've been unable to exorcise what happened from my head. Waking or sleeping I've found myself disturbed by - let us just say, a dark nexus of thoughts. A labyrinth in the wreckage of my former certainties. The more I try to think my way out of it the more lost I become. Maybe there is no way out. And you are never quite alone in a labyrinth – there is always the echo of footsteps behind you. I feel like I beat my head against a propositional calculus with no solution. Perhaps that is what the World is – a vast equation that will not come out - an edifice of broken logic. As for the other things that have been coming into my mind, I will not write them down. On the basis of eye witnesses the coroner recorded the time of death as about half past midnight.'

In the Wood of the Suicides

'One who is supposed to be a warrior
considers it his foremost concern
to keep death in mind at all times,
every day and every night'

Bushido Shoshinshu

Escape from the Floating World

The first light of dawn spread in languid mauves across the bay from Shimosa. Filtering through mists which lay in ranks above the rice fields, it picked out here and there small orchards of cherry, pear, and persimmon. Between these crouched the arch of the last bridge in Edo. Its decayed wooden shape was a little too steep for true elegance, but the rickety joists and scuffed paintwork lent it something of the picturesque, as its mass loomed dark against the early morning sky. At the top of its span, with a certain air of nonchalance, a figure was leaning on the railing. As he approached it, Saigo Motonari slowed his horse to a walk and half fumbled at the hilt of his katana.

'Who's there?' he called out. He noticed he was struggling to keep the desperation from his voice.

'Go easy,' laughed the man on the bridge, with no suggestion of deference. His clothes were simple and a little scruffy, and he had a pronounced stoop. He did not appear to be armed, though there was something slung over his shoulder.

'Are you going to challenge me? Or will you let me pass?'

Motonari was ashamed as he said it, but there was no time for a less clumsy speech.

'Who am I: Benkei?' the man replied. 'I'm a commoner. And I carry no weapon. How could I harm a samurai like you? You can search me all you want.'

Indeed the man had nothing on him except a small lacquered box: black, finely crafted, and light enough to hold with one hand. It was rather an exquisite object.

'What's in that?' asked Motonari.

'You don't want to know.'

There was something unsettling in the man's self-assurance.

'How dare you! What's in the box?'

'You won't ask about the box - I won't ask why you're running away.'

'What did you say?' cried Motonari, struggling to maintain a sense of authority. He was quite aware of the danger of sounding ridiculous.

'I can be your guide if you want', the man answered, in a conciliatory tone. 'I know the safe way into the hills. Then you can re-join the Koshu-Kaido beyond Monkey Bridge. Once you're that far from Edo the roads will be safe. And you can turn onto the Nakasendo at Shimosuwa if you want to go on to Kyoto.'

'Why do you say I'm running away?'

'A samurai rides out of town on his own in the dark, and takes the bridge over the old canal. Even a blind man could see you're avoiding the curfew - and the guard on the stations on the toll roads. But I'm not here to judge you. As they say: you can do that for yourself.'

Motonari decided to ignore this insolence. He needed all the help he could get. He pictured himself giving the man a good beating when he had no further use for him.

'You have a horse?' he asked.

'Yes: tied up over there. She cost me everything I made at the market.'

'How much do you want, to show me the way and keep your mouth shut?'

'Oh nothing, Sir. Even the back roads are dangerous. I'd be glad of a samurai for company.'

Motonari grunted. The man must be some buffoon of a merchant from the sticks, but he would still serve his purpose if he knew the way. He looked around him as the trader hurried over the bridge to untie his horse. The sleeping city was spread out behind him, lit up all about by lanterns. In the pleasure quarters the last of his friends would be making their way to their homes. Here and there smoke rose from chimneys and seeped into the gentle haze. Above the capital the first hints of pink were catching the base of high clouds. For a moment he was half hypnotised. What a fine prospect, he thought – how awful that he might never see it again.

But for heaven's sake, this was no time to stand around admiring the view. His friends thought this melancholic languor was an affectation, and indeed apathy and ennui were rather fashionable at that time. But in truth all his life he had been too distracted by the World's beauty. It had held him back from ever quite realising his potential, or from taking decisive action when it was needed. And now only decisive action could save him. He would force himself to think like a samurai. He spurred on over the bridge to where the trader was mounting his horse. If the man slowed him down he could always kill him and take his ride. He kicked his own horse and they galloped off into the mist.

They rode fast in silence along the road between the paddy fields. It was getting lighter now, so that they would soon be clearly visible from a distance. After an hour they came to a crossroad with a punishment board. A family of crows, indignant at the disturbance, rose up from it as one. As they did they revealed the body of a man who had been crucified several days earlier.

'The punishment for those travelling without papers', said the trader.

'I had no idea.'

'Don't worry, that's only for peasants, it doesn't affect merchants or samurai.'

Motonari circled round the dead man, fascinated. This vignette would make a wonderful woodcut, he thought, especially with Fuji in the background like that. 'Strange Sight on the Road from Edo', you would call it. In his head he tried to frame the best view.

But he was soon interrupted:

'Come on, Sir, we mustn't stop.'

They rode on. Soon – mercifully - the road began to rise under them as it hit the first of the wooded hills that clambered over each other to the West. From now on at least they were afforded some cover. Scrolled clouds began to roll over them and released a thin but incessant rain. They continued on rough and muddy tracks that wound their way up into forested mountains. Around lunchtime they passed a small village. A handful of houses clustered in a plateaued clearing, their steep thatched roofs tapering down to the ground. Some peasants looked up at them warily. But no-one challenged them, and they pressed on for another few miles. Then they came to a ford by a river cascading across boulders. On the further bank a young child sat sobbing softly. There was no one else about.

'What are you doing here?' Motonari asked. The child was too young to answer.

'She must have been left here by her parents,' said the trader.

'Why would they do such a thing?'

'The rice tax is a heavy burden for the peasants. They're starving. They expose their daughters, then their younger sons.'

Motonari shook his head sadly. He thought for a minute and recited:

''*The ancient poet*
Who pitied monkeys for their cries,
What would he say, if he saw
This child crying in the autumn wind?'

It's a hard World. I wish I could sit and contemplate this scene. But there's no time - we have to press on.'

They rode hard all afternoon until the sun, which had never quite managed to break through - so that it might as well have been twilight all day - at last gave up the fight and retreated behind the Western peaks. They were well into the hills now. Whenever a vista opened up they could see low shreds of cloud drifting between them and the wooded slopes beyond. As it started to get darker the woods changed too: they grew somehow thicker and more tangled, denser with darker-leaved trees and completely choked with undergrowth. Large green and yellow spiders hung motionless in the air, suspended between the branches on webs that were only visible where they had caught the rain. Other than that there was no sign of animal or bird life. On either side the great green wilderness blanketed the landscape and there was nothing but a silent sea of trees.

'Don't you know what these forests are?' said the trader, as he contemplated the dismal prospect. 'This is Aokigahara - the Wood of the Suicides. People won't go near these woods if they don't have to – they say that if you go in you never come out. Even Basho wouldn't come this way. The villagers in these parts have a tradition: when they get too old to work their families bring them up here. Then they leave them out in the woods to die.'

'Why would they do that?'

'You can't conceive of death for the good of others? And you call yourself a samurai! You've clearly never lived in the country. They've been starving in these mountains since the days of Tokugawa Ieyasu. The masters take all the food to feed the likes of you, so you can sit around in luxury and never work. There are bodies and bones of suicides scattered all through these woods. Also of babies that are unwanted or deformed. The place is infested with their angry spirits. I'm surprised you've never heard about it. And it's not just peasants: sometimes artisans come all the way from Edo to kill themselves here, when life or the authorities get too hard to bear. Not all of us have the luxury of *hara-kiri*.'

'That is a 'luxury' I have no intention of indulging in', said Motonari. Then he added: 'Even if it might be best for everyone else involved.'

'Are you frightened?'

'A samurai is never frightened of death.'

'They say the physically brave can be moral cowards.'

'Yes,' replied Motonari, 'though the opposite can also be true. I'm no coward, but I don't fancy dying just now – not for ideals that I don't share. Will the 58 Wrathful Deities weigh up the white and black pebbles of my deeds? Who knows? Who cares? I live in *this* world. And in this world people should look to themselves first of all. Now come on, we need to get further away from the city.'

He urged his horse on and for another hour they rode into the hills. Eventually the horses could go no further and the trader, who had been moaning for some time, insisted that they dismount to have a rest. By the side of the road there was a small stone lantern covered in moss. Behind it there was what might be a path, but then again might not be. Apart from that and a couple more toppled stone pagodas, there was nothing else to be seen - except the dark green shadows of the forest closing in on them from either side.

Suddenly the trader cocked his head to listen.

'There's someone coming up behind us,' he said.

Motonari strained to catch anything but the oppressive silence that had grown almost unbearable now they were still.

'I can't hear anything.'

'Three horses at least,' the trader insisted. 'What do we do?'

'We need to get off the road – quick now!'

'Won't you fight them?'

'Don't be absurd!' Motonari smiled at the trader's simplicity. He had led a life of lassitude and unsullied beauty. He had consorted with gamblers and courtesans, and - even worse - with poets. There was a delicious irony in that, he thought to himself with a smile: he was a member of a warrior caste, but he had never once been in a fight.

Leading his horse by the reigns he plunged down the half-track into the trees at the side of the road. They scrambled down the slope for some time, pushing through undergrowth and switching direction whenever they could, until anyone following them must have lost their bearings as completely as Motonari had lost his. He realised with a vague amusement that they were now quite lost in these woods. Every so often he stopped and crouched to listen. There was no sound at all except the light patter of rain on the leaves above. In fact he could not remember ever being anywhere so silent. There seemed to be no birds in this forest. Still he insisted they press on deeper into it. Finally he seemed satisfied that they could not have been followed. Then, soaked through and muddy, he threw himself down on the ground with a gesture of theatrical despair:

'I was wrong – going to the country is *worse* than suicide.'

'We mustn't stay here too long, Sir. It will be dark soon. A man could die out here in these woods.'

‘I’m too hungry to think about dying. I’d do anything for a mouthful of rice. Or some sour plums. Or a few *wagashi* sweets.’

The other man sighed. This was doubtless the prelude to an agonising description of the delights of Edo’s teahouses. Now he tried another approach:

‘If we stay here much longer we’re almost bound to be attacked by monsters.’

‘Monsters? What monsters?’ laughed Motonari.

‘Oh there any number of them out here: *Yokai*, mountain hags, kappas, whore-spiders, *Heikegani* ghost crabs, *Obake* shape-shifters, badgers, *Mononoke*, *Jubboko* vampire trees, dragons, tengus, fox spirits, Yanari floorboard-creakers, bridge demons, gate demons, one-eyed demons, sake-drinking *Shojo* demons, *Oni* mountain ogres, giant *Gashadokuro* skeletons, hundred-year-old animated sake jars, cadaver-eating *Jikininki...*’

Motonari looked at him with an expression of amused contempt. But the man was oblivious and continued:

‘And even if we’re not, we’re certain to be haunted by all sorts of *Yurei*: hungry *Gaki* ghosts, vengeful *Onryo* ghosts, footless warrior-monk ghosts, *Noppera-bo* faceless ghosts, *Nukekubi* head-detatchers, *Rokurokubi* neck-stretchers, *Nuribotoke* eye-danglers, and double-mouthed *Futakuchi-onna* corpse-munchers.’

‘You seem to be something of an expert’, observed Motonari, dryly.

The trader shrugged; ‘I’ve read the ‘Guide to the Forms and Habits of All 11,520 Types of Supernatural Creatures in the World, As Dictated by the Monster Bai Ze to the Yellow Emperor. I know what I’m talking about.’

‘Well I’m not afraid...’ Motonari started to say. ‘I’m too hungry. I’ve never been so hungry in my life. Are you sure you have no food?’

‘None, Sir.’

‘What about whatever you’ve got in that box? How do I know you aren’t hoarding supplies?’

The trader threw his head back and let out a forlorn laugh.

‘If you knew what I have in here I don’t think you’d want to eat it, however hungry you got,’

'Try me,' said Motonari, 'in Yoshiwara they still talk about the time when for a bet I once ate a whole…'

But he petered out as something first caught his attention and then absorbed it entirely. With renewed energy that made a mockery of his previous collapse, he leaped across the rough path and into some nearby trees, followed by the cursing trader. There, on the twisted trunk of a dying and half-rotted tree, sat large clump of mushrooms. Indeed, now that he had seen them, he could see others too. Whole clans of them were scattered amongst the tangled roots of the forest floor. They were unlike any he had seen before: slender, with round conical heads. They reminded him of elegant ladies crossing *Edobashi* bridge wearing bamboo hats against the rain. Delighted, he started to pick them and throw them into his satchel.

'I don't recognise this type,' said the trader. 'We should be careful.'

'Why? What's worse than starving to death?'

'I once heard a story about a monk in Shikoku who ate some strange mushrooms. He fell asleep and when he woke up he'd turned into a racoon.'

'Oh shut up and start a fire, or I'll beat you black and blue.'

'Yes Sir!'

Twenty minutes later they were lying by the remains of their supper, prodding more wet branches onto a smoky fire.

'Are you going to tell me what you've got in that box?'

'Are you going to tell me why you had to leave Edo so fast in the middle of the night?'

Motonari stretched out and yawned, then said, in a quiet voice:

'All right. I wrote a poem I should never have written… to a woman I should never have loved.'

'Oh yeah? Did you screw her?' asked the trader (he was curiously insistent).

'Don't be coarse.'

'In other words, 'yes'.'

Motonari smiled.

The trader was silent for a minute. His usual high spirits seem to desert him and he said, in an awe-struck tone:

'What was she like?'

'Oh,' grinned Motonari, 'not the best I've had... But not too bad for a novice.'

There was another silence.

'Who was she?'

'Unfortunately she was the niece of the Daimyo, my master.'

'Oh dear!' it was the trader's turn to smile.

'He extended to me the privilege of suicide. The '*privilege*'! Well, I wasn't going to do that, not even for her. If there's one thing I've learned in life it's this: no woman is worth killing yourself for.'

'And if you wouldn't?'

Motonari's face fell and he lowered his voice:

'He said he'd commission Hideharu Fuma for my head.'

'Hideharu Fuma?!'

'He's one of the three best assassins in Edo.'

'I know. I heard he was the best. He kills differently each time, they say: he's quite the artist. Once he's supposed to have assassinated a man using nothing but a fishing rod. How the hell do you kill someone with a fishing rod? I don't know but he always gets his man. Oh, sorry...'

'It's worse than that. I heard a rumour he was also in love with my woman. So there's no way he wouldn't accept the commission.'

'Hmmm. Then there's not much point running away.'

'I'll hide out in the wilds until things cool off. Then I'll go to ground in Kyoto – I have relatives there. He'll never find me.'

'You think so? I'm pretty sure he *will* find you.'

Motonari spat with defiance and went off to relieve himself behind some trees. But he didn't go far. There was an atmosphere to this place that made him nervous. And he already knew how easy it was to get lost here. He was trying not think about how they would find the road again. He strode back to where the horses were tied up. He was almost comforted to see the guileless face of his companion, who now opened his mouth and said:

‘Why not consider the obvious option?’

‘What’s that?’

‘Kill yourself.’

‘Never!’

‘Why not? It would be better for your soul. The spirits of those killed by assassins seldom rest quiet. Bai Ze says-’

‘I don’t believe in spirits and I don’t believe in suicide. In this floating life of ours there is pain and there is pleasure. That’s all. Free men can run away from the one and into the arms of the other.’

‘Hoo! What impiety. If only a monk could hear you.’

‘A monk? Pfa! You shouldn’t believe everything *they* tell you. Most of the monks I’ve met are happy to visit a geisha house if they can. And when did you ever hear of one of them killing himself?’

‘You’ve never heard of the living mummies of Dewa Province?’ asked the trader. ‘They practice self-mortification until they achieve enlightenment. The way it works is this: they retreat to a hole in the ground and bury themselves inside it, with only a thin tube to connect to the air. Then they self-mummify by meditating for weeks, eating nothing but teak and salt… ’

‘What an affectation!’ said Motonari. ‘They probably only do it because their disciples tell them not to. The entire veneer of holiness comes from being paradoxical. Anyway, isn’t taking action against nature supposed to be a gross impiety?’

‘If that’s true then we’re guilty every time we go to a doctor.’

‘Well, I leave religion to others.’

‘But as a samurai you must at least believe in honour?’ the trader insisted. ‘And surely committing *seppuku* is the essence of honour. What about Masahide? Or those forty seven retainers?’

‘I’m fed up of hearing about them,’ said Motonari. ‘Why should we have to die just to satisfy the whims of our masters? It’s never *them* who have to kill themselves. You can keep your honour and give me freedom.’

‘There can be no greater freedom than to die at your own choosing…’

‘Suicide is the opposite of freedom. Your living actions are free. By killing yourself you destroy the possibility of future acts. So you destroy all future freedom.’

‘No, Sir’, said the trader: he seemed almost hurt. ‘Death and the fear of Death are the greatest enemies of freedom. To leave something as important as dying to old age or disease or the hand of another is to be beaten by Death. The only escape from that fear is to embrace it willingly at the time that is right for you.’

Motonari looked wearily at him.

‘Well, perhaps the time isn’t yet right for me. You don’t know – I might still get my life back.’

Out here, away from the city that was his life, he sounded weak and uncertain.

‘So you wouldn’t even kill yourself for love?’ Asked the trader, at last. ‘Every Bunraku play I’ve seen has been about some love-suicide or other. You can’t really have loved this woman, if you can stand the thought of never seeing her again.’

At this Motonari was once more in a rage.

‘What did you say? Say it again!’

‘Calm down! Let me tell you some stories to explain what I mean.’

Kwaidan

And with that the merchant started to tell his *kwaidan* – his strange stories. They were, Motonari thought, rather beautifully told. True, some were familiar - or at least of a type. But never so well constructed or so well delivered. This man had something of a talent. Soon Motonari was lying back in the damp dead leaves of the forest, huddled between the gnarled mossy roots. He stared up at the rain which fell towards him through the tangled canopy of branches. He had all but forgotten where he was and why.

The first story was that of the great bell of Suzhou, and how the bell-maker's daughter had thrown herself into the cast to give it its perfect tone. The second was the story of the Painting of Hell, and how the artist's sister had allowed herself to be burned alive so that he could paint her suffering from the life. The third was a version of the tale of the Peony Lantern: how the wife of the sake merchant, who had disfigured her face with a corrosive cosmetic given to her by a rival, had killed herself - and how her husband had later slept with a woman who looked like her, only to be found dead in the morning, entwined with her putrefied corpse.

When the trader had finished Motonari grimaced. There was a silence, broken only by the cracking of a log on the fire.

The Work of Art

'You tell these stories well', said Motonari in a soft voice. 'Though there are parts of them that I have heard before. Which means that I don't believe them – they are nothing but folk tales. In real life people don't die for love. I wish they did but the World is too ugly for that.'

'I agree. But our ancestors turned suicide into an art-form. We must not let the decline in standards corrupt that as well. A man of true artistic sensibility should see this. And a true artist in your position would not hesitate to kill himself: a protest at the corruption of love and the death of his loved one, Hotaru.'

'Wait!' Motonari jumped up. He stepped forward towards the trader. 'How do you know her name?'

'You have been honest with me, so it's time I was honest with you. You wanted to know what's in the box.'

'How do you know her name? How dare you speak to me like this! What *have* you got in that damned box?'

The trader picked up the box and passed it to him. Appalled, Motonari took off the lid. A mass of black hair cascaded out. Taking out the hair he looked underneath it. Then he recoiled in horror. The trader continued, implacably:

'Hotaru's heart', he said. 'She died very beautifully – in the old way. When I found her she had tied her legs together and slit her throat. Her death poem asked that she be buried in Yamanote. But it said that her heart and a lock of her hair should be given to you before your suicide. Here it is.'

Motonari cried out, dropped the box, and scrambled away through the undergrowth. The trader stood up to his full height. His stoop was gone. There was a sudden nobility in his bearing. He walked slowly after Motonari, who came to rest with his back to a tree.

'You can see now what I mean,' said the trader. 'You'll never forgive yourself any more than his Lordship will ever forgive you. Your life, even if you could hold onto it, wouldn't be worth living. Her last act was to beg you to do it. If not for honour or freedom then do it for love, and if not for love then do it for beauty. There is no point making your life a work of art if you can't do the same for your death.'

Motonari lowered his head and slowly nodded. Taking one last long look at the box he now knelt forward. He unsheathed his *wakizashi* and shrugged off his kimono. He placed the blade of his short sword to his stomach and took three short breaths. Then – quickly raising his arms – he brought it down in a brutal stab that pierced straight through his stomach and liver. Gasping at the pain he dragged the blade sideways in a wide jagged gash. Whimpering now he twisted it round and managed to make the second cut - that went upwards and inwards – before falling face forward into the damp leaves in front of him. The other man declined to decapitate him as custom dictated. The agony would no doubt continue for some hours, but there could be only one end.

Hideharu Fuma, having as promised performed his mission with all suitable elegance, - and using nothing but an actor's wig and some pig's offal he had bought from a butcher - saluted the dying man in front of him. Then he turned to make his way back to the City and his reckoning with the Daimyo's niece.

Chinese Whispers

Contents

Chinese Whispers

'Heaven sends forth innumerable things to nurture man.
Man has little good to send to Heaven in repayment.
Kill. Kill. Kill. Kill. Kill. Kill. Kill.'

King Zhang Xianzhong, c.1647

'[The First Emperor] Qin Shi Huang buried 460 scholars alive. We have buried forty-six thousand scholars alive... You intellectuals revile us for being Qin Shi Huangs. You are wrong. We have surpassed him a hundredfold.'

Mao Zedong, 1969

Lost in a Chinese Archive

What follows was found in the newly opened Party Archives in Beijing, in what is still the People's Republic of China. It was discovered by a sinologist colleague of mine. She was researching a book on 'the Effects of the Cultural Revolution in Shanxi Province'. These papers were too strange and macabre to be of any use to her. She found nothing else in the archives that shed any more light on the matter. Nor does she know of any other trace of the great book created (though not written) by the immortal scholar Wei Xu. There is one possible reference in a Qing Dynasty commentary on the Strange Stories of Pu Songling, in which the learned commentator promises a further volume (which does not appear to survive) on a work he calls 'Dark Tales from a Scholar's Studio', which he claims surpasses the work of Pu Songling as 'The Dream of the Red Chamber' surpasses 'The Plum in the Golden Vase'.

My colleague, then, was unable to use these papers. But, knowing my interest in such things, she translated them and passed them to me. The more I have read them the more subtle and provoking I have found them. It has inspired me to add to them myself, and to encourage others to do the same. So that in some small, imperfect way, a fragment of a possible interpretation of the impossible vision of Wei Xu would not be entirely lost in the vast ruin of time.

The Report of Comrade Wu

Report by Comrade Wu of the 3rd division of the people's red guard brigade of Taiyuan district, Shaanxi province, on 6th December 1966, into the strange occurences in plum-blossom village, Wutai county, and the failed investigation of comrade li.

My concerns about the idealogical soundness and even the sanity of my friend, Li Lijuan, began when I discovered that she had hidden a large bundle of papers from amongst the forbidden luxuries confiscated from the bourgeois elements in Xinghualing prefecture. Furthermore, she had written her own notes in the margins of some of these papers. When I later demanded that she hand them over she resisted, and she made statements suggesting that she had been influenced by revisionist mindsets and reactionary ideas. The events in plum-blossom village in the north of Jinge valley confirmed that my suspicions were correct. Mindful of the call by the party to 'sweep away all monsters and demons', I refer the matter to the commisar attached to 134th brigade of the red army. I include Li's own notes, and a copy of that part of the book she had taken which she explicitly refers to, together with my own comments. Here are Li's notes:

The Marginal Notes of Li Lijuan (with More Marginal Notes by Comrade Wu)

I am not a learned scholar like the great Wei Xu, or his many followers down the ages since his awful fate. I studied languages at college in Taiyuan; but I have never sat an examination for the Imperial School of the Sons of State, nor memorised the plots of the four great classic novels, nor written an 'eight-legged' essay. All these things have been swept away forever. There are many things in Xu's book that I don't understand.

[Wu] I can confirm this is true: Li was a second-class student and had to re-sit two of her papers.

Yet I feel I must try to add something, however humble, to the huge edifice of art built by the cultured people of the past. I have a duty to record the impossible things I have witnessed. For I see now that, if the last years in China have proved anything, it is that everything you think is true is also a lie - and at the same time there is nothing, however monstrous, that is not also true.

And if there's no-one left to keep the light of Wei Xu alive, then it falls to us – however weak we are – to guard it and keep it burning for others who come after.

[Wu] Many of the following details I can confirm as true, as I was attached to the same unit, though I dissociate myself from all superstition and any treasonous rightist sentiments expressed.

I first came out to Jinge Valley in the north of our prefecture with our comrades from the 3rd Division of the Red Guard Brigade of Taiyuan District. We were to ensure that the class struggle was being successfully waged, and the tenets of Marxist-Leninist-Mao Zedong Thought being followed in the remoter rural areas. Disturbing reports had reached party headquarters of disappearances and subversive elements in some of the villages high in the mountains. This year the spectres of sinister secret societies, and counter-revolutionary plots, have seemed to be lurking everywhere in the shadows. Although I am young, I have already witnessed much violence and conspiracy while protecting the Revolution. But nothing prepared me for what happened in Wutai county.

Fortunately, I had already at this time started reading Wei Xu's book. I had found it three weeks previously, when my Red Guard Unit had been called to resolve a dispute in a small town up in Xinghualing. An old lady who had been a schoolteacher was denounced as a bourgeois lickspittle by other local women. These had not forgiven her for some minor and ancient land dispute, from before the town fields were collectivised. They said she had treasure hidden in the study of her house, and some of the superstitious old folk whispered that she was a witch. Her house was the biggest in the area, having once belonged to her father, who'd been a mandarin and local governor, back in the time of the Empress Dowager. He had been an educated man, and kept an extensive library in his studio. He had died decades earlier during the time of troubles. And his daughter, the old lady (who he had educated himself) had taken over the house. She had run the village school for many years.

She lived in some squalor, and our hopes of finding much worthy of confiscation or destruction seemed in vain. It was as if she'd taken care to get rid of all the feudal or renegade objects in her possession. Even her father's studio at the back of the small courtyard had been emptied of all its curios and books. All we could find was one box. This the old woman would not give up. She was forced to in the end, when she was made to drink the customary bottle of ink and given the customary beating. We confiscated her house for re-distribution amongst the larger local families, and we pulled down the studio. I asked her why she had refused to cooperate for the sake of one old box. I shall always remember what she said, quivering in the dust on her knees, with black ink vomiting from her mouth as she looked up at me: 'You will know, when you have opened it'.

[Wu] This old bourgeois was properly punished, and has been sent for re-education.

We had not yet encountered such fanaticism, though we'd been warned about it, and I took the box away for interrogation. It was made of old, blackened lacquer, on which were the faded remnants of painted dragons, contorted into fantastic shapes. For its size it was surprisingly heavy. There was no obvious way of opening it.

My friends were all for smashing the box, but I insisted on puzzling it out, and took it away with me. I spent hours that night searching for the box's secrets. Turning it this way and that, pressing and knocking on it – whatever I tried had no effect. I was beginning to think it was some bizarre sort of joke, and that it didn't open at all. At last I noticed that the corners on one side were slightly lose. Or rather – they could be wiggled, so that the thinnest of gaps opened up between them and the rest of the box. I slipped a finger nail into these gaps. With some effort, I now saw they could be moved out slightly to the side. This in turn revealed a small section of wooden panel, which itself could be slid to reveal a second panel. Finally, pressing this second panel caused a hidden mechanism to spring back and the lid of the box to open. Ecstatic at this discovery, and intrigued as to what had been hidden with such care and ingenuity, I lifted the lid further open and peeked inside.

To my initial disappointment, inside the box there was nothing but an old book. It was bound in thick yellow paper. It was a single folio, loose-leaved and very battered, with old papers of different sizes, barely held together between ancient covers.

I thought it was important to know to which school of rightist traitors the old woman belonged. But to my surprise the book was not a political treatise. It was called 'Dark Tales from a Scholar's Study'. And from what I could make out it was exactly that. I searched for hidden meanings and coded references. The search was in vain; because the book was full of them by the thousand. But none, it seemed to me, that had any political or social force or contemporary relevance.

Instead it was a labyrinth of strange stories and antiquarian jottings, with poems, quotes, comments, and notes by many hands. It was constructed from stories within stories within stories, nestled together like a Chinese box. Some connected clearly to each other. The links with others were more obscure. Some digressed before they resolved. Others seemed to link out to other stories that were not there. They were ludicrous, monstrous, occasionally satirical, sometimes obscene, mostly uncanny, or at least open to possible mysterious interpretations. They varied in length from single paragraphs and comments to convoluted narratives the length of novellas. Some were written as fiction, some presented as true. Through all of them there ran a dark fascination with the supernatural. In quality, it must be said they varied greatly, from weird childish accounts about fox spirits and dragons, to strange stories about Buddhist monks and Taoist magicians, and *wokou* dwarf pirates battling monsters, and mad drunk poets having intercourse with spirits, to learned visions of sex and of death and subtle explorations of evil, whose full meanings I was often quite unable to fathom.

There were stories in both classical and in vernacular Chinese, in different dialects - even occasionally different languages, including one or two in Tibetan, perhaps extracts from the Book of the Dead, several in what looked like Sanskrit, a long one in Russian, and one in old-style Japanese that I've attempted to translate (I read this first, fearing a fascist message. Though from what I am able to tell it is simply a story of suicide and murder, set in the Edo period, purporting - according to a commentary – to be a re-telling of a true event, though hard enough to credit). The links between them sometimes created infinite loops. A narrator in one story might turn up, impossibly, as a character in another. The tales were set, and apparently originally written, in many different eras, as the dynasties of the past rose and fell. Many had been re-written with scholar's notes in later centuries. A Song Dynasty commentary claimed that the stories contained within its sub-narrative had once been written out in poisoned ink and presented by a bitter rival to the Senior Grand Secretary at Court, successfully guessing that he would become so engrossed in it that he would read himself to death. It is true that not all books are good for you to read. The oldest content I could date was apparently from the early Han Dynasty. It claimed to be an otherwise un-known entry from the records of the Grand Historian, and I believe it is the key that unlocks the whole.

[Wu] I attach the section referred at the end of this report [see below]

The rest of the book contained plenty that helped me to understand the things I was later to witness with my own eyes in Plum-Blossom Village - and much else besides. Fortunately, I had already read much of it when I was told to investigate the strange production figures from Wutai County.

These Wutai production figures were extremely disappointing, particularly from the more mountainous areas. In addition, there were anomalies in the rationing quotas, so that some communes were claiming back almost as much food as they were producing. Finally, we had had passed to us an anonymous cryptic message, apparently received from one village in the area, that said simply as follows:

'*COMRADE HUANG STILL EATS.*'

This was particularly odd. Comrade Huang was the local party representative for Plum-Blossom commune. According to the Party office he had been dead for three months.

Huang had been one of a number of promising men sent out from the local HQ to bring revolutionary methods to the backward areas, and had had a particularly assiduous reputation. He reported record production and sent a surplus, even as many neighbouring areas claimed to be suffering severe shortages and problems with the harvest. He also uncovered and punished several traitors in the region. Part of the problem was no doubt the bureaucratic confusion that was resulting from the revolutionary struggle. Answering the Chairman's call, the students and younger workers of Taiyuan city had successfully seized control of much of the government machinery from the older party cadres, which we were told had been corrupted by anti-socialist revisionism and Khrushevism. This was how I, though a mere girl of twenty-two, had come to be charged with solving the problems of the remote parts of Shanxi province, together with several other students from my dormitory, including my best friends Zhang and Wu. But it must be admitted that much chaos had been created in the process.

[Wu] I admit to knowing comrade li as a classmate and through family links, but would like to dispute this description. All temporary confusion arising from the necessary assault on revisionist elements in HQ is in the process of being eliminated.

It was here that I first found help from Wei Xu. There was an interesting short entry of commentary on the story of the 'heavenly candles'.

The True Story of the Heavenly Candles

This was an incident in Sichuan province at the end of the Ming period, during the rule of the proto-revolutionary King Zhang Xianzhong. This man, having proclaimed himself King of the West, had become obsessed with his mistress's ankles, which were unusually small. Eventually he got so distracted by them that he ordered all the other young women of the city to have their feet cut off. These he had placed in two huge piles in the square in front of his palace. Then he himself carefully cut off his mistresses' feet, above the ankles, and placed one on top of each pile. He had the piles doused in oil and lit as an offer of thanks to heaven. This sent him into such raptures that he then seems to have lost his mind, and conducted such terrible massacres that all order broke down and the Manchus invaded. After the subsequent fighting, resulting famine, and the ravages of disease, the survivors were apparently picked off by depredations of *shanxiao* monsters, tigers and other wild beasts, which came down from the mountains to live in the ruins of the towns and villages, until the whole of Sichuan province was completely abandoned, and had to be re-populated by outsiders from Fujian and Hubei.

The commentator says, in answer to those who dispute the truth of this, that he himself compared the census entries for the province for the years before and after Xianzhong's reign, and could confirm that they showed only 16,096 adult men in Sichuan after his rule, compared to 3,102,073 registered there a few years before.

The Marginal Notes of Li Lijuan Continued (with Further Marginal Notes by Comrade Wu)

This gave me the idea of checking the modern census data for Wutai county, and cross-checking it against the commune head-counts for the rationing quotas.

It was a glorious winter day when I made my way to the archive office - on my own initiative. What Xu's book would describe as 'auspicious clouds' were piling up in the East. The rest of the sky was clear enough, above the smoke rising from book fires as high as nearby houses. These had been burning for 3 days now, with eager volunteers working round the clock to bring more fuel from the bookshop quarter and the University library. In Yingze park stood 300 pianos, confiscated from bourgeois elements. School kids wearing red armbands played mad tunes on them and smashed them with hammers.

I cycled to the party archives. These were supposed to be off-limits to all but senior officials. But the archivists seemed terrified of me – a mere student – because I wore the red armband. I was ushered to a bare and airless room where I sat all afternoon as they brought me the party records for Wutai county. Most was administrative paperwork of no interest to anyone. But after an hour or two I had found what I was looking for: the local census records for the region, both the most recent and the previous one, which had been conducted shortly after the war. For completism, I also looked at reports from the older censuses. Soon a pattern emerged, with the numbers of households staying roughly stable decade by decade, all the way back to the late Manchu period. There was a substantial drop in the 1930's and 1940's, which was little surprise. The mountains had seen fighting between warlords, and then between our heroic forces and the Fascist foreign devils (the forces resisting the invaders also included Nationalist units, which themselves later had to be defeated). The Japanese had dropped plague rats and gas bombs on some villages. And, after they captured most of the region, they brought in their infamous 'Unit 731', which conducted human vivisections and other strange experiments on their prisoners.

The figures to this point corresponded exactly with what you would expect. But then they became more puzzling.

The first post-war census, far from indicating a recovery to previous levels, showed a further dramatic drop. And worse still, the most recent figures, which the glorious breakthroughs in agriculture and local industry suggested should have rebounded, showed another precipitate decline. Whichever way you cut the figures, it was clear there were hundreds – perhaps thousands - of souls *missing* from the villages in the Jinge valley. It was as if some fantastic horror had unfolded up in Wutai, that for some reason was not reflected in the worker quotas or the death registrations, and so also not in the food rationing quotas.

As the shadows started to lengthen towards evening, I asked for equivalent census reports for the rest of the province. This was as a comparison, and to ensure there had been no change in the methodology by which the censuses had been conducted. At this point the archivists became hostile and refused to cooperate any further.

The next day I set out with Comrades Wu and Zhang towards the Wutai mountains. The countryside beyond the city was in uproar. Long lines of students were making their way into the country, to be re-educated with the peasants, through productive toil on the land. Abandoned steel foundries were everywhere in the fields. Mass de-forestation had left the hills above Taiyuan muddy and bare. As we drove through one market town we saw rows of tiny children conducting bayonet practice. They were shouting over and over: 'Kill the traitors!'. In another we saw a group of twenty or thirty children stoning an old man. The roads were clogged with vehicles transporting undesirable elements and excess producers away to help fulfil the proletariat quotas.

As we got further from the main centres of population, however, things grew quieter and less frantic. The peasants in the paddies looked much as they must have done for centuries. Above Doucunzhen the country rises sharply and becomes a lot more rugged. The road is soon little more than a dusty track, winding up precariously, dog-legging back on itself, hugging the cliffs, between rice terraces and patches of woodland, towards the peaks of the Wutai. These mountains are constantly shrouded in clouds. The villages become poorer and more spread out. Little wooden temples can be seen in clearings and on the lower peaks. Pathways up crumbling stairways cut into cliffs lead to ruined shrines high in the mists. The whole region looks like something from old landscape prints, like those we had removed from the grand houses back in town. Coming up here in the remote parts of the mountains was like stepping back into feudal China - before the revolution. It was a relief to see occasional signs of progress: here an electricity generator, there some posters with party slogans denouncing traitors. The people we encountered were dirty, thin, and sullen. They moved and talked sluggishly. The children, though, looked old: they had swollen bellies and some of them beards. These were clear signs that there was malnutrition. None would talk to us. We dropped off Comrade Wu in a small town at the foot of the valley.

[Wu] I can confirm all the details up to this point, when I was dropped off. Over the next two days I conducted a successful re-education campaign and uncovered several bourgeois elements and punished them.

On the second day out from Taiyuan I said goodbye to Comrade Zhang. I left him in another village, where he was to investigate, whilst I covered the smaller settlements further up the valley. From there on I drove myself in our commandeered truck. The roads were very bad. After an hour to two I broke a wheel on a rock on a tight right turn. It was clear the truck could go no further. But I reckoned that by now I was a short walk from my destination: a decayed village at the very top of the valley, near the source of the river. I followed a rutted track along the side of this river, heading up-stream until I finally reached the settlement. Its buildings were mostly large, communal wooden houses. These were of the old style, with steep-pitched roofs constructed, not of tiles, but of thatch. On some of the slopes above the village, patches of last winter's snow could still be seen, even this late in the year.

The villagers were waiting for me, watching in silence as I approached. Delighted to have reached habitation in daylight, I greeted them warmly. I immediately demanded to speak to the acting party representative, Comrade Wang. In the chaos of recent months he had been appointed by the village commune, though he had not yet been confirmed by Party HQ. They sent someone to find him. Soon they returned with a gaunt, bespectacled man of perhaps 50, who politely welcomed me to the village. He addressed me rather haltingly, with slogans so out of date that they would have put him under immediate suspicion down in the city. But he seemed a good man. No-one in Plum-Blossom village had travel permits, and it was a long way from the nearest party office. Indeed, it was a long way from anywhere.

A small crowd gathered round us as I spoke to him, exchanging glances. It was late, and I was shown to the only available accommodation: a draughty wooden shack. It had once been an inn for pilgrims and travellers crossing the high passes, and was now used as the village's party office at the front - and by the Wang family in shuttered, alcoved rooms round the sides and the back. I was shown to a wooden-screened alcove off the three-storey communal space that made up the middle of the building, which contained the family kitchen and fire, the smoke from which rose up through the house's centre to a chimney high up in the rafters. It was a simple and very old-fashioned place, though it certainly had a sort of cosiness. Wang's family consisted of him and his wife, two late adolescent children (they had older children too, I believe), a sister-in-law, an aunt, and his aged mother, who showed at least some signs of senility. They served me a basic dinner with great efforts at friendliness, and it was a relief to witness the warmth and simple generosity of these country people, who had nothing but shared everything. It was surely this spirit that was behind the great leader's exhortation that we should seek education from the peasants. But at the same time I was conscious of several whispered conversations, and a sense of tension in all my dealings with them and the rest of the villagers, so that I got the impression I wasn't welcome. We'd all heard stories of forced marriages and rapes, of beatings and of murders, committed by peasants on re-located students (though these were all word of mouth: they never appeared in the papers). I was suddenly painfully aware that I was a long way from home, barely older than a schoolgirl, with no transport and little to protect me. I only had my fervour for the Party, and the vague suggestion that my red guard comrades might shortly join me - though I was told the telephone lines were down, and in truth I had no means to contact them.

That afternoon, as planned, I immediately organised a 'struggle session', in which I was to call together all the adults of the village, up-date them on the latest Party thinking, and encourage them to confront each other - and themselves - with any crimes they might have committed against the state. In other villages I had seen this quickly lead to denouncements of class traitors and undesirable elements. Here, though, I was alone. And I faced a community in which there was an apparently united front. Speaking in the thick mountain dialect, with a great show of being friendly and helpful, and using similar turns of phrase, they all repeated the same message. They had fulfilled all they could, given their numbers. Their output had declined because of the harvest. There was no food. One girl about my own age blurted out that things had been different before Comrade Huang had died. She was told to keep quiet by several of the older men, who re-iterated with profuse apologies that the harvest was terrible, and there were not enough peasants to produce any more, but too many mouths to feed.

At this point I asked for a head-count. There was a more hostile silence. Then several people started making comments about how some of the farmers were away in the distant high pastures (which seemed odd, given the lateness of the year, but I'm no expert on farming; and I supposed this made sense of the fact that I had seen no livestock). I asked how quickly I could gather together everyone from the commune, but it seemed that this would be difficult – and certainly impossible for many days. I asked what had happened to Comrade Huang. I was told he had met with a strange accident: his body had been found, face-down, in the river, and that he seemed to have slipped, somehow hit his head, and sadly died of a terrible injury to his brain. He had been a widower, and had no immediate family. Somewhat unsure of myself, but not wishing to reveal my uncertainty, I called an end to the session for that day. Then I returned to the old inn, where I did some pointless paperwork, and made a show of seeming that I knew what I was doing. It was clear that something had happened here. But also that it would be hard to get them to tell me what it was.

An hour or so later there was a knock on the door. A young woman came in. I recognised her as the girl who had tried to speak up at the meeting. Shy at first, and apparently frightened, she looked around her and shouted:

'You are welcome here Comrade! Let me embrace you!' Then she came forward and, gripping me tightly, whispered 'You aren't safe here – get out – or they will kill you!'

'Who will?'

Her voice dropped still further. I struggled to hear anything at all as she pressed her lips to my ear and started to speak. I only caught three words. Just then one of the older women of the house came into the room, apparently busying herself clearing up some bowls. The girl retreated and simply said: 'Thank you Comrade Li. I will endeavour to be more like Comrade Lei Feng! Death to the capitalist roaders and anti-socialist cabals!'

Then she scurried away. I was left baffled and, for the first time since my arrival, genuinely shaken. Had I heard it right? The dialect was thick and her throat was half-closed with fear, so that it had come out in the barest whisper. But I was pretty sure what she had started to say was:

'The blood drinkers-'

The Wang family were extremely polite and did their best to make me feel at home. They were full of apologies about the simplicity of their food – it seemed the villagers had nothing left to eat but cabbages, potatoes, and beets – but we had a very pleasant evening eating round the fire, in the centre of the old inn that was now their home. They were full of questions about the city, and what had been happening in China over the last few months. I did my best to educate them about the great progress the revolution was making at casting off residual bourgeois habits of thought. It seemed harder to explain out here, without my comrades around me. I made sure to repeat how important the leaders knew the peasantry was, as the bedrock of the people.

That night, long after my hosts had gone to bed, I was struggling to sleep in the quiet of the countryside. There was something oppressive about that deep silence. The only noises were the occasional creaks of the wooden roof above me, the tiny sounds of logs settling on the fire and, some time after one, the distinct noise of someone hawking and spitting outside – a sound that got closer and then gradually disappeared into the distance.

In retrospect, it was strange that someone was out so late, but I didn't think about it at the time and at last fell asleep.

The next day was what used to be called 'ghost day' in Shanxi. I was surprised to see that the villagers still marked the occasion. They even left simple offerings to the dead in the cemetery – mostly food (though they had precious little themselves) and cigarettes. They also released little lotus lanterns in the river. We watched the lights float down the clear, dark, fast-flowing water, until they disappeared in the mist that lay about the valley. One of the women made a comment about whether the dead would forgive them and rest in peace. Her husband glanced at her. I wondered if there was a warning in his eyes.

Three young children – two boys of around seven or eight and a girl of maybe five – were playing rather listlessly with sticks in a field by the river. I stopped to ask them what they were doing. 'We're running away from hungry ghosts', said one of the boys. At this the young girl started crying. I picked her up to comfort her. She weighed nothing in my arms.

'Don't be afraid of paper tigers,' I said, rather self-consciously, 'there's no such thing as ghosts.'

'Yes there are,' the girl sobbed, 'I've seen them.'

'No you haven't', I said, soothing her. But she was inconsolable, insisting that she had seem them from her bedroom window, wandering in the cemetery at night.

'Just a nightmare,' I said.

‘No,’ said one of the older boys, ‘I’ve seen them too – we all have.’

What was chilling was the matter-of-fact tone of his voice, as if this nonsense was obvious.

‘What do you mean?’ I asked.

The other boy hit the first and said ‘Daddy says we mustn’t talk about it.’

I took a chance and, crouching down, I grabbed one of the boys and asked him: ‘Who are the ‘blood drinkers’?’

The boys looked at each other. The little girl said simply, through renewed tears: ‘the old ones – they say we can’t talk about it.’ Then the boys laughed mischievously, the one I was holding wriggled out of my grasp, and they ran away.

That afternoon I made little more progress getting any sense from my hosts about the precise numbers of the villagers who could be assembled and by when. All my enquiries were met with the same combination of politeness, incomprehension, and evasion. I asked to see the young lady who had come to me the previous day, but of course I didn’t know her name. I looked out for her but didn’t see her. I spent most of the day just trying to arrange to get a message out of the village. Eventually Mr Wang found one of the farmers, who said he was intending to cycle down the valley next day, and agreed to carry with him a message from me to Comrade Zhang. The message told Zhang about what had happened to the truck, and asked him to come and help me as soon as possible. I hinted I would be particularly grateful for his assistance. In case the message was read on the way, however, I decided not to put in any stronger suggestion that I was starting to sense that, in my village, all might not be quite as it had at first seemed, and to feel thwarted at every turn, and dangerously out of my depth.

That night I slept even more fitfully. My mind was racing between all sorts of dark and confused thoughts. It didn’t help that I hadn’t had a full stomach now for several days. At some point in the early hours I was woken again by the sound of spitting. Again, it was very late for someone to be outside on normal business, particularly amongst this population of farmers, who tended to go to bed early and rise with the sun. Also, I now realised, the noise was coming from the direction of the village, but from the fields just beyond the stream that bordered it. Once again it came closer - right along the side of the house, on the other side of the wall from where I lay. It was disgusting and gutteral. Like someone trying to get rid of some phlegm or noxious bile that they could never shift. Determined to find out who it was, I pulled my clothes on and crept to the door of the house. Stepping out into the shock of the cold winter air, I looked around. There was no sign of anyone about. I went around to the side of the house from where I had heard the spitting. Since this was the side away from the village centre, this was deep in shadow. I slipped over on some mud and fell to my knees with a curse. Just then I thought I heard a sound from the field beyond – something between a gasp and an exhalation, like a startled animal. By the time I had managed to pick myself up and look around, there was nothing to see. I stood there and made myself count to 60, then do it again more slowly. But still there was nothing. Shivering, I picked my way back into the warmth of the old inn.

The next morning I went out to the field from which I had heard the noise. In the daylight things looked different, but I now realised that it was the village cemetery. There were plenty of footprints, presumably from the previous day. And, treading my way carefully between the graves, I noticed that the soil around some of the newer ones was slightly scuffed. Of course this was easily explained by the ceremonies the day before. I also noticed, though, that some of the offerings seemed to have been disturbed in the night, and were strewn or missing. Some wild animals, I guessed, had also played their part in this barbaric old feudal custom. That could, I reasoned, explain what I had heard the previous nights. Just about.

Returning to the village, I asked Mr Wang about the noises I had heard. He looked at me in shock, but said he had no idea what I was thinking about. His grizzled old mother, sitting in the corner, looked up and tutted. Mr Wang stood up and left. His mother shuffled over to me, took my face in her dirty, wrinkled hands, and said with a sad laugh: 'The dead are hungry, like the living.'

That afternoon, I tried again to confront Mr Wang. He interrupted and said he had some bad news for me. The farmer who had gone to the lower village had arrived to find Zhang already gone, having apparently left to return to the city. He said that, if I wanted to leave, he would personally arrange for transport the following day. This would have been very tempting, if the news had not been so strange and so unwelcome. I couldn't imagine why Zhang would have left the other village so soon, without sending for me or coming to pick me up, or – if it wasn't true – what Mr Wang and his messenger meant or intended. I had started to fear that I couldn't trust them and that they wanted to get rid of me as soon as possible. Whatever the truth of it, I had little choice but to agree. I was now entirely on my own, with no prospect of outside help, and effectively at the mercy of a village that seemed to have closed ranks against me.

That night I stayed up late reading Wei Xu's book in the swirling smoke of an old charcoal fire, until my head was swimming with all that I'd read. There had been several interlinked stories about secret sects, from vampiric Triad societies to Thai necromantic cults, that roast the bodies of unborn babies and cover them all over in gold leaf and occult tattoos.

I stepped outside to clear my mind. There was no sign of whoever or whatever had been making the spitting noise. Above me, between the dark ridges rising high on either side, was an incredible canopy of stars. I had never seen so many or with such exquisite clarity. I realised how much the air of the city had obscured from sight. I thought of a phrase of poetry I had just read in Xu's book about 'harmony under heaven'. Around me the village was asleep. Smoke rose from chimneys that were little more than holes in the thatch of the larger family houses. Beyond there was a deeper blackness where the wooded slopes rose high on either side. It was then that I spotted a single light – distant but clear – twinkling in the blackness, high on one of the ridges above the village. I realised it must have been coming from the tiny temple above the cliff. I had previously been assured that this temple was derelict. The thought that this was a lie was frightening. But by now I had realised that, if there was indeed a subversive conspiracy going on, and if the peasants were truly against me, I wasn't safe where I was in the village in any case.

Eager to take what might be my only chance to get to the bottom of whatever was happening, I plucked up the courage to take a lantern and set off towards the temple. I made my way cautiously up a path between houses and allotments, over a small wooden bridge that crossed the stream, and finally to the foot of a long path of log steps, that criss-crossed up towards the temple. Quickly reaching the snow-line I could see footprints leading up before me. The path rose steeply and I soon emerged, panting somewhat, above the thickest of the forest, to a spot where the path narrowed and – protected only by an insubstantial-looking wooden railing – skirted a windy blackness that I knew was the cliff-edge. The little temple was clearly visible in front of me now, and I could see the light that shone under the doorway between two couchant lion statues. Coloured dragons and fantastic beasts were crudely-carved into the trabeated wooden beams below the roof.

Eager to discover the truth, I marched up to the door and, taking a deep breath, stepped into the sudden warmth of the temple. The air inside was thick and heady. Fires burned in blackened braziers. Scented sticks smouldered in bronze bowls. A bald old man in dirty old clothes was leaning over some papers, smoking a long pipe, and muttering. Whether he was consulting the Hexagrams of the Book of Changes or reading a copy of the People's Daily, I was unable to see.

'"Speak of Cao Cao and Cao Cao arrives" – I was just talking about you,' he said.

'Who were you talking to?'

'To myself of course. Why, who else is there here? Do you think there are hungry ghosts listening?'

'Why did you say that? You aren't the first person here to talk about them today.'

'Oh really? Well it's been the time of year for it, I suppose. But we live in an age of 'scientific materialism'. You yourself are here to remind us of this fact. And, though I used to be a monk, I renounced my supernatural beliefs like a good revolutionary. It is many years since locals or pilgrims used this temple. I am only here because I have nowhere else to live. So I should plead, as Master Kong once did, that I refuse to talk about ghosts.'

'But I want you to tell me about them!' I surprised myself as I said it.

'How much do you want to know? Go away and read up on it. Assuming you can find a book that hasn't been burned.'

'Come on, you must be able to tell me something. People here seem still to believe. Back when you were a monk, did the villagers ever ask you to perform exorcisms?'

'Me? Bah! I prayed for the dead, of course. But if ever any village needed something like that they would get in a specialist Taoist ghost-buster.'

'You mean like Zhong Kui, in the stories?'

The old man gave me a curious look 'I thought those sorts of stories were now frowned upon.'

A sudden spasm of terror gripped me.

'Don't worry!' the old man laughed, 'I won't inform on you. You're just – well - not quite what I expected. It sounds like you already know rather a lot yourself?'

I paused for a second then said: 'The discredited superstitions of Buddhism and Taoism claimed that hungry ghosts can return from the 40,000 hells to plague the living, if we neglect the spirits of our ancestors, or forget the old rights that propitiate them, or desecrate their burials. But such feudal practices have been swept away across the whole of China. Some used to believe', I added, rather pleased to show off the knowledge of such matters I had gleaned from the many ghost stories in Xu's book, 'that those who died tragic deaths, or who sinned against the state, or who seek vengeance against the living, can also return from hell to walk among us. They seek to feed on the spiritual powers of the living, and the flesh of corpses.'

'Ah, the flesh of corpses – that most exquisite and terrible source of sustenance – that really would stick in the throat. Imagine what insatiable, raging hunger could drive a soul to that. Imagine what awful satiation it would feel afterwards, and what insane horror - particularly if they had feasted on someone they knew.' He glanced toward the shuttered windows, painted in once-lurid colours, now somewhat faded.

'What has been happening here? What do you know? Why all this talk of hungry ghosts?'

'China is a land of ghosts. This attempt by our great leader to exorcise them has created many millions more. And did your reading also tell you about *jian*? Ghosts of ghosts. After their death, men used to say, a person becomes a ghost. After *its* death, a ghost becomes a *jian*. A paradox, of course. But perhaps there is wisdom hidden in that superstition too. Much more tragic. And much more dangerous. Most people can no longer see ghosts amongst us and we forget everything. A society's memory is its soul, just as a person's memory is. If a person exorcises their memory they will become nothing but a soulless lunatic. And if a nation exorcises its memory it too will go insane.'

'Careful - you could be killed for that.' I didn't mean it as a threat.

'Chuang Tzu once said: 'Life is desirable and death undesirable only from the point of view of the living. How do we know that the reverse is not true from the point of view of the dead?' If there are hungry ghosts, perhaps that is why they try to harm us. For our own good.

'Life here has been very hard. Many have died, and there are one or two who have gone mad with grief. I am an old man now and the world has lost its beauty for me. Perhaps I would be happier dead. That is why I smoke this. Would you like some? Go on!'

It was quite out of my character, but I was entranced by this old man, who seemed like something from Xu's book. My curiosity got the better of me. I took that pipe and breathed in deeply. The smoke was not acrid, but sweet. At first it had no noticeable effect.

'I find that smoking this pipe can allow you to see things you would not normally see.'

'So you have seen… things?'

'Yes. I've seen things you couldn't possibly believe. I saw my first ghost when I was studying the Way with Master Hao. My hair stood up on end – or at least, it would have done, if I had had any hair to stand up! And the God of

Dreams has since opened my eyes to many things. But it sounds like you are yourself not unacquainted with ghost stories.

Strange Stories in a Taoist Temple: Liu Shisi, Fatty Ding, and the Monk from Luoyang

Have you heard the tales of the great courtesan Liu Shishi, who the Emperor used most unnaturally, who wore too many pearls and not enough silks, which led to her accumulating too much yin, so she started to see ghosts and it sent her mad? Or Fatty Ding, who collected Burmese jade, and realised he could see the plague-carriers, the un-dead who come into people's houses when they're asleep, and when they breathe on someone that person will die – he was paid to lie awake in rich men's houses, and keep a look out for these monsters; but one night he ate so much he fell asleep and he was himself breathed on and died of the red fever? Or that monk from Luoyang, who drank too much green tea in an attempt to prevent lascivious dreams, and found he was soon plagued by insatiable fox spirits. Fortunately, (and please forgive the lewdness of this story Miss) he was as well-endowed as Lao Ai, whose huge member had given such satisfaction to the Queen Dowager of Qin. He was able to screw those horny foxes until they died of exhaustion, and after a few years of being bed-ridden, he eventually made a complete recovery. Though he could never again abide the sight of foxes…'

By now we were both laughing, and my head was beginning to swim.

'So you don't deny that this place is being plagued with ghosts?'

'The questions *you* should be asking', he said, suddenly serious and grave, 'is: "Why? And *why are they hungry?*"

A Further Continuation of the Marginal Notes of Li Lijuan (with Yet Further Marginal Notes by Comrade Wu)

My head was spinning like a paper lantern in a typhoon. Strange shapes and colours swirled before my eyes. I felt a terrible sense of dread, though I could hear myself laughing insanely. After some time – I cannot tell how long – I left the old man and stumbled outside into the snow, though I remember feeling no cold. Somehow I must have made my way back down towards the village. I have confused memories of standing by the cliff, and shouting out defiantly into the void. I shudder to think how close I came to falling into the abyss. I somehow picked my way back down through the trees in the darkness, until I was back amongst the dark houses of the sleeping village. In the dark and my confusion it seemed strangely hard to find the right building.

Eventually I did. I was just reaching for the latch when I heard a dragging sound somewhere off in the darkness to my right. I froze and strained my ears. There was nothing. I started to repeat my counting trick from the previous night. I had only got as far as twenty when I heard it – the unmistakeable noise of spitting. It was coming, as before, from beyond the house on the other side. It must have already gone along the side of the building, and was now behind me, to the right, in the burial ground.

The thought of going straight inside and curling up in bed with my fingers in my ears was very tempting. But I felt compelled and emboldened to find out once and for all what was going on. I crouched down and listened again. There it was again – a gargling, retching sound, more human than animal, but deeply unnatural. Creeping forwards in the darkness on my hands and knees, I reached a low wall that marked the boundary of the yard. I crouched beneath it for what seemed an age, straining to hear. At first there was nothing. Then there was a low muttering that at last resolved into a sound of retching, followed by a despairing, gutteral laugh. I steeled myself and stood up. I wish I had not. At the far end of the village cemetery, crouched over, there was a *figure*. It looked more than anything like a haggish old woman, wearing nothing but rags. It spun round, glaring at me with mad wide eyes that caught a reflected light from the village. Then it loped off with surprising speed and disappeared into the darkness.

I turned and fled. I somehow must have got back into the house and into bed. There I fell into a sleep, tormented by vivid dreams, until I finally awoke the next morning with a thumping headache, and spewed my guts up.

As I lay, too sick and weak to get up, Mr Wang came up to see me.

'You were seen out walking last night', he said crossly. 'This is very bad – you should have told me. Now you can't get a lift down the valley. You will have to stay here.'

It wasn't clear if he was referring to the fact that I was too sick to move, or was simply stating that he was going to keep me here, effectively, as a prisoner. Seriously frightened now, I decided to play along with the understanding that it was the former. I guessed that at least this would make us both feel better.

'You're right,' I said, 'I'm sorry. I can't go anywhere today. Perhaps tomorrow I can leave. Thank you for being so understanding.'

I lay there all morning, weighing up my options as my head slowly cleared. I was desperate not to spend another night in the place. But it was at least a full day's walk to the next village. That was assuming I could find the way. And of course, I had no reason to think that the villagers there weren't part of the same conspiracy. For all I knew they might even have got rid of Comrade Zhang. Any way I looked at it I was trapped.

I lay there for hours, half wondering if I was safe in my bed. Then suddenly I heard a thrilling sound reverberating up the valley, unexpected but unmistakable, and the best thing I could have wished for: a motorcar. Lurching up and downstairs I arrived in the village square at the same time as it came to a halt and out got my saviour - it was Zhang.

I took him to the old inn and introduced him to Mr Wang and his family. As soon as we were alone, I told him – as much as I could make sense of it myself – everything that had happened to me, I asked him what we should do. I was appalled to hear he agreed with my earlier suspicion, that there might be some sort of conspiracy here. Indeed, he had come to warn me that he had uncovered a secret society at work behind the scenes. And he had himself been physically threatened by some of the villagers. He had had to take dozens of names. Far from accusing each other, the villagers were covering each other's backs. Even worse, though, he had no intention of driving us both out of there. Instead he told Mr Wang he would be calling another struggle session, to confront my villagers head-on. 'It is our duty to stamp out this nest of reactionaries!' I remember him saying. Of what I had seen the night before, I was somewhat more vague, though I did tell him the basic details.

'What are we going to do?' I asked.

'Cabals and secret conspiracies are treason against the people – remember the criminal Dragon Head leader of the Single Hearted Celestial Principle Dragon-flower Sacred Religion Society! Learn the lesson of his reactionary plot to proclaim himself Emperor after the revolution, and its glorious defeat by the proletarian vanguards!'

'That's all very well,' I said, 'but I think there's something else going on here. I don't believe the villagers are to blame – they are good people at heart, just frightened.'

He looked at me suspiciously.

'Is it true you asked to see the census records for the whole province?'

This came as a terrible shock, particularly coming from Zhang. The tone of accusation in his voice was all too clear.

'Yes, why?'

He made a note in his notebook.

'Tell me what to do,' I said, desperate to get back into his good opinion.

'If you want to be a good comrade and help uncover this conspiracy, show me where you saw this… old woman.'

'Ok,' I said, uncertainly, 'but I'm not exactly sure…'

'We'll soon find out what they're up to,' he said.

We dined with our hosts and made every appearance of going to bed. Then, as pre-arranged, after darkness had fallen and everyone had retired, we crept downstairs, took two lanterns, and picked our way to the cemetery to the spot where I had seen the strange thing the previous night. Gathering some spades and other farming implements from a nearby shed, we started to dig down into one of the fresher family graves, where the scuff marks were most concentrated. The grave marker said it contained a man and two young children, and that they had died recently.

'What are we looking for?' I asked.

'I don't know. Weapons, perhaps, or forbidden propaganda. Whatever these people are hiding here must be pretty important.'

I stood by the side of the hole for what seemed like an age, shivering in the cold of the winter night. Zhang worked slowly, anxious not to make too much noise, though we were some way from the houses and a thick mist had swathed the valley, which deadened the sound. After an hour or so a light swirling snow began to fall. I continually looked round to see if there was any sign of whether we had been seen, or worse still whether there was anyone – or anything – creeping up on us. After digging about three feet down Zhang finally found something, gasped, and dropped to scramble at the earth with his hands. Then - with a sudden cry - he fell backwards and scrambled desperately out of the hole. I looked over in the direction he was pointing. There, at the foot of it, was a large mass of human hair.

'Go and get a sheet or something,' he gasped. Looking closer, poking out of the soil, the hair was clearly obscuring the remains of a face.

I didn't like walking off into the fog on my own, but on the other hand I was relieved to get away from that pit. I went back to the shed and found a tarpaulin and hurried back to the burial ground, where I could soon see the round yellow halo, glowing from Zhang's lantern in the mist. I could see that for some reason Zhang had climbed back into the excavation, and re-commenced digging. Steeling myself, I crept back to the edge of the hole and peered over the side.

I could now see the source of the hair. There were three heads in the trench, one large and two small, lying close together, still with semi-putrid flesh on them, each sprouting a full head of black hair, clogged with clay. What was even worse was this: there were no other remains to be seen. But I could also see why Zhang had kept digging. For he had also uncovered the top of a wooden box – too small and square to be a normal coffin - directly under where the heads had been placed. I must have said something, for Zhang – who clearly had not heard me return until that moment – screamed out in shock and span round. We stood in silence for a moment, straining to tell if we had been over-heard. Then, now desperate to finish the grisly task as soon as possible, Zhang gingerly used the shovel to scrape the heads onto the tarpaulin, and started to prize open the lid of the box with his spade.

On opening this box, things were clear enough. It contained what must have been three full sets of human bones, deliberately arranged, entirely without flesh, but covered everywhere with cut marks.

Zhang gasped. We looked at each other for a long time in silence. Then he said: 'go and fetch my bag from the house.'

'But why?' I asked, appalled.

'Just do it!'

Desperate now to get away from the ghastly scene in the field, I fled back to the inn, where I crept around until I found Zhang's bag. Then I steeled myself to return once more to the burial ground. Just as I got to the gate at its far edge, I heard a sort of coughing sound from the direction of the grave. The fog had thickened, and the effect of Zhang's remaining lantern in the hole cast grotesque shadows through its sickly light. But I could not at first see Zhang. I called out to him – partly as a warning this time that I was coming, and partly because I was scared. I didn't hear anything from the excavations, except perhaps a fall of earth.

I could not see Zhang until I arrived at the spot. He was lying face-down in the trench. Turning him over, gently, I saw that his eyes stared out in shock, his fine features distorted into a wild grin. On the other side: a sticky white mess where his head was completely caved in.

I turned and somehow scrambled back to the village, as fast as I could go in the fog. I was conscious that I must have been watched. I went into the inn and grabbed my few possessions, including the book of Wei Xu. But I couldn't find Zhang's keys to the truck. Cursing, I forced myself back to the graveyard, to search for them on his body. I tried not to look at his face. It was a ghastly job. It was also a fruitless one – they certainly weren't in his pockets. I raced to where the truck was parked, in case the keys were somewhere in that. As I was frantically searching for them, and no doubt making quite a noise doing it, I'm sure I heard a twig snap somewhere nearby. There was nothing else I could do. I jumped out and simply ran straight down the path towards the road out of the village. I didn't look back.

I walked all night and all the next day down the valley, taking as wide a detour as I dared around the village Zhang had been in, and kept going. Finally, as the sun was sinking behind the tree-lined ridges that evening, I stumbled exhausted into the small town at the mouth of the valley where we had left Wu. As far as I could tell I did not appear to have been followed. I soon was found and taken to Wu. We were able to find a working vehicle. We paid our remaining currency to its owner, and drove back onto the plain that night. I shall never go back to Wutai and, after filing the sort of report that will disturb no one at HQ, I will never speak to anyone of what happened there. At last it was clear to me what horror had occurred in the mountains; and why we were wrong to stop believing in hungry ghosts.

[Wu] Comrade li appeared as she described, told me that Zhang was dead, and insisted on leaving the area immediately. I could get no further real sense out of her, and the meaning of these last lines of her notes is unclear to me. For what it's worth, I include the section of the book to which li previously referred:

Dark Tales from a Scholar's Study

My genitals were cut off by men who do not appreciate good writing. I wear them, pickled, in a jar about my neck. Not, as men say, as a reminder of my disgrace. Rather as a symbol of my fecundity. Condemned for defending an innocent man, General Ling, when the rest of the Imperial Court had rallied against him, I, Sima Qian, the Hereditary Grand Historiographer, was offered the choice of dismissal or castration. Conscious of my filial duties, and despite still being childless, I naturally chose the more shameful punishment. It was the only way to finish my books – the Annals of the Grand Historian - and so preserve for posterity the work begun by my father and what it records: everything that remains of the old traditions of the world which have been scattered and lost. I wished to examine all that concerns heaven and man, to penetrate the mysteries of the past and so to explain the present, so that people of the future might understand it and themselves. My father on his deathbed begged me to complete his work. Our ancestors have been official recorders for a thousand years, since the time of the Duke of Chou. He told me it was my duty to the descendants I would beget to keep the tradition alive. He did not explain what I should do when faced with a choice between carrying on the work and carrying on the family. In making the terrible choice, between killing my unborn children and losing access to the state archives, I had always before me the example of my great predecessor, Lord Xu of Wei.

Xu was, as all the educated know, Prime Minister of the Duke of Wei at the end of the Age of the Warring States. When the King of Qin conquered the other states and made himself the first Emperor of all China, he became obsessed with the quest for eternal life and the destruction of all ideas with which he disagreed. In particular he hated books, which he said shortened life, by taking the reader out of the real world whilst they were reading. He therefore decreed that all the books in the world that did not pertain to agriculture, divination, or alchemy, should be banned. He did not understand that, though books may not contain the recipe of immortality, they can at least be the best way to achieve it. In particular, all poetry (which he abhorred), all the histories of all the other states apart from Qin, and all the works of the 100 Schools of Philosophy (apart from the strict Legalism that he favoured), were to be collected and burned, except one copy of each, to be preserved in the Imperial library. To defy this order carried a sentence of death. 460 Confucian scholars chose to defy it, and were executed in a most cruel manner. And many metaphysicians, doctors, and other learned men were also condemned in the Emperor's futile quest for an elixir of immortality, his reasoning being that they would produce it to save themselves, or, if they could not, were of no use to the Middle Kingdom. These infamous crimes are often described as worse than the burning of books. But books and minds are just the strongholds of ideas. Ideas are at war with each other and will seek to destroy each other's strongholds. So, to my mind, burning books is as bad as burning people, because people are only more valuable than animals to the extent that they carry ideas. Indeed, burning books can be worse, if they contain more irreplaceable ideas than do human victims. Sure enough the Imperial archives, which was now sole repository of all human knowledge since the beginning of time, itself was burned in the conflagration that destroyed the Imperial Library after the revolt of Liu Bang.

All this is well known thanks to my father's Annals. What is not well known is the actions of Xu. Alone foreseeing the catastrophe, he gathered twelve hundred scholars from the courts of Wei, Han, and Zhao. Each clerk was given the task of memorising three books from the libraries of the Duke of Wei: one of poetry, one of philosophy, and one of history.

Unfortunately, Xu had no time to consider how the books should be divided up between his scholars – either the combination of the three works, or their suitability to the individual characters of the scholars. The act of learning the great books by heart gave rise to great new ideas in the minds of some of these learned men. Others it drove mad. Some it converted into patriots for foreign nations that no longer existed. Others into metaphysical poets. Others still became converts to some of the obscure schools of ethics and religion, quite outside their own background, and committed strange acts of asceticism and self-mutilation.

When the forces of Qin finally diverted the Yellow River and so conquered the impregnable fortress city of Daliang and broke into the Ducal palace, they found the shelves of the library utterly empty. Ordered to burn the books, they discovered that the books had all been hidden. But many of the scholars, trained not to wear their learning lightly, could not help travelling about quoting from the books they had memorised. It was as if the words and phrases of the great masters had a life of their own and refused the narrow confines in which they had been locked up. And some of those driven mad began to say what Xu had ordered them to do. Soon enough news got back to the Emperor that his orders had been defied. He sent men to track down all the scholars of Wei and invited Xu to watch as his men cut out the brains of all the ones they could find and burned them on the same pyres that they burned the books.

Then he demanded that Xu tell him which books he, Xu, had memorised himself. Xu said that, as an old man, his memory was too weak for such a feat. He therefore had himself taken responsibility for only one book, and that was not hidden in his memory. The Emperor demanded that he produce it, on pain of death. Xu refused, saying that this would not be possible. The Emperor threatened him, saying that if he did not produce it he would be subjected to the most exquisite punishment of all: the death of 'the 1,000 and the 9'. The '1,000' is the death of 1,000 cuts, starting with the eyes, followed by the extremities, followed by deeper cuts of flesh that were careful to avoid major arteries or organs. A skilled executioner (and Xu knew that the Emperor's were the most skilled in the known world) could extend the punishment for up to three days, with the victim conscious throughout. And even at the final cut the tortured soul would find no relief, for they would be tormented at that moment of ecstatic release by the knowledge that all their known relatives, for 9 degrees of consanguinity, would also be killed, and that their entire family would thus be wiped forever from the face of the Earth.

Xu must have known that the Emperor would follow through with his threat. Yet still he refused to give up the book. Incredulous, the Emperor asked why not.

'Because', answered Xu, 'it has not yet been written.'

Puzzled by this answer, the Emperor asked him what he meant.

'Your Highness', said Xu, 'I knew as soon as your men diverted the river, and it broke through the Phoenix Gate of Daliang, that I was destined for death. And after what you have done to learning I have no wish to remain alive. I would save my remaining relatives if I could, but I am unable to produce my book, even if it were in your power to grant me another lifetime to write it. My book, The Book of Dark Tales from a Scholar's Study, is the work of many lifetimes. It will be the record of all the ghosts in the world, including my own, and of all the many incredible things that men know and will continue to tell each other, even if you burn every book on Earth. You will be unable to stop it, even if you succeed in your mad quest to live forever, unless you kill the entire human race.'

'And who', scoffed the Emperor, 'will be foolish enough to defy my orders and create this book after you are dead?'

Xu laughed and said: 'You will.'

Then he was given to the executioners.

For many years the Emperor told this story at dinner, to anyone who would listen. He would scoff at the madness of Xu in imagining that he, the ruler of all under heaven, would give him the posthumous satisfaction of ever creating such a thing, and his stupidity in giving up his life for a book, let alone one that did not exist. As a result, of course, as Xu must have foreseen, the anecdote became famous. I myself came across it when I took over the universal history from my Father. Like all stories, it may have changed in the telling. I therefore have spent my life in the shadow of Xu's dedication to learning, which cost his life and that of everyone he cared for, turning over in my mind exactly what he meant by it.

My Grandfather was the first I know who interpreted the meaning of Xu's last speech. He was the first to confirm that what Xu meant was that the Emperor would ultimately fail to wipe out all the learning that had gone before. Like ghosts, the great ideas of the past would still be found in the land of the living. That even if the Emperor found and killed every one of Xu's 1,200 scholars, many would have had enough opportunity to pass on at least parts of the books inside them to others they would speak to. And that besides this, there were fragments of all the great poems and histories and philosophical texts in the minds of many millions of people up and down China. They would be passed from person to person, changing as they passed, but often retaining the core ideas. And that after the Emperor's death, scholars of the future would travel the whole world, and dedicate their whole lives to piecing back together as much of the lost learning as they could find. That they would reconstruct the histories and the insights of the 100 Great Schools of Learning, and would season their annals with all those fragments of poetry that were surely the most memorable, since they would be the very ones that were remembered. It was this hereditary calling that I inherited as Grand Historiographer from my father before me. As you know, I have made it one half of my life's work.

But the other half I have spent creating another book. For, perhaps distorted as it was by the re-telling, it always seemed to me that there was another possible meaning to Xu's final comment. Perhaps he meant it more literally. That he would achieve immortality as a sort of ghost, by creating a book about ghosts and marvels, in this vast land of ghosts and marvels.

For Xu would have known, as I do, that the wisdom of the people exists in their stories as much as in their official records. Indeed the former, though fantastic, often contain more un-manipulated truth and wisdom than the latter. And unlike official historians, folk story tellers do not lie.

I have therefore spent all the time, when not on official duties, gathering and recording all the accounts of strange and wonderful things that I can discover, from asking anyone I have talked to in my travels and my researches. It is full of the sort of ephemera that is produced around the sides of serious study, or collected by scholars to entertain them late at night, as they sit with a cup of tea or wine in their studies and warm themselves by a fire. And when I die I will pass this book –

the book you are reading now – on to others, who will themselves edit it, comment on it, and add to it. So that Xu's book of dark tales, that the Emperor inadvertently helped to create by boasting of how he would never do so, now has real existence, and will continue to live and change and grow for many generations, for as long as people care about what has happened and are interested in strange and wonderful things.

[Wu] In addition to the above, comrade li had added typed a translation of a story of feudal deviance from the fascist oppressors of japan, which I have also enclosed. As well as hiding subversive literature, li clearly abandoned her duties in Wutai and refused to condemn the villagers in an official report or explain what happened in plum-blossom village beyond the note you have just read. She has refused re-education and was eliminated on 5th December at 15:40. I recommend that her family, who are known to me, be spared from the usual sanctions applied to relatives of subversive elements, but the authorities may feel otherwise, and this is of course a matter for them. The lying book of Wei Xu we have otherwise entirely destroyed.

Epilogue

Leviathan

The incident at Dyatlov Pass was real, and remains unsolved. The rest of what is contained in this book is unverified. Many incidental details, though, are certainly confirmed elsewhere.

Baikal is as described. It holds a fifth of all the World's fresh water. It is indeed home to some 60,000 seals, that eat salmon and grayling and golomyanka. What eats the seals is a mystery. Still to this day they bring up from the lake monstrous fish quite unknown to science. In the depths there are Kaluga sturgeons that grow to obscene size (eighteen footers are common, and they grow even bigger than that). No monsters have been found, of course. But the local Buryats did indeed worship and fear the 'Vegohzi'. Many great lakes in northern climes have had stories of lake monsters associated with them. The chronicles tell us that Batu Khan's Mongol horde turned back when they reached Lake Brosno, because a beast called the Brosnya came out of the lake and started to eat men and horses whole.

Akademgorodok is real. There are no records of a murderers' city (though much was kept secret in those days). The thieves' guild is certainly real, and shares many characteristics with the murderers' 'union' referred to in the book. Russia adopted the metric system in 1924, but Gorobets mostly uses the old Imperial measurements. A verst is about two thirds of a mile.

People had been exiled to Siberia for centuries before the First World War, although in nothing like the numbers they were later on. Their crimes ranged from the many political assassinations, in the years before the Revolution, to the often absurdly minor or trumped-up misdemeanours that condemned so many after it. It is estimated that 18 million people were sent to the gulags under Stalin alone, with millions more forced into starving exile. Our picture is still very unclear, but it seems likely that at least 10 or 12 million were killed in the camps and the wider Soviet Terrors.

The City of Dreadful Night

There exists no other reference to the 'Pala recension' of the fable of King Vikram and the *vetala.* But that famous fable itself is both a meta-story and a sub-story within the vast edifice of the 'Ocean of the Sea of Stories' – the endless and endlessly changing architecture of Indian supernatural tales, which link to and sit within and beneath each other in various well-known collections. The old British cemetery is much as described. There is at least one 'bleeding tomb', and there certainly were several Company men very like Hawkins in Kolkata.

It is inconceivable that any of the staff at the Oberoi would ever bring the wrong drink. The Chowringhee bar cannot be recommended enough – though perhaps you should be careful whom you fall into conversation with there.

Kolkata is yet to benefit much from the rising prosperity of India, though things have changed since Kipling called it 'the City of Dreadful Night'. Nowhere else in the World has such learned and outspoken taxi drivers. The city is still full of reminders of 'John Company'. After all, it was the ensigns, agents, and writers of the Honourable East India Company that first caused it to be built. The Great Bengal Famine of the 1770s may have killed eleven million, after the monsoons failed for several seasons running. It is not clear whether the same number would have died under local rulers, or if it was the consequence of the Company's policies. But even Adam Smith criticised the Company for exacerbating the tragedy. In Bengali, the word 'Bhoot' means both 'ghost' and 'the Past'. If so it is another haunted region.

The Black Sands

There is no other source for Al-Shirazi. The ruins of Merv are still much as described. The Mongol invasion of Khorezm happened just as set out in his notes. It destroyed a civilisation famous for, amongst other things, the inventor of algebra and the algorithm (the very word is a corruption of his name, 'Al-Khorezmi' or 'the Khorezmian'). The Caliph's plan - if he did have a hand in it - of calling barbarian hordes into the lands of Khorezm, certainly destroyed the Empire of his enemy the Shah. But it did nothing to restore the Caliphate, which was itself destroyed when the Mongols later carried on west and sacked Baghdad. One by one the great Muslim cities were wiped out, in perhaps the most complete massacres in History, with pyramids of skulls, streets slippery with human fat, and rivers coloured by blood and ink. The Arab world took centuries to recover.

There is no other record of a Captain Fitzwilliam. Brave Englishmen did venture into the cruel and secret Kingdoms of Tartary. There they fought a cold war against the Russians that was known as the 'Great Game' or the 'Tournament of Shadows'. Fitzwilliam's ride to Khiva looks like a prelude to the invasion of Afghanistan. This was the first of four wars the British have lost there, and the worst disaster of them all. Ten thousand men marched through the Khyber and only one came out alive. The tortures described, from bug pits to scaphism (also known as 'the boats'), are traditional ones for the region, whose rulers to this day are notorious for acid baths and other dark practices, and where some say the Great Game is still played.

The Mummy Returns

As Selma says, everyone loves a good mummy. The Egyptological details of this story, from the Book of the Dead to brain-scramblers, will be familiar to everyone with a passing awareness of the subject. What is less well known, perhaps, is the attraction Egyptology had to superstitious eccentrics. Sir Ernest Alfred Thompson Wallace Budge was just one example. The leading Egypt expert at the British Museum from the 1880's to 1920's, he was also a famous occultist. His protégé Dorothy Eady was convinced she was the reincarnation of a lover of Seti I, and tried to have herself interred in an Egyptian-style tomb. Budge's cat, Mike, was a famous figure at the Museum, and even had an obituary in the Evening Standard.

The Museum of Egyptian Antiquities stands on Tahrir Square. At the time of writing, sadly, history is still very much happening in the oldest city on Earth.

The Cleansing of the Temple

The Hittites were entirely destroyed in the Late Bronze Age Collapse. They have left us little but thousands of cuneiform tablets. King Suppiluliumas II was their ruler at the time of their mysterious destruction. The other details given by Professor Finlayson are mostly accurate. In common with most bronze-age societies, the Hittites would have valued meteoric iron. God-stealing was indeed something of a Hittite pastime. Their literate class would have been tiny and, as such, irreplaceable.

Although no written records survive to explain the catastrophe which wiped them out, some intriguing oral echoes may have done. Homer's Iliad and the Odyssey were composed perhaps 500 years after the events they describe. They have seemed to some scholars to contain confused memories of the vast destruction that signalled the end of the Bronze Age, and perhaps of the voyages of the 'sea peoples'. The Greeks knew that before their Age of Iron there had been an Age of Bronze, and they saw these sweeps of History as decline from an initial Golden Age. Perhaps Homer's contemporaries retained distant memories of civilisations that would to them have seemed very sophisticated. Tantalisingly, the Hittite records from Hattusas contain names which are very close to some of those in the Greek myths. Was the Hittite 'Ahhiyawa' the same as the Greek word for their country: 'Achaea'? Was their 'Truwisa' Troy? If so, it seems that some memory of the momentous events of the Bronze Age Collapse may have survived after all, in the oldest legends of our later, baser civilisation.

The details of the disastrous crusade of 1101 are certainly historical. It was destroyed within the geographic heart of the old Hittite Kingdom. The Knights Templar, who founded the Temple Church in what is now London's legal quarter, were indeed purged for blasphemy. Under torture several confessed to idolatry before the image of the mysterious idol 'Baphomet'. The ancient Liberties of the Honourable Societies of Inner and Middle Temple, and the other Inns of Court, together with their history and folklore, are as described. Anyone who has worked in Lincoln's Inn knows that the truth can be more horrible than fiction.

In the Wood of the Suicides

The Wood of the Suicides, also known as Demon Forest, or the Dark Sea of Trees, is a real place in the foothills near Mt Fuji. It is not far from Tokyo, the modern name of old Edo, famous for its leisured samurai class and the 'Floating World' of their pleasure quarters. The forest was traditionally associated with the practice of *obasute*, by which the elderly were exposed to die, and with their angry ghosts who were supposed to haunt the place. It remains the most famous suicide spot in Japan and still claims hundreds of victims each year in a nation that can turn anything – even suicide – into an art.

Chinese Whispers

The editorial of the China Daily on 1st July 1966, exhorting the people to 'sweep away all monsters and demons', marked the start of the Cultural Revolution, which destroyed millions of lives, and the material culture of one of the greatest civilisations on Earth. Books, buildings, paintings, and artefacts were burned, and intellectuals made to swallow ink. Violence, rape, and murder were endemic on a massive scale, as the regime mobilised the young to declare total war on the past.

This followed Mao's Great Leap Forward, which itself caused massive violence and famine. Across China, victims were drowned in ponds and wells, stripped naked and exposed to the elements, doused in boiling water, forced to eat human excrement, and subjected to mutilation and torture. Central planning broke down under the pressure to report inflated production statistics, and the death registration system collapsed in the face of a disaster that could not be admitted - indeed, assiduous census statistitians were shot. Many deaths were unreported so family members could keep drawing the dead's rations. Some parents were forced by party officials to bury their children alive, others to sell them for food. Cannibalism was common - and even, in some areas, encouraged - by the local party leaders. There were in all senses many hungry ghosts. The period of Mao's leadership caused the death of perhaps some fifty or sixty million people – the greatest single holocaust in human history.

King Zhang Xianzhong, of the 'heavenly candles' and the inscription on the 'Seven Kill Stele', followed his own exhortation so thoroughly in 17th Century Sichuan that the province was totally depopulated – indeed the genocide was complete enough to have earned him some praise from later Communist revisionist scholars. Like so many catastrophes in Chinese history, the huge population decline in the census was the best evidence for what happened. Bureaucracies are never efficient at hiding the disasters they cause. Had Comrade Li followed through with her investigations, she might have found a similar picture across the country.

Throughout Chinese history, and particularly in troubled times, there have been many secret societies, often combining supernatural rituals with resistance to oppressive rule: White Turbans, Mazdeist Fire worshippers, Manicheans, Boxers, and Triads. Many still exist. It is believed some drink each other's blood as part of their initiation rites.

Sima Qian, 'The Grand Historiographer' of the First Emperor, did compose his histories in the manner described, fulfilling his pledge to his father, and in spite of the punishment of castration. It is to him we owe much of our knowledge of ancient Chinese history. For the First Emperor was indeed responsible, Sima Qian tells us, for the burning of books and the burial alive of scholars. These were his attempt to destroy all the past that did not suit him and his ideas.

There is no other mention of Lord Xu, or his dark and unlucky book, though similar collections exist – including the Strange Stories of Pu Songling, with their accretion of learned marginal notes. Hopefully people will continue to write them, for knowledge and entertainment - and as tempting amusements, diversions, and tests - which is why I have made another beginning here...

30028036R00144

Printed in Great Britain
by Amazon